Face in the Shadows

R. J. Stevens

Published by R.J. Stevens, 2024.

This is a work of fiction. Similarities to real people, places, or events are entirely coincidental.

FACE IN THE SHADOWS

First edition. July 7, 2024.

Copyright © 2024 R. J. Stevens.

ISBN: 979-8227699756

Written by R. J. Stevens.

To my friend Judy E.

Prologue

On Abby O'Malley's first night alone in her new home, lightning flashed outside as the wind howled, and hail pelted the windows. A scream ripped from her lips when the clap of thunder vibrated her tiny cottage. Memories of the night her parents died in a fire caused by a dangerous thunderstorm flashed before her eyes.

That traumatic experience haunted her in the most unusual way. Each time she suffered through a lightning storm something bad would happen in her life. Abby made a mistake of telling one of her foster parents about the incidents, so they took her to a therapist. Because of that, she had to stay in a mental institution for a time, since the so-called therapist thought her fear was all in her head. That's when she learned to keep things to herself.

The next flash of lightening killed the lights in her home. She turned the flashlight on that she gripped in her hands. The beam of light cut like a knife through the inky blackness revealing the one thing she feared the most.

TRENT WINTHROP SAT behind the large mahogany desk in the study of the O'Malley mansion. Jacob O'Malley Sr. had been laid to rest in the family cemetery overlooking the ocean earlier in the day.

The guests in attendance of the funeral had finally left for the mainland. Now he would begin fulfilling the promise he had made to the old man. Trent sighed as though the weight of the world rested on his shoulders.

The ranch foreman, Lance Elliot, knocked on the heavy wooden door drawing his attention and he asked, "Did the last boat leave?"

"They just left. If there's nothing else, Gina and I are going home." Lance replied.

"Did you know Mr. O'Malley has a granddaughter?" Trent asked with a sigh.

"I suppose it's possible. His son and new bride moved to the States after a huge argument." Lance answered.

"Well, he does, and she'll arrive next week." Trent's frown deepened.

"Should we be concerned?" Lance asked.

"I don't know." Trent replied hesitantly. "We have one week to make sure everything is running smoothly."

"We can talk about this tomorrow. It's late and we all need some rest." Gina, Lance's wife beckoned from the doorway.

Trent watched the two people who were more like a mother and father to him than employees. It didn't matter that they weren't his biological parents, he loved them all the same.

Reluctantly going upstairs to his room, he knew sleep would elude him. The worry of keeping his promise to Mr. O'Malley rested heavily on his mind. He had no idea where to start the investigation the old man asked him to do on his deathbed. Sometimes he hated that he valued his honor and word above all else. But in doing so, he was a well-respected man.

Chapter One

Abby O'Malley leaned against the balcony railing filling her lungs with fragrant fresh air. The magnificent view enchanted her with its fields of lavender peeking through the light fog swirling playfully in the cool morning breeze.

A knock on the door to her elaborate suite drew her back inside. Reluctantly, she called out, "Come in."

The door slowly opened to reveal an older woman with dull gray hair pinned into a tight bun. "Miss O'Malley, breakfast is ready in the dining room."

"Thank you, but I couldn't eat anything just now." She declined.

"As you wish. Mr. Winthrop is waiting for you in the study when you're ready." The woman frowned. "My name is Barbara should you require anything else."

"I'll be down after I freshen up." She moved toward the in-suite bathroom.

"I'll inform Mr. Winthrop." Barbara said and closed the door behind her.

Abby quickly changed into a pair of blue jeans, yellow tank top and new tennis shoes. Her excitement continued to build as she ran a brush through her thick red tresses.

The recent event that brought her to O'Malley Island, left her feeling as if she slipped into an alternate universe. Today, the legacy of her grandfather, Jacob O'Malley would be turned over to her. Although she had no idea what that entailed, or what she faced in the future, her hope of a new, better life would make her current dismal existence a long-forgotten memory.

Rushing out of her bedroom, she made her way downstairs thinking about that day one week ago when everything changed. Even now she pinched herself to make sure this wasn't a dream.

After the initial shock of learning she not only had a grandfather, but that he had also left his entire estate to her, filled her with anticipation. Harold Carson, her guardian's attorney explained she was the last living descendant of the O'Malley line leaving her embarrassingly rich.

When she discovered her guardian knew about her grandfather and he had sent money for her care, she became furious with him.

"How long have you known? She demanded.

"Deidra searched a long time for your family after you came to live with us. When we contacted your grandfather, he swore us to secrecy and sent money for your care."

In that moment, Abby's heart fractured into a million pieces, and she asked with tears in her eyes, "Why didn't he want me?"

"He never said. My only instructions were to care for you until his death. My attorney made a visit and received his will to be read when the time came." Walter explained. "Did he mention my grandmother?" She held a small strand of hope in her heart.

"No, he didn't. I assume she had already passed away." Walter replied. "I assume you'll be leaving for the island soon."

"Yes, will you make the arrangements for me?" Abby asked overwhelmed with too many emotions to think at that point.

"The estate manager already made the arrangements for your travel and sent along a credit card for your expenses." Walter handed her a small manila envelope.

She accepted the packet and went to her room. Inside she found the credit card, a passport, cash, and a list of necessary items for staying on the island.

Abby's eyes clouded with tears. She couldn't help but remember that fateful night when she became an orphan at eight years old. Her parents kissed her goodnight and went to bed themselves.

Awakened from a sound sleep by lightning and thunder, she screamed into a mask someone put on her face. She felt arms lifting her from the bed. The heat from the fire was so intense her parents perished leaving her all alone in the world.

From that moment on, the broken system she found herself in placed her in one home after another. When she screamed in terror from the occasional storm, they sent her to therapy and eventually a few months in a mental health institution. That's when she learned how to read people and became an expert at hiding in plain sight.

Forcing her memories back into the box they had escaped from, she stepped into the huge foyer and moved toward the large open wooden doors to what she assumed was the study. She stopped for a moment, took a deep breath, and slowly let it out. It was time to meet the estate manager, Mr. Winthrop.

The wonderful aromas of old books, fine leather, expensive cigars, and burning wood wrapped around her like a warm fuzzy blanket as she stepped into the room. Oblivious to the man standing by the large desk, she allowed her fondest memories to surface. Her father would sit with her near their fireplace and read to her before bedtime.

"Miss O'Malley?" A rich baritone voice broke through the euphoria she drifted into.

She turned her mesmerizing green eyes to meet his intense dark chocolate eyes filled with curiosity.

"I'm Trent Winthrop." He offered his hand.

When she extended her small soft hand, he brushed his lips across her knuckles, setting a swarm of butterflies to flight in her stomach.

"It's an honor to meet you." He watched her face flush a pretty pink. "I trust you slept well?"

"I did thank you. The room is quite comfortable as was the bed." She replied.

"I'm sure you're aware that your grandfather hired me as the manager of his vast estate." He released her hand. "It seems now that I'm tasked with acquainting you with your inheritance, Miss O'Malley."

"Please, call me Abby." She insisted nervously.

"The housekeeper will give you a tour of your new home after we review the financial records." His eyes turned serious. "We will begin at your leisure."

"I would prefer to wait for my guardian and his attorney to arrive before we go over the estate records." She said. "I'm quite anxious to see what my grandfather left me."

"Barbara!" He bellowed startling her. "I do have some business in the fields that need my attention. By the time you've finished the tour, I'll be back to show you the rest of your estate."

"Sir?" Barbara stepped into the room.

"Show Miss O'Malley her new home." He ordered curtly. "I'll return within the hour."

"Yes sir." Barbara replied then turned to Abby. "Follow me Miss."

Trent's eyes followed the young woman as she trailed behind the housekeeper while expressing her appreciation for the exquisite surroundings.

"Snap out of it Trent!" He mumbled tearing his eyes away from her.

The emotional storm brewing from the moment he kissed her hand surprised him. From the soft scent of her perfume to her kissable ruby red lips intensified his strong reaction to her.

Miss Abby O'Malley reminded him of a perfect Irish Rose. Beautiful and pure rising above a garden of less perfect ones. Deep down, he suspected she possessed some extremely sharp thorns hiding beneath the surface.

Chapter Two

Room by room, Abby marveled over the luxurious furnishings. Each room displayed a perfect mix of mahogany and marble. From the finest furnishings to the window treatments and exquisite hand-woven rugs, all of it spoke of how wealthy her grandfather really was. The study, formal living room, large ballroom with a grand piano situated near the enormous doors that led to a small patio. The grand foyer highlighted the ornate mahogany staircase. The dining room table sat twelve people and the kitchen was a caterers dream.

The second story was made up of four suites on each side of the hall with the master suite at the end. Each just as beautiful as the last.

When the tour was finished, Abby followed Barbara back downstairs and commented, "I feel like royalty will step out of a room at any moment."

"Mr. Winthrop will be along shortly." Barbara stopped at the study door.

"Thank you for the tour." Abby smiled at the woman as she left for the kitchen.

The amazing aroma of the study brought wonderful feelings back to her. Immersed in the fond memories of her childhood, Abby ran her fingers along the spines of the books carefully organized on the floor to ceiling bookshelves lining the walls.

One question plagued her, *"Why hadn't anyone ever mentioned her grandmother?"*

The desire to learn everything about her family topped her list of things she wanted to accomplish.

A chill ran down her spine when she felt eyes land on her. The sound of footsteps behind her intensified the fear as she slowly turned holding her breath.

Relief engulfed her when an older man with kind eyes smiled at her. From his balding head to his weather worn boots, she sensed an air of authority.

"Miss O'Malley?" His pleasant smile put her at ease.

"Yes, may I help you?" She returned his smile.

"Begging your pardon ma'am, I'm Lance Elliot, your estate foreman. Mr. Winthrop sends his apologies, but he's been detained in the fields. I have been instructed to give you the tour of the grounds." He said tapping his cowboy hat against his leg.

"That's great. I'm ready when you are." She replied eagerly.

As Abby followed him toward the stables, the closer the building came, the more her anxiety grew. Stepping inside the enormous stable, Lance took the reins of a beautiful Paint and held them out to her. Observing the color drain from her face he asked, "Are you well Miss O'Malley?"

"I've never been on a horse before. I loved the carrousel horses when I was little, but I don't think it will be the same riding this one." She said nervously.

"Not to worry, Miss O'Malley. Princess is the gentlest horse you own. I promise you'll be safe since I'll be with you." He assured her. "Put your hand out and let her get acquainted with you."

Tentatively holding her hand out, the horse gently sniffed her hand before nuzzling its velvety nose against her. Gently rubbing the animals soft muzzle, her fear melted away. Its gentle eyes drew her under its spell.

Lance helped her into the saddle, giving her a few instructions. After the ranch hand brought Darwin, a high-spirited black stallion for Lance, he swung into the saddle and led her out of the stable.

The older man impressed her with the ease of his control over the animal. To Abby's relief, Princess followed with little prompting from her.

Lance led her past several large hay fields ready for cutting, and others with lush green alfalfa and oats ripening for the winter months.

Workers came into view stacking large bales of hay on trucks for transport to the enormous hay barns.

To her surprise, Mr. Winthrop tossed the bales alongside the men. Admiration for his bulging muscles through his sweat soaked t-shirt brought heat to her cheeks.

Lance suppressed a smile when he caught her ogling his boss while leading her past a helicopter sitting on a pad. He explained it was for emergency use only. Three more pads were for visiting friends who didn't want to travel by boat.

The smell of rich wet earth reached her nose just before she heard the sound of water. Lance stopped at the edge of the beautiful stream separating the estate from the dense forest that lie on the other side.

When he turned away from the stream Abby asked, "Why are we turning back?"

"Mr. Winthrop's orders ma'am. He forbade me to enter the forest. There's some mighty aggressive animals lurking beyond those trees." He explained. "We wouldn't want you to be injured or killed so soon after your arrival on the island."

"While I appreciate you loyalty to Mr. Winthrop, may I remind you of the fact that I am now your boss as well. My wishes and orders will always supersede his." She tried to sound authoritative. "I must insist you show me the rest of the island."

"I'm sorry, but I didn't bring my rifle and you aren't an experienced rider. There are too many dangers beyond the stream. May I suggest you take it up with Mr. Winthrop?" He respectfully declined.

Abby's lips thinned in anger as her cheeks flushed, *"Apparently Mr. Winthrop's word is law around here."* She muttered. "I apologize for making you uncomfortable."

Lance continued back toward the mansion past fields of lavender with workers harvesting the mature plants while she muttered under her breath. *"How dare he! The man had no right denying me access to any part of my island. I'll teach him who's in charge."*

Lance pretended she hadn't said anything while smiling.

After turning the horses over to the groomers, Lance escorted her through the smaller stock yards and the garden area.

When the large gazebo overlooking the ocean came into view her eyes lit up. She definitely would spend a lot of time there.

On the way back to her new home, she observed a well house and more beautiful landscaping.

Everything was so lovely, Abby had no words to describe her estate. Obviously, her grandfather cared a great deal about the natural beauty of nature by using the resources of the island.

The sun just touched the horizon when Lance said, "I hope you enjoyed the tour. Good evening, Miss O'Malley."

"Mr. Elliot, you may call me Abby. I've enjoyed your company today and I thank you for your time." She replied with a sunny smile.

Lance tipped his hat and turned to leave smiling to himself. *"Trent is in trouble with Miss O'Malley. The woman was stubborn and had what he would call an Irish temper. The coming days are going to be quite entertaining when the fireworks start."*

Chapter Three

Abby's stomach rumbled when she stepped into the fragrant kitchen. Barbara informed her dinner was ready, so she hurried upstairs to freshen up and change.

Slipping into a cool dress and running a brush through her hair, she hurried downstairs. Lost in thought, a squeak of surprise slipped from her lips when she collided with a hard chest.

Strong arms encircled her to keep her from falling as she heard, "Oof."

Her eyes followed up the buttons to his squared jaw and into his heated eyes. There was no stopping the heat flowing into her cheeks.

"Miss O'Malley, it would be wise to watch where you're going." His eyes bore into hers. "And stop daydreaming of a passing adventure."

"What do you mean by a passing adventure?" She asked confused.

"Surely, you will want to sell what your grandfather left you. I'm quite sure you have no experience in running a household, let alone an estate as vast as this one." He smirked.

"Why would you assume that?" She raised a suspicious brow. "Are you such a man that you'd cheat me out of my inheritance?"

Trent watched her grandfather's temper shine brightly from her eyes. However, the sweet innocence of her youth softened the bite of fury. "I'm evaluating my opponent, Miss O'Malley. I'm positive if I were to offer you the right price, you wouldn't hesitate to sell."

"Don't hold your breath, Mister. I learn long ago how to take care of myself. The day I learned of my grandfather, my goal in life changed to find out all about him." She informed him defiantly. "I feel if I live his life here, I can get to know him."

Trent watched tears glimmer in her eyes unprepared for the feeling of remorse hitting his heart for being a jerk.

"Take care, Mr. Winthrop, if anyone including you tries to stand in my way, it would be a grave error in judgement." She glared at him. 'While I admire your dedication to my grandfather, I suggest you let me discover how he lived without interfering."

Abby knew he was angry since his jaw clenched. He might be an arrogant bully, but he was handsome.

"Mr. Winthrop, Miss O'Malley, dinner is served." Barbara announced.

Abby moved to step around him when his voice cut through the tense atmosphere. "Be careful what you wish for, Miss O'Malley. This island possesses dangerous secrets that should remain undisturbed. Trust me that path should be left alone. Especially when you don't know where it will lead."

"I don't understand." Her brows furrowed.

"Many times in life, things aren't what they seem. I'm curious as to why your parents never mentioned your grandfather." He paused a moment. "My guess is, they were afraid and hid it from you. However, if you'll forget this little adventure of yours, I'm quite sure we can reach an amicable agreement."

"Mr. Winthrop, your primary function at the moment it to educate me on the condition of my estate. As your employer, may I trust you to teach me how everything operates, or should I find someone else to take your place?" She glared at him with her arms crossed defiantly.

Out of desperation to hide his smile, he bowed. "As your employee, I'll fulfill the duties your grandfather hired me for. Be aware, Miss O'Malley, I'm keeping a close eye on you."

ABBY YANKED THE CURTAINS open allowing the early morning light to chase the shadows of night away. The sun warmed her chilled skin while she admired the island she had quickly fallen in love with.

Dark heavy clouds boiled on the horizon, emitting flashes of lightening as it slowly approached the island. Abby shuddered afraid of what may happened when it arrived.

Slowly dressing for the day, she looked into the mirror. Her innocent beauty reflected back at her, unaware of how others viewed her youthful appearance.

After a spritz of expensive perfume she splurged on, and a gloss on her ruby red lips, she deemed herself ready for the day. Dare she hope Mr. Winthrop would see her as a woman instead of a child? Would he grant her permission to see the rest of her island?

Carefully stepping into the foyer, she wanted to avoid crashing into Mr. Winthrop. When she stepped into the dining room, the aromas of fresh coffee and sweet pastries brought a sense of comfort.

Mr. Winthrop immediately stood to help seat her, then he sat back down to finish his breakfast.

"At least he has impeccable manners." She thought, remaining silent.

"Did you sleep well, Miss O'Malley?" He asked.

"I did, thank you." She replied.

"Good. What plans have you made for the day?" He watched her with suspicion.

"I want to see the rest of the island, with your permission of course." She said impatiently. "Apparently, you wouldn't allow Mr. Elliot to take me into the forest."

"No." He rejected her request. "The forest is off limits to you."

"That is unacceptable! What are you hiding from me?" She hissed in anger.

"The forest is challenging to the most seasoned rider, and you Miss O'Malley are the definition of a greenhorn." He growled in annoyance. "For your own safety, it's best you stay close to home."

"Need I remind you that I now own this island? I have every right to inspect my property. I'm also your employer and expect you to make it possible." She argued. "I only asked as a courtesy."

"No! You will refrain from putting one foot in that forest!" His voice held an invisible threat. "If you do, I'll..."

"You'll what? Turn me over your knee and spank me? I'm not a child!" She challenged.

"I'll do whatever is necessary to keep you from harm. Consider yourself warned Miss O'Malley!" He snarled as he tossed his napkin on the table and stormed from the room.

Abby slumped into her chair utterly defeated.

Although she would have to accept his rules for now, she was determined to get what she wanted. With a sigh she decided to start investigating her grandfather's life starting in his room.

Leisurely strolling down the hall to his room, she studied the portraits of her ancestors going back one hundred fifty years. When she reached the portrait of her father, a shroud of sadness enveloped her. She had long sense come to realize no matter how bad she wanted her parents to live again, nothing would bring them back.

"Who cares what Mr. Winthrop thinks?" She snorted pushing the door to her grandfather's room open. A fresh wave of admiration washed over her when she stepped inside.

The light streaming in the large balcony windows bathed the room in a warm glow. From the mahogany paneled walls to the exquisitely carved furniture, everything spoke of comfort.

She crossed the room and opened the balcony doors allowing the fresh island air to rush inside. The scent of rain from the approaching storm caught her attention as the sun's rays began to fade in the dark clouds.

After she closed the doors, she noticed an elaborate writing desk begging to be searched. The soft leather office chair cradled her as she began opening the drawers.

A bundle of letters with a string holding them together sat just inside the bottom drawer. Her breath caught when she recognized her father's handwriting.

After removing the string, she opened the first one and pulled out the letter. A picture of her as a newborn fell onto the desk. Curious, she began reading.

Father,

I hope you and mother are well. Even though I understand you won't respond to this, I want you to know you have a granddaughter. Her name is Abigail Jane after mother. I've enclosed a picture of her, so you'll know what she looks like.

Despite our differences, I offer you the invitation to be in her life. If you refuse, I hope you know it will be because of your own issues and not mine.

It is clear that you don't care, but I still love you and mother.

Your son.

Jake.

Abby swiped tears trailing down her cheeks as she looked at the baby picture enclosed with the tear-stained letter. Grief slammed into her as she wondered whose tears they were, her father's or her grandfather's.

She put the envelope to the side and reached for another when she froze hearing a noise from behind her.

Chapter Four

She swallowed her fear and slowly turned to find her clearly upset housekeeper. "Miss O'Malley, you shouldn't be in here."

"Why?" Abby masked her annoyance of the interruption.

"Did Mr. Winthrop give you permission to go through your grandfather's things?" Barbara wrung her hands together nervously.

"I don't need his permission to do anything." She huffed.

"Mr. Winthrop won't be pleased." Barbara warned her.

"That's his problem, and I don't care." She retorted waving her off. "You should go take care of your duties."

"Don't say I didn't warn you." Barbara backed out of the room. "He won't be pleased."

After the door closed, Abby returned to the letters. Each one contained an updated picture of her and ended with: *"It is clear that you don't care, but I still love you and mother.*

Your son, Jake."

Questions filled her mind, *"What happened between the two of them? Why would her grandfather disown his own son?"*

Abby became so engrossed in the letters, she didn't know Trent had entered the room until his angry voice pierced the silence. "What are you doing Miss O'Malley?"

She nearly jumped out of the seat as she turned with a gasp. "Although it's none of your business, I'm exploring my grandfather's life."

"No one is allowed in this room, not even you!" He growled. "You cannot be in here!"

"You have no right to deny me access to any part of my home! I don't want or need permission to do anything I want!" She hissed.

Clearly fighting to rein in his temper, he replied. "Miss O'Malley, you must understand, this room hasn't been touched since your grandfather's demise. If you desire to know your grandfather, I'll be more than happy to answer your questions."

"You don't understand! I don't want you to tell me anything about him! You've already forbidden me from seeing the rest of the island, you won't take this from me!" She shouted. "You've already admitted you want to swindle me out of my inheritance. Why would I believe anything you tell me? Leave me alone!"

She whirled back to the letters with a flip of her hair over her shoulder.

"You will leave this room immediately, Miss O'Malley!" He roared. "If necessary I'll pick you up and carry you out!"

Tension hung heavy in the room like a thick cloud of steam. He took a menacing step toward her and snarled. "Well?"

She knew she'd lost this round so she picked up the letters and moved toward the door when he stopped her by grabbing her arm.

"Leave those letters here!" He ordered.

"These letters were written by my father. Like it or not, I'm going to read them. If you want me to leave this room they go with me!" She stomped her foot.

"Fine, just get out of here!" He ushered her into the hallway.

While he shut and locked the door, she stole a glance at the angry man thinking, *Well I won! It may not have been a big win, but I still won.*

"Your guardian and his attorney arrived a few moments ago. Shall we?" He waved his arm toward the staircase.

"Let me drop these off in my room." She quickly ducked inside and put them on her dresser and hurried back into the hall.

Trent waited impatiently in the hall to accompany her downstairs. He didn't trust her to begin with and now his trust level dropped even lower.

The minute Walter came into view, Abby called out from behind Trent, "Walter! How are you?"

Her guardian looked up in time to see her stumble halfway down the staircase. Mr. Winthrop scooped her into his arms averting a nasty tumble. He carried her the rest of the way. When he set her on her feet, her crimson face made a smile tug at the corners of his mouth.

"Abby? Are you okay?" Walter asked concerned.

"Yes, thanks to Mr. Winthrop." She said quietly turning her attention to the attorney. "It's nice to see you again Harold. Did you have a good trip?"

"Yes ma'am." He replied with amusement dancing in his eyes.

"Lunch is ready if you'll follow me." Trent turned with a smile fascinated by Abby's reaction.

Abby grabbed Walter's arm like a lifeline while they followed Trent.

Walter happily told Trent stories of Abby's silly stunts after he became her guardian. Abby wished he would stop because Mr. Winthrop didn't need any more ammunition to use against her.

After lunch they retired to the study to go over the estate's legal issues and finances. When they finished, Abby had a headache trying to absorb all the information. It didn't help that her estate manager stood so close while explaining things.

Abby hugged Walter before he and Harold left for the mainland. She watched the helicopter fade from sight before returning to the mansion. She closed the door wiping tears from her flushed cheeks.

Trent stepped from the shadow of the study and asked if she wanted a drink.

"I suppose one won't hurt." She sniffed.

After seating her on the oversized leather sofa, he gave her a glass and sat across from her in one of two matching leather chairs.

She sputtered after her first sip, unused to the strong liquor. Wine coolers were her preferred drink, and even one of those made her tipsy. The drink tasted good leaving a trail of warmth in its wake.

"So, your relationship with Mr. Hartford was more intimate than his guardianship?" He asked presumptuously.

"What? No! Walter and his wife became my guardians when I turned twelve. My parents perished in a fire caused by a thunderstorm when I was eight. After four years in the foster system, I was placed in their care."

"I'm sorry for your loss, Miss O'Malley." He sounded genuinely sympathetic. "I suspect there's more to your story, isn't there?"

"If it weren't for Walter and his wife Deidra, I'd have been on the streets. The foster homes they placed me in were, well..." She stopped for a sip of her drink. "Since my parents died, I've had a difficult time during thunderstorms. If not for the fireman who rescued me, I'd have died too."

The fiery liquid warmed her insides while relaxing her mind and mouth. "Even with my psychological problems, Walter and Deidra have been kind to me."

Trent filed the psychological comment away to examine later and said, "It sounds like you've had a rough go of it. Tell me, why didn't you reach out to your grandfather after the death of your parents? Surely there was some information about him among your parents belongings."

"Everything was destroyed in the fire. I had no idea he existed until Harold contacted me with his will. For some reason, my parents never spoke of him." She slurred her words.

"That explains a lot." He commented.

'I should go to bed. I'm feeling quite sleepy." She yawned. "Whatever this drink is has relaxed me enough, I think I may actually sleep well tonight.

When she stood to leave, she stumbled over the coffee table. Once again Trent swept her off her feet as she lost herself in his dark chocolate eyes full of compassion.

After he entered her room, he kissed her plump red lips. Then he put her on the bed and quickly left the room.

He closed the door behind him with a deep sigh, he shouldn't have done that. But he couldn't resist.

Chapter Five

Trent punched his pillow again before rolling over, yet nothing worked. He still couldn't sleep.

Abby O'Malley surprised him. The young woman was nothing like he expected which made her a big distraction. He made a colossal mistake when he kissed her. Apparently, she'd wormed her way into his heart without warning.

She was young, infuriating, defiant, and beautiful. Thus, his torment. Abby terrified and enticed him to no end.

What made it all worse, he'd never had feelings like this toward any other woman and he didn't know how to deal with her. The moment Abby O'Malley set foot on the island; his world flipped upside down. Without a doubt, he would have to watch himself around her, for both their sakes.

His number one priority, keep the secrets of the island away from Abby or the consequences would be devastating. Failure was not an option.

Just before he fell asleep, lightning lit up his room followed by a clap of thunder so loud it rattled the windows. The scream that reached his ears caused him to bolt from his bed and scramble down the hall to Abby's room.

THE BRIGHT LIGHTENING awoke Abby just before thunder shook the mansion. Her eyes focused across the room when something moved in the shadows. A tremor of fear shot from her toes to her head as she screamed.

"How did he find me so quickly?" She thought as the black clothed body with the hideous face moved toward her.

Each time the lightening lit up the room, she saw he was moving closer.

Her door flew open drawing her attention away from the apparition as Trent burst into the room.

"Abby? Are you okay? What's wrong?" He asked breathlessly.

When she looked back toward the shadow of the room, it was gone. Unable to speak out of fear, tears fell from her cheeks.

Trent cautiously approached her as if he would a frightened filly. "Miss Abby?"

"D-did you see?" She turned terrified eyes on him.

"See what?" He asked as his heart filled with worry.

"You didn't see him did you?" She trembled.

Trent gently eased her into his arms to comfort her, wondering if the curse on her family had reappeared after seven years. Outside the storm raged against the island relentlessly for hours.

Abby clung to him in fear of the apparition appearing again. Somehow she felt safe in his arms, yet she knew the fiend wouldn't appear until she was alone in the dark with the storm howling outside.

Finally, the storm abated, but Abby wouldn't let him go in her sleep. Instinctively, he knew the effects of the terror she experienced would linger long after the incident.

Unable to free himself from her grip, he settled against the headboard and held her while she slept.

Abby snuggled deeper into the warmth surrounding her. It occurred to her that someone held her when arms tightened around her. Slowly opening her eyes, she observed Trent resting peacefully with her in his arms.

"Why is he in my bed?" She wondered. The last thing she remembered was taking the drink he offered her.

While studying him as he slept, his boyishly innocent expression didn't fool her. The man admitted he had every intention of stealing her inheritance.

Butterflies took flight in her stomach with the thought, Whomever he fell in love with would be a lucky woman.

Trent stirred and looked into her emerald, green eyes, "Well, this isn't awkward at all."

"I have two questions, what happened last night and why are you in my bed?" She asked clearly confused.

"Would you like the truth?" He asked with a mischievous glint in his eyes.

"Of course, I want the truth. Why would you want to lie?" Her eyes held a challenge.

"You're no fun. A thunderstorm rolled in..." He began when she held up her hand.

"I wish you'd have lied. I'm sorry, thunderstorms terrify me." She didn't mention being haunted for fear he would think she was crazy.

"No worries, it's over so forget it." He could see she hadn't told him everything.

Unable to resist, he kissed her. When she responded with the eagerness of inexperience, he pulled away. "I need to go, are you okay now?" He released her.

"I'm fine." She replied as her face heated.

"I'll see you at breakfast." He said on his way out of her room.

She watched the door close behind him thinking about how much she liked his kisses, yet the feelings he stirred in her were baffling.

Then the fact he was human one minute and the next he became a tyrant added to her confusion.

Inspired by the reality that he had kissed her she felt at the very least maybe she could get some answers from him now.

Abby stepped off the stairway into the foyer armed with her prettiest dress, softest perfume, and lightly applied makeup.

Voices coming from the study drew her attention. Quietly slipping across the foyer, she peered through the slightly opened door. Her eyes fell on Trent arguing with a beautiful, tall, slender woman with coal black hair glaring at him.

"I'm sorry Milly, I gave you my answer weeks ago." He growled. "I haven't changed my mind, nor will I."

"You don't have a choice! Your father promised my family you'd marry me before he died." Milly whined.

Before he could move, she wound her arms around his neck and kissed him fiercely.

Shoving her away, he wiped his mouth with the back of his hand. "The answer is still no! Nothing will change how I feel. I don't love you and I never will! I refuse to marry someone because of a promise made by a dead man, even if he was my father."

Abby hurried into the dining room unwilling to hear more. As she took her first sip of the steaming hot coffee, Trent entered the room and sat down.

Even though he was furious, he didn't miss the soft fragrance of her perfume mixed with the enticing aroma of the breakfast food and coffee.

Tension filled the air while she slowly ate feeling guilty for eavesdropping.

"Her name is Milly Boudreau." He said startling her. "She fancies herself proper wife material for me."

"I wasn't asking. That's your personal business and none of mine." She avoided his gaze.

"Good. I'll leave it at that." He grunted in no mood for a discussion.

When the silence became uncomfortable, she spoke up, "Mr. Winthrop?"

"Please call me Trent. After all we just spent the night together." He teased.

"Okay... Trent, may I have permission to look through my grandfather's room again?" She asked hopefully.

"No. There's nothing in that room that concerns you." He shook his head stubbornly.

"Those letters concerned me. How do you know there aren't other things he wanted me to find there?" She asked. "I want to know where he came from, how he grew up, who my grandmother was and why my father left the island."

"You won't have time today. I'm taking you to the mainland. There is someone on the mainland you should meet. She'll have the answers to all your questions." He told her.

With mixed emotions she slumped into the chair. Trent would never allow her to search on her own.

"You should pack an overnight bag and bring a heavy coat." He instructed her.

Excitement filled her while she packed. Who was this person? When she entered the foyer, Trent was waiting patiently.

Chapter Six

Trent led her to the dock and helped her onto the boat awaiting their arrival. When she saw Millie Boudreau sitting near the bow, she moved toward the stern, but Miss Boudreau quickly blocked her way.

"So, you're Abby O'Malley. I'm Milly Boudreau." The woman introduced herself smugly.

"I'm pleased to meet you Miss Boudreau." Abby instantly knew the woman was a wolf in sheep's clothing.

"Call me Milly, all my friends do. So, how do you like our little island?" She asked arrogantly.

"I'm pleased with the beauty of my grandfather's estate." Abby smiled resisting the urge to slap the sneer off the woman's face. "The mansion is outstandingly beautiful and what I've seen of the island is breathtaking. I'll be quite happy living on my island."

Milly's eyes narrowed as she sputtered. "My mistake, I was under the impression that you wouldn't want your inheritance."

"The thought crossed my mind when I first learned of my grandfather's will. However, since my arrival I've had a change of heart." Abby replied.

Milly's eyes flashed hot with anger and Abby could swear she saw steam come out of her ears. The woman had no idea who she was trifling with. After the death of her parents, Abby learned quickly how to be tough in the face of adversity early on.

"It seems I've made another mistake. No one informed me you had decided to stay. You should know it's not all fun and games on that island." Milly warned her with a snarky smile.

"I may be young, but I know that nothing in life is easy Miss Boudreau." Abby responded. "I assure you nothing or no one will stop me from living my life on my island."

Milly reminded her of the spoiled rich kids who constantly bullied her.

Milly huffed off to the bow of the boat and sat sulking that Abby wasn't leaving as she'd hoped.

Trent stood with the captain as he guided the boat out of the shallow water into the open sea. He couldn't help but shamefully eavesdrop on the two women's conversation.

Abby impressed him in how she expertly turned the tables on Milly. Obviously, there was more to Miss Abby than he realized with a grin on his lips.

From that moment on, the trip turned into quite a show for Abby. She watched Milly make her intentions toward Trent known at every opportunity.

Occasionally she had to bite her cheek to keep from laughing out loud at the woman's pathetic attempts to keep his attention on her. Thankfully, she was spared hearing the woman's efforts to seduce someone who clearly had no interest in her.

Two hours later, in an attempt to warm herself, Abby crossed her arms, but the frigid wind coming off the water chilled her through the heavy coat she wore.

Ever watchful, Trent noticed her trying to warm herself. He grabbed a warm blanket and a thermos of hot coffee to give to her.

Milly had other ideas. She latched onto his arm as he passed by and tried to pull him into the seat next to her. The look he shot her could have frozen a live volcano. She immediately released his arm and sat down with a huff.

Abby quickly looked away to hide the smile that appeared on her lips.

Trent wrapped the blanket around her and poured a cup of hot coffee for her.

The heat from the cup warmed her frozen hands, then the hot beverage spread warmth to her insides.

Shivering she thanked him. Then he surprised her by gathering her into his arms allowing the warmth of his body to permeate hers.

Snuggling closer to his heat, she cast a discrete glance at Milly. The look on the woman's face almost made her laugh out loud.

"You shouldn't leave your guest unattended Trent." She pointed out enjoying his predicament.

"There is an old proverb, Miss Abby, beauty is in the eye of the beholder." He retorted. "Sometimes an inner darkness spoils the beauty on the outside."

Abby knew exactly what he was saying. Her second encounter with him put her off immediately, but now? She wondered.

Trent stayed by Abby's side asking about her life in America. Wary of his sudden interest, she wondered if she could trust him.

What about Milly? The poor woman sulked in the cold all alone. Was Trent using her to get rid of the woman who desperately inserted herself into his life?

Whatever his intentions, she felt unsettled since he was almost unreadable. It was apparent that she would have to be on her guard around this wonderful, infuriating, and gorgeous man.

Trent released her when the boat entered the marina. She immediately missed his warmth as the cold air blasted through the open blanket when he stood.

After he helped secure the boat to the dock, he disembarked and waited for the two women to follow. Abby allowed Milly to go ahead of her to ease the disgruntled woman's feelings.

Trent offered his hand to help her but in her anger, she refused his help and nearly fell into the water. Thanks to his quick actions, he averted the accident.

Abby had to give the woman credit, Milly's plan was well executed, unfortunately it wasn't well received. Trent made sure she was steady on her feet, then immediately turned his attention to Abby.

He grasped her around her tiny waist as she grasped his shoulders in surprise. When her feet touched the dock, he held her a bit longer than necessary. Heat suffused her cheeks as she smiled looking into his chocolate eyes.

Everyone on the dock heard Milly fly into a fit of rage. The scene she created wouldn't soon be forgotten.

Trent, however, found it amusing to embarrass Abby even though it was difficult to keep his wits about him. Miss O'Malley's presence proved to be sweet torture as he desperately tried to keep his heart in check. The moment he looked into her emerald, green eyes, he knew his heart was in danger of being stolen.

Trent led her to the parking area where a limo waited for their arrival. When they were settled inside, the driver pulled onto the road.

Memories of the day of her parent's funeral flooded her mind before she could stop them. Tears gathered in her eyes as she relived every detail.

Eight years old was too young to be alone in the world, yet that's what happened to her. Oh, she knew younger children suffered the agony of being orphans and she felt for them too.

Abby closed her eyes and visualized that awful day. She found herself walking down the long aisle toward the two caskets draped with beautiful, fragrant flowers. Two enlarged portraits of her parents positioned on each side of the caskets that contained everything she held dear.

Trent's gentle touch on her arm brought her back to the present. When she opened her eyes, tears escaped trickling down her cheeks. Quickly wiping them away, she managed to smile up at him.

"Are you well Miss Abby?' His concern touched her.

"Yes, I was reliving a bad memory. It's really nothing." She stammered.

Sensing she was unwilling to say more, he let it go. With a concerned smile he gently wiped away another stray tear from her cheek. Abby sniffed as he put his arm around her pulling her into his side.

Confused by his sudden attitude change, she snuggled closer accepting the comfort he offered.

Chapter Seven

Almost an hour later, the limo parked in front of a quaint little cottage. Trent helped her from the car then turned to get their luggage.

Abby inhaled the fresh air scented with fall flowers carried on the cool evening breeze kissing her cheeks. She relaxed to the sounds of crickets chirping and the rustle of the fallen leaves.

Trent took her arm and guided her to the front door and knocked while she became lost in her surroundings.

Presently, the door opened to reveal a tiny old woman. A toothless smile split her weather worn face when she looked up at Trent. "Master Trent! Come in, come in!"

Her gaze fell on Abby when Trent drew her forward. The old woman's eyes held a hint of recognition.

"Grandmother Abigail, I'd like to introduce you to Miss Abby O'Malley." Trent said with a smile.

Shock transformed the old woman's face as she looked up at Trent. "Did you say Abby O'Malley?"

"Yes, Grandmother Abigail. Abby is your granddaughter." Trent replied waiting for Abby's reaction.

Surprise and confusion turned to anger when she realized what he had said. *"How dare he keep her in the dark about her grandmother!"*

"My grandmother? Why didn't you tell me sooner?" She asked as her eyes flashed with fury.

Tears fell freely from her grandmother's eyes as she asked, "Are you Jacob's daughter? Is he coming to visit too?"

"Yes ma'am, Jacob was my father." Abby answered softly as her throat swelled. "My parents won't be joining us."

"Why not?" Her grandmother asked in confusion.

Trent stepped in to break the news for Abby. "Jacob and his wife were killed in a house fire."

Grandmother Abigail took hold of Abby's arm to draw her into the large living room and said. "Tell me everything child."

Abby explained what happened to her parents and her grandmother insisted she tell her about her life. Abby told her the important parts of her existence, leaving the dark lonely days she had endured while in the foster care system.

"If I had known, I could have done something." Abigail patted her hand. "Now that you're here, we'll take good care of you."

Trent nodded his understanding when Grandmother Abigail's eyes caught his. "May we stay the night?"

"Master Trent, you know you're always welcome to stay. Now that my granddaughter is here it's my pleasure to welcome you into my home anytime you wish to visit." She scowled at him.

"I also believe it's time for you to return home. You've been away too long. It will also give you and Miss Abby time to get acquainted with one another. I know Miss Abby has a million questions that only you can answer." He smiled affectionately at her.

"Yes, I agree. Now that my granddaughter has found me, I want to know everything about her." She smiled with tears in her eyes.

It was settled, the next morning the three of them and her nurse Steven, would travel back to the island together.

Trent left them to talk while he carried their luggage upstairs. Soon after he sat down in the living room, Grandmother Abigail retired for the evening.

Trent led Abby to the room she would occupy for the night. Abby shoved him inside when he opened her door and slammed it behind her.

"Why didn't you tell me my grandmother was alive?" She hissed.

"Pardon me, but I believe that's what I just did." He chuckled while twin daggers of anger shot from her eyes.

"It would've been nice to have some warning!" She exclaimed. "You had no right to spring something so important on either of us."

"I wasn't keeping her a secret. You expressed a desire to know about your family, so I obliged." He shrugged. "I thought you'd be happy, but apparently I was wrong."

"Give me a break! You knew I longed to have a relative. I'm upset because you didn't tell me before introducing us." She crossed her arms angrily. "I don't like surprises when it's this important!"

He moved closer and said, "Sorry, next time I'll tell you and keep you in suspense for a few days."

"You're the most..." She began when Trent grabbed her capturing her mouth in a fiery kiss.

At first she struggled, but as his kiss deepened, new feelings sparked to life threatening to drown her.

Trent stopped with a look of something she didn't understand in his eyes.

"Goodnight, Miss O'Malley." He sidestepped her leaving her dazed and confused.

After the door closed, she struggled to calm the storm of emotions bombarding her. Unconsciously dressing for bed, she wondered if it had been a dream. Of course, it wasn't. The lingering feeling of his lips on hers was too real. Eventually, she fell asleep dreaming of him.

TRENT FLOPPED ONTO the bed after stripping down to his briefs. Miss O'Malley had no idea how much the fire in her eyes affected him. What had the little vixen done to him? His last thought before drifting into a fitful sleep was, *"I'm in deep trouble."*

Chapter Eight

Abby sat up with her heart racing as someone knocked on her bedroom door. She slipped out of bed and asked who was on the other side.

"It's your grandmother, child." The old woman answered.

Abby opened the door to allow her inside. From the puffiness around her red rimmed eyes, she knew her grandmother had not slept well.

"What's wrong Grandmother?" Abby's worry laced her voice.

"I... Would you allow me to give you a hug?" She wrung her wrinkled hand as tears spilled from her tired eyes.

Abby threw her arms around her grandmother. The joy of finding each other filled a deep empty hole in both of their hearts and they thanked God while crying tears of happiness.

TRENT STEPPED FROM his room just as Grandmother Abigail went into Abby's room. The door didn't completely close enticing him to shamelessly listen to their short conversation.

He smiled to himself pleased to have completed phase one of his plans. However, phase two had already proven to be elusive, but he would give it his all. Unwilling to disturb them, he slipped downstairs to make coffee.

He just sat with his first cup when Abby came in and poured her own cup and sat across from him. From her stiff posture and the angry furrow of her brows, oh yeah, she was still put out with him. Was she angry over his kisses as well?

Abby remained silent in an emotional whirlwind. The events over the last few weeks seemed to crash over her all at once. Now she had to wonder if the man sitting across from her actually liked her or was he using her to rid himself of a leech. The bigger question was, is he playing her to get her inheritance?

Right now, the only thing he had going for him was he'd brought her grandmother into her life.

"Good morning." He greeted her casually.

She replied avoiding eye contact, "Good morning."

With the help of her nurse, Steven, Grandmother ambled into the room looking a good twenty years younger. It had been ages since Trent had seen such a carefree smile on her weathered face.

For years, he had worried about her, now it seemed as though Abby's presence breathed life into the only other woman besides Gina who treated him like a son.

Five years into his employment with Mr. O'Malley, Grandmother Abigail left the island. All he knew about the situation was she resented her husband for driving away their only child. Everyone speculated she couldn't live with what he had done. After she left, Mr. O'Malley became a bitter, lonely old man.

Trent visited her weekly to give her the stipend Mr. O'Malley afforded her. With every visit, her life seemed to fade a little more as depression settled into her heart. It was hard to watch her slowly lose her will to live.

The minute he found out about Abby he made plans to bring them together. The one thing he hadn't foreseen was the effect the young innocent woman would have on him.

Time quickly slipped away as they prepared to leave. The driver loaded a mountain of luggage while Trent and Steven helped Grandmother Abigail into the limo.

Abby slipped in from the other side before Trent could offer his hand. Protecting her heart was difficult where he was concerned. She resolved to steer clear of the ruggedly handsome man.

Trent sat across from her wondering if he had pushed her too far the night before. He had an uneasy feeling he did and knew he couldn't let himself be alone with her again.

Now with Grandmother there, it should be easy to do. Hopefully, she would keep Abby occupied leaving him free to do his job and work on phase two of his plan.

Grandmother Abigail shook his arm and asked, "Master Trent? Are you listening to me? I want to know if you have enough blankets for me. You know how much the ocean air affects me."

"Yes, ma'am. Everything is prepared exactly as you like it." Trent answered fondly. "Steven will stay below deck with you to ensure your comfort."

Abby quietly observed the tenderness he used while caring for her grandmother. Intuition told her he would never do anything to hurt her, including using her granddaughter to drive someone else away and more importantly try to rob her of her inheritance.

By the time they reached the ship, all the excitement took its toll upon her grandmother. Trent and Steven settled her below deck before they got underway.

Abby sat at the stern of the ship as a cold chill raced down her spine. Storm clouds slowly approached from the direction they were heading. Realistically, the spirit that haunted her during stormy nights wouldn't show up on the ship with so many witnesses.

She watched Trent speaking with the captain with mixed emotions. With her limited experience where men were concerned she felt vulnerable. She avoided dealing with men out of fear.

Like most girls she dreamed of getting married someday, however getting to that point was a complete mystery to her.

Being tossed from home to home in the foster care system, dating was impossible, much less making friends. School was a nightmare since her clothes were hand me downs or thrift store specials. What made things worse was she learned early on that she was nothing but a paycheck to most of those tasked with caring for her.

Trent watched the approaching storm and decided to keep Abby company in case she needed him. At least that's what he told himself while strolling to the stern where she sat.

The wind began to pick up as he sat down next to her. He draped a blanket over her as lightening flashed and the first clap of thunder made her jump.

"It's okay Miss Abby." He said as the first of many raindrops began to fall.

"Thank you." She snuggled into his arms trembling.

With each flash of lightening, she stiffened in anticipation of the clap of thunder that followed. Never in her life was she so grateful for someone to hold her. Usually, she had to weather the storms by herself. In those times the apparition tormented her from the shadows of whatever room she was in.

Finally, the storm passed leaving Abby exhausted. Trent was thankful Steven cared for her grandmother so he could be there for Abby.

His gaze found her green eyes full of gratefulness, yet this time she didn't seem to be quite so fearful. He wondered why.

The pull of her innocent eyes made him realize the fire she ignited in him wouldn't be easily quenched.

In another time or place, he would sweep her off her feet and marry her. How cruel life was to bring such a beautiful woman into his life, yet circumstances kept her just out of his reach. Yes, he was foolish for feeling this way after only meeting her four days ago.

"Thank you for staying with me." She smiled as heat flooded her cheeks.

"It was my pleasure." He said calmly.

Abby's heart fought confusing feelings she'd never felt before. The mixed signals Trent sent out baffled her to the point where she vowed to keep her distance for her own self-preservation. At least until she could figure him out.

Trent remained silent by her side, yet she could feel his gaze on her. With a smile she turned to look at him hoping her true feelings weren't showing.

The smile she turned on him stole his breath. It took every ounce of strength to keep his hands to himself. If he were honest, he knew he was already in love with her.

Chapter Nine

Trent left her to check on Grandmother Abigail to put some distance between them.

Abby watched his retreating back wondering what she did wrong. Deep down she wished she were more experienced in dealing with men.

Her mind traveled back in time to her days in the foster care system. Traumatized by her parents death, she had become quiet and withdrawn. Those two traits made her a perfect candidate for bullying at school. She counted herself blessed the foster parents weren't perverts like some she had heard of.

On the one-year anniversary of her parents demise, he showed up. For one moment, she was back in the bedroom listening to the storm outside. Already afraid of the lightening, when the face appeared in the shadow of the room she froze in terror.

Unable to move, a cold sweat formed over her body as he hovered just inside the shadows. His hideously disfigured face and dark eyes burned into her brain. Another flash of lightening flooded the room with light, and he disappeared.

That was the beginning of his torment of appearing every time it stormed. Walter hired a psychologist to help her manage her fear, but it didn't help. In the end, she suffered in silence letting the adults think she had conquered her fear.

When Harold informed her of her grandfather's death she thought it strange he passed away on the same night her parents did.

Lost in her memories, she didn't hear Trent return. When he gently touched her shoulder, she squeaked in fear.

"I'm sorry for startling you. Are you well?" He asked with concern in his eyes.

Her frustration in being unable to read him grew. The man was a mystery that was impossible to solve.

He brushed her hair behind her ear and wiped the stray tear slipping down her cheek.

"I'm fine. I was just thinking." She managed to answer.

"Why don't you go below and see your grandmother. I'm sure she'd love the company." He suggested.

Quickly mopping her face on her sleeve, she straightened her hair. When she stood to leave her foot became entangled in a rope that fell during the storm.

Once again, Trent came to her aid by catching her before she fell. After she was steady on her feet, he led her to the stairs that went below deck. When she descended, he walked away brooding.

"There's my lovely granddaughter!" Her grandmother smiled.

"Are you feeling better grandmother?" Abby asked with a forced smile.

"What's wrong child?" She asked sensing her turmoil.

"Nothing really. I was just remembering some things from the past." Abby answered as a lone tear slipped down her cheek.

"Tell me about them. What kind of memory would make you sad." She patted the seat next to her.

Before Abby knew it, she'd told her grandmother almost everything, However, she left out the ghost haunting her.

"How I wish I could've been there for you child, but thanks to Trent I'm here now." She squeezed Abby's hand.

Abby melted into her grandmother's embrace finally letting the losses she suffered go. She realized Grandmother Abigail comforted her in a way no one else could.

Trent stood near enough to hear most of the conversation. He'd already been informed of some of her circumstances, but listening to what she revealed to her grandmother broke his heart. How had she survived losing her parents and being bullied everywhere she went. Abby deserved better and he vowed to end her suffering.

In that moment he regretted one of the promises he made to her grandfather.

When the boat pulled up to the boat slip on the island, he noticed another boat tied to the dock. Swearing under his breath, he knew Milly had returned with company.

While Abby helped Steven get her grandmother settled in the room she shared with her grandfather, Trent asked Lance to have some of the ranch hands help unload the luggage. Slowly and reluctantly, he went to the study where Milly and her brothers waited.

Lord, God in Heaven, how he wished she would give up and leave him alone. Unfortunately, Milly Boudreau would die before giving up on something she set her sights on.

ABBY CHANGED FROM HER damp clothes into clean ones. Hunger drove her to go downstairs in search of a snack before dinner.

When she closed her door, loud voices could be heard downstairs. Abby slipped to the banister and hid in the shadow of the hall. Trent and Milly were arguing while two men stood close by. It was obvious they were related to Milly.

"Your father promised before he died, Trent!" She shrieked. "You have to honor his word!"

"I told you; I refuse to marry someone I don't love Milly! That's my final word on it!" He growled in anger.

"Since you won't listen to reason, my brothers will have to convince you!" She put her fisted hands on her hips.

"They can try, but my mind is made up and nothing will change it." His voice held a menacing tone.

"You should really think about what you're saying, darling." She hissed. "Miss Abby or her grandmother could meet with an unfortunate accident."

Trent got into her face and snarled, "Don't ever threaten Grandmother Abigail or Miss Abby again, Milly. That would be the worst mistake you'll ever make. A very dangerous mistake. Do I make myself clear?"

Milly's face grew red with rage as she slapped Trent hard enough to leave a perfect handprint on his cheek.

She moved to do it again, but Trent caught her hand, and her brothers jumped him. One managed to hold him while the other punched his midsection.

Trent headbutted the man holding him with the back of his head freeing himself. The fight was over when the other man dropped unconscious from an uppercut.

Milly stood to the side with her mouth hanging open when Trent turned toward her. Her eyes widened with fear when she realized she'd pushed him too far.

"Miss Boudreau, you've worn out your welcome, take your brothers and get off this island. Now!" Trent barked scaring her into action. "Oh, and don't come back!"

Abby watched the defeated family hurry out the door. She glance back at Trent noticing his bloody lip and nose. Hurrying to her room, she grabbed a damp cool cloth and ran downstairs to help him.

She found him in the study pouring himself a drink.

"What do you want?" He growled angrily.

Abby crossed the room and gently dabbed the cloth on his bleeding lip.

"You should learn to duck." She teased.

"I take it you saw what happened." He winced.

"Yeah, couldn't have missed it, although I was quite impressed with the way you handled the situation." She said with a twinkle in her eyes.

When she checked the cloth, his lip was still bleeding steadily so she replaced it.

"You might need a stitch or two, that's a pretty bad cut." She said with concern furrowing her brows.

"I'm a big boy and haven't needed a mother in a long time." He snapped taking the cloth from her.

"That's no way to treat someone who's trying to help." She scowled at him. "Maybe I should let you take care of yourself."

"Sorry." He apologized contritely.

"Would you like some ice for your eye?" She asked sympathetically.

"If you don't mind." He replied squashing the feelings rising in his chest.

When Abby left the room, he sat on the sofa and leaned his head back with his eyes closed.

"This is a fine mess you've left for me dad. O'Malley is no better with the promises he forced me to make."

Abby returned with a towel and a small baggie of ice. He winced when she placed it over his eye and informed him dinner would be ready in a few minutes leaving him to make himself presentable.

Chapter Ten

Steven Wilson, R.N., escorted Grandmother Abigail into the dining room as Abby followed close behind. She liked Steven the minute she met him. Not only was he committed to his job, but he was easy on the eyes.

Trent arrived as Steven seated her grandmother. After he seated Abby, he sat down aware of Grandmother Abigail's scrutiny.

"Master Trent? What on earth happened to your face?" The old woman exclaimed.

"The Boudreau's paid me a visit." He muttered.

"So that parasite is still after you?" She asked with disgust.

"Yes, Ma'am." He replied still angry.

"Did you kick their backsides?" She asked with a twinkle in her eyes.

Abby couldn't resist entering the conversation. "I saw the whole thing. Trent handled the situation pretty well I think. The only advice I could give him is he should learn to duck."

Her grandmother chuckled so hard she choked herself. Steven immediately assisted her without a word.

Trent shot her a surly look, but when his eyes locked with hers, the anger turned to want making everything worse.

Abby quickly turned to the old woman. "Grandmother, would you join me for tea in the gazebo for a little while?"

"Why yes, child. I'd love to sit in the fresh air for a time." The old woman's smile warmed her heart.

Trent excused himself to catch up with the paperwork left for him, but truth be told, he needed to put a lot of space between him and Abby.

Steven escorted Grandmother to the gazebo. Barbara had already laid out the tea for them to enjoy.

They sat in companionable silence sipping their tea while listening to the harmonic sounds of nature.

Fluffy white clouds drifted lazily across the darkening sky as the sun slowly sank seemingly into the ocean. Animals scurried to and fro as the scent of fresh cut hay on the cool breeze wrapped them in a cocoon of peace.

"Grandmother, would you tell me about grandfather?" Abby asked breaking the calm silence.

"Surely. Jacob was a difficult man who never accepted the word no for an answer." She smiled. "When I met him he swept me off my feet. Before I knew it we were married, and I had little Jake.

Abby listened as tears slipped from her grandmother's eyes.

"This island has been passed down from one generation to the next for over a hundred years. Although when Miles O'Malley died, none of your ancestors lived here until your grandfather inherited it. Master Trent arrive six months after Jacob took possession of the island.

Not long after, the mysteries of the island became an obsession with Jacob. He began neglecting his obligations to his family. Your father saw what it did to him when he brought your mother to meet us for the first time.

Your grandfather didn't approve of her, yet he wouldn't give a reason why. Whatever it was he took it to his grave."

Steven arrived to get Grandmother as Abby notice the tiredness in her eyes.

After kissing her goodnight, Abby closed her eyes soaking in a peace she thought was lost to her.

The feeling of eyes on her shook her from the blissful place she had gone to. As the light faded and shadows grew long, she picked up the tray to take inside.

"Snap!"

Whirling around to what made the noise, she squinted to see if someone was hiding close by. Fear quickly flooded her system traveling from her toes to the top of her head.

She move to take the tray to the mansion, and something caught her eye. A scream stuck in her throat when she saw him hiding in the shadows.

The minute she turned to run, she rammed into Trent spilling the tray. One look at the terror in her eyes, he knew something had frightened her.

"Woah! What's wrong Abby?" He asked scanning the area for danger.

"I heard a noise and there was a face in the shadows of the barn watching me." She managed to say with a trembling voice.

"Let's get you inside. Then I'll have Lance look around." He said as he helped pick up the tea service.

He tried to ignore the huge knot that formed in his stomach. With a protective arm around her, he continued to scan the area, but nothing was moving. In fact, the animals had gone unusually silent.

Clearly whatever had disturbed the area had scared Abby. The need to protect her hit him squarely in the chest. He hoped she was imagining things from any stories she'd heard about the island and her family.

Lance stepped out of the bunkhouse on his way to the cottage where his wife had dinner waiting for him. When he saw Trent and Abby together, he couldn't help but think they were perfect for each other.

"Lance!" Trent called when he saw him.

"What can I do for you Trent?" He called walking toward them.

"Something scared Abby. Gather the men and find out what's prowling around the area." He ordered.

"Sure thing." Lance agreed. "Can you tell me what it looks like?"

"All I saw was a man in the shadow of the barn watching me." She managed to tell him.

"Don't worry, Miss O'Malley. We'll find him." Lance assured her turning to leave. As he walked away worry washed over him. He hoped the legends of the island hadn't come back to haunt them again. The last time, seven years ago, the little child it took had never been found.

Chapter Eleven

Trent led her into the study and seated her on the sofa while he poured her a drink.

"Here." He insisted. "Drink this, it will calm you down."

"But I don't..." She said as he shoved the glass in her hand.

"Drink it!" He ordered with a look that she better comply.

Rather than fight him, she took a drink feeling the warmth spread through her body.

"Tell me exactly what you saw Miss Abby." He demanded after she emptied the glass.

"I saw the outline of a man standing in the shadow of the barn." She told him as he refilled her glass.

"Have you ever seen the man before?" He asked.

"Yes... I mean no." She replied feeling the effects of the alcohol.

"What do you mean? Either you saw him, or you didn't." Trent's brows furrowed in confusion.

"One year to the day after my parents died, another thunderstorm blew through where I lived. That night he appeared in the window of the foster home I was in at midnight." She slurred her words. "No matter where I was, when it stormed, he would appear in the window. I hoped he hadn't followed me here."

Trent pushed the urge to hold her in his arms again. One moment before his resolve crumbled, Lance knocked on the door.

"Trent, you need to see this." He looked at Abby with fear in his eyes.

"Miss Abby, I'll be right back." Trent moved to go with Lance.

Abby took another sip of the drink not caring what Lance had found. Her mind felt numb, and her body was following close behind.

TRENT FOLLOWED LANCE wondering what he had found while his stomach twisted with worry. What if the one thing that could destroy Abby O'Malley had returned to the island? The thought of losing her hit him hard in the chest. No, he couldn't allow himself to believe it.

Lance stopped to show him a pair of fresh boot prints in the soft ground by the barn. Trent followed the tracks with his eyes to find they let toward the forest.

Trent's face turned stony as his jaw twitched.

"Do you think he's returned?" Lance asked.

"Don't be absurd Lance, there's no way he can come back. He's dead." Trent insisted.

"We never found his body, maybe..." Lance closed his mouth.

"After this long, with no sign of a body, no sightings, nothing. He's dead and that's the last I want to hear of it." Trent's icy stare made Lance take a step back. "Tomorrow, I'll follow the tracks and find out where they lead."

"You ain't going alone, I'll come with you." Lance insisted. "It's too dangerous to go into the forest alone."

"Be ready after breakfast, right now I need to get some answers from Abby." He said turning to go back to the mansion. "Goodnight."

"I'll put a couple of men on watch overnight. I'll see you in the morning," Lance said determined to keep watch over Abby.

Something fishy was going on and he wouldn't let anything happen to the young woman. She reminded him of his little Grace. Even after all these years, the memory of his baby girl still held enough power to break his heart all over again.

Neither he nor Gina had any idea their child would be born with Tay-Sachs disease. It was hard to watch their baby's life gradually deteriorate until she died at five years old.

The similarity of Abby to little Grace was uncanny. Their eyes were the same shade of green. Grace's hair was a shade lighter than Abby's. In his mind's eye, his little Gracie would have grown to look like Abby. The young woman may not be his child, but as a father, he resolved to protect her as if she were his own.

ABBY LEANED BACK WITH her eyes closed feeling relaxed and sleepy. Even in her state of drunkenness, memories better left in the past bombarded her mind.

Trent stopped to observe her before gently touching her shoulder. "Miss Abby?"

"Mm?" She murmured.

"Can you tell me more about this man?" He asked knowing he most likely wouldn't get any more answers.

"It doesn't matter, it's all in my head anyways." She muttered. "At least that's what the psychiatrists all told me. Let's talk about something more pleasant."

With a sigh, he knew there would be nothing more from her tonight. Disappointed, he picked her up and carried her to her room.

He gently sat her on the bed, realizing she couldn't sleep in her wet tea-stained clothes. Barbara had already retired to her cottage, Gina was at home with Lance, and Grandmother Abigail couldn't help if she wanted to.

Quickly undressing her he finally whipped the covers back and started to lay her down when she kissed him. To his surprise, she whispered in his ear.

With every ounce of will power he had, he put her in the bed and covered her. Satisfied she was okay; he quickly left the room.

He went downstairs to lock everything up thinking about his promise to her grandfather. He'd never break a promise to anyone. If his suspicions were right he may have to.

Nevertheless, in the morning he and Lance would set out to find the owner of the boot prints. Hopefully, they would have the answer to the mystery that had plagued not only him for seven years, but also the O'Malley family for over a hundred years.

SUNLIGHT SLOWLY CRAWLED across the bed into Abby's eyes burying a spike in her head. Unable to stay in bed like she wanted to, she took her time dressing for the day. Eventually, she made it downstairs just after everyone sat down for breakfast.

"There you are child, are you well?" Grandmother asked noting the dark circles under her eyes.

"I will be after a cup of coffee." She said shooting a loathing look at Trent. "It must've been something I drank last night."

"Well, let's get some coffee in you. I'm sure it will cure what ails you." Grandmother didn't miss the look.

"I have things to do, if you'll excuse me." Trent dropped his napkin onto his plate.

"What's so important that you can't finish your breakfast, Master Trent?" Grandmother asked with a disapproving look.

"I'm going to hunt down something in the forest." He answered honestly.

"What's going on?" Abby asked when her grandmother stiffened.

"I'm hunting the animal that scared you last night." He said. He wasn't lying about the man being an animal if his suspicions were accurate.

"Master Trent, please be careful. You know what dangers lurk in that forest." Grandmother reminded him with worry and fear marring her weathered face.

"Lance and three of the best ranch hands are going with me." He promised. "We'll be careful."

Lance arrived as he moved toward the door. "We're ready when you are."

The two men left the room to join the men waiting with their horses. Each man was well armed and had chosen their best horses to ride.

Lance kept his thoughts to himself, but he couldn't help but be truly worried about the boot prints and their owner. If it was who he suspected, he feared for Abby's safety and Grandmother Abigail's peace of mind.

Trent could feel the anxiety rolling off of Lance in waves. "He's dead."

"Until I see his body, I'll always have doubts." Lance replied. "If he isn't Miss Abby's life is in danger, and I fear Grandmother Abigail won't handle things well if anything happens to her."

"I told you he's dead! Let it go!" Trent growled. "It's most likely one of the natives who lost his way. Besides after this long, he'd be nothing but old bleached out bones."

"If it were a native, we could all be in danger. What Miss Abby's ancestor's did to them is still a sore spot even after one hundred years." Lance reminded him. "Should they find out Abby is the sole heir to the O'Malley legacy, well I don't have to tell you what could happen. We both know if you hadn't convinced them you were taking over the island, O'Malley would've suffered their wrath."

"Why would they know about her unless someone tells them? Now that O'Malley's gone, they believe I own the island. That's the way it has to be. Right now, we need to focus on the owner of those tracks." Trent said.

"I just hope we don't find what I fear we will." Lance grumbled.

"He's DEAD!" Trent barked at him.

ABBY'S HEADACHE EASED some, but her body was sluggish from the hangover Trent caused. Her grandmother, bless her heart couldn't stop mothering her. She truly didn't mind, but it was beginning to annoy her a little bit.

The minute she noticed the fatigue in her grandmother's eyes, she suggested Steven take her upstairs for a little nap. To say her grandmother was stubborn was an understatement. After an argument with Steven, she finally relented. Abby gave him a grateful smile as he escorted her from the room.

Silence filled the study, and she sank blissfully into the soft overstuffed sofa. Unfortunately, the peace ended when the study door flew open and the one person she didn't want to deal with sashayed uninvited into the room as if she owned the place. Milly Boudreau stood at the end of the sofa glaring at her.

"Great, just what I need to top off my day. Some bimbo gold-digger invading my space." She sighed as she sat up.

"May I help you Miss Boudreau?" Abby asked barely controlling her temper.

Milly plopped into the other chair and snarled. "I see you're making yourself right at home."

"Why not? I happen to own it." She calmly retorted.

"Not for long. Do you think Trent is attracted to you? I happen to know he's planning to take everything you own, then he's going to marry me. I shall have this entire island for my own." Milly scoffed.

"Why should I believe a gold-digger like you? I witnessed your altercations with Trent. I know he doesn't love you, so the question is, why are you trying to force yourself into a loveless marriage?" Abby asked with a raised brow. "You have to be desperate, or stupid. On the other hand, is it possible you have nothing between your ears but hot air?"

That comment pushed Milly over the edge. The woman jumped to her feet and began screaming in white hot fury. "You think you know everything don't you! Well Miss Smarty-pants, go ahead and fall for him, let him bed you, but you'll never have him! Before his father died he made a promise to my family Trent would marry me! Trent can't weasel out of it!" She stopped to take a breath. "He'll get you to hand over every dime of your inheritance, then he'll toss you aside! You'll leave here brokenhearted and alone, pining away for a man who took you for everything you own!"

With strength she didn't know she had, Abby remained calm, even though Milly's words cut deep into her heart.

"Miss Boudreau, this is my home, on my island. I'll thank you to leave and never return. However, should you happen to venture back, you will be met with, shall we say, a more fitting greeting for someone of your obvious breeding. Like a bullet between those over made-up eyes."

Abby stopped to let that sink in then continued. "Furthermore, as far as I'm concerned, Miss Boudreau, you may have Mr. Winthrop with my blessing. There is absolutely nothing between us, and as for my inheritance, that is none of your concern. You should know that nothing will entice me to sell what my grandfather gave me. It's all I have left of my family and it's worth more to me than all the gold in the world. Nobody, Mr. Winthrop, you, or anyone else will ever take it away from me as long as I have breath in my body."

Milly face blanched as she tried to hide the fear shining in her wide eyes when she realized Abby meant every word she said.

"Good day, Miss Boudreau!" Abby said crossing her arms to keep from hitting the woman.

Milly left on shaky legs in shock because no one ever stood up to her, until now."

When Abby was sure she was alone, she sat down and buried her face in her hands while tears of frustration broke free. *Could Milly be right? Was*

Trent playing her? At that moment she wished she'd never heard of O'Malley Island.

Abby quickly wiped away her tears when someone knocked on the door. "Come in."

Steven's head appeared around the door ensuring she was alone. He entered the room with concern furrowing his brows.

"Miss Abby? Are you well?" He asked noting her red eyes. "I heard an awful commotion down here."

"I'll be fine, now that our uninvited guest is gone." She said with a weak smile. "Thank you for asking."

"No, Miss Abby, You are not okay. If you'd like to talk about it, I've got some mighty broad shoulders if you need one."

"That's sweet of you Steven, I appreciate it, but this is something I'll have to deal with on my own." She shook her head.

"Well, the offer stands, whenever you need a shoulder to cry on." He said unhappily. "If you need anything at all, just give a shout. I'll come running."

"I'm quite sure you'll hear me if I yell." She forced a smile.

When he closed the door behind him he made up his mind, *"That is one woman I'm definitely going to get to know. She's gorgeous."*

The quiet of the room now made Abby restless so she decided a long walk was in order. The gardens behind the mansion would ease her soul with the soft scents of the flowers.

When she strolled through the kitchen she noticed Barbara putting fresh rolls in the oven. Upon seeing Abby, she asked, "May I help you, Miss Abby?"

"May I have a cup of hot tea? If it isn't too much trouble." Abby replied.

It's no trouble." Barbara assured her noting the sadness in her eyes. "Are you well?"

"Nothing I can't handle." She shrugged.

"Does it have anything to do with Miss Boudreau?" Barbara asked.

"Would you be surprised if it was?" She asked missing the slight smile tug at the corners of the woman's mouth.

"No. She's been after Mr. Winthrop since they were in high school. Trent's father took a liking to her. I think she was the daughter he never had." Barbara said. "Trent was an only child after his mother died in childbirth. Mr. Winthrop blamed Trent for her death. He mistreated Trent most of his life. After graduating high school, Mr. O'Malley hired him. He is so smart, Mr. O'Malley made him estate manager in a year. His father wasn't through torturing him and promised the Boudreau family his son would marry Milly. Not too long afterward, despite Mr. O'Malley's warnings, he disappeared into the forest to find Trent while he was on the other side of the island. No one ever saw him again. Trent and the ranch hands searched for weeks with no sigh of him. Some say he's still out there waiting for who knows what."

Abby took her cup and made her escape unwilling to hear any more. Sadness hovered over her for Trent after finding how badly his life had gone. She could empathize with him since she endured the foster care system. Even as her heart went out to him, Milly's words, already haunting her, rang out clearly in her mind.

Chapter Twelve

Abby tried to relax with the hot cup of tea, but her mind kept rehashing Milly's harsh tirade. Then empathy for Trent's hardship growing up followed close behind.

Weary of the emotional turmoil her life had become, she leaned back in the comfy lounge chair and closed her eyes. Memories of her own hardships forced their way to the head of the bevy of her current ones. Oh, what she would give to have those memories fade into the nothingness of space.

More than once, she thanked God for protecting her from some of the more heinous abuses in those homes. She kept to herself and obeyed without question. Having developed the talent of hiding in plain sight became her saving grace.

Shoving those thoughts aside, her thoughts turned to the fact that the face in the shadows seemed to follow her wherever she went. The ghostly appearance during storms terrified her while staring at her from the shadows of her room.

The afternoon Harold informed her of her grandfather's will, hope chased away the doldrum of the life she'd made for herself. Six nights ago, she stepped onto the island dreaming of a better life. Now she wondered what she'd gotten herself into by coming to O'Malley island.

In all the bad memories flooding her mind, one bright spot was the only reason why she wouldn't leave. Grandmother Abigail. Although she'd just met her yesterday, their attachment was strong. At times, she would see her father looking at her through her grandmother's eyes. Her heart warmed realizing the kind gentle woman was her father's first love.

TRENT CALLED OFF THE search an hour after they lost the trail. The men were keenly aware of the danger they faced entering the dense forest.

Nearing the edge of the forest, two feral wolves attacked them from the top of the boulders lining the stream. Billy, the best shooter of the bunch, shot one of them. The other knocked Trent off his horse and buried its fangs in his shoulder when they hit the ground.

Lance tried to wrestle it off of him, but the animal sank its teeth into his arm. Trent grabbed the loose skin of the wolf's neck struggling to hold on while it continued its attack on him.

Charlie jumped behind the animal and slit its throat before Trent lost his grip. Lance's arm was serious, but Trent suffered from deep gaping scratches on his chest, but the bite the wolf had taken of his shoulder bled profusely.

Sam brought the first aid kit from Lance's pack and Billy went to work bandaging Trent up while Charlie took care of Lance. Billy finished with a grim face. The blood had already soaked the bandage on Trent's shoulder. He jumped on his horse while Sam and Charlie helped Trent into the saddle in front of Billy. The men spurred their horses through the tree line spraying water as they galloped across the stream.

ABBY HEARD THE HORSES when they galloped past the barn toward the back door of the mansion. The moment her eyes landed on Trent's bloody body; the color drained from her face. She ran ahead of them into the mansion to get Steven.

The minute she and Steven returned he immediately began working on Trent and barking orders.

"Miss Barbara, I need hot water and towels. Miss Abby get the big med kit from your grandmother's room." He noticed Lance's injury. "How's your arm?"

Lance's wife Gina told him she'd take care of it because Trent needed his full attention.

When Abby returned with the med kit, she stood back while Billy helped take care of Trent. Her eyes fell on Lance and the lovely woman cleaning his arm. The love she witnessed between them pierced her heart with longing. "What's with the long face Abby?" Trent whispered weakly.

"I'm worried about you and Lance." She said as Milly's words echoed through her mind.

"I'm sure Steven will take good care of us." He winced.

Steven worked quickly and efficiently with a frown, "Do you keep extra blood on hand for emergencies?"

When Abby didn't answer, Lance said, "In the medical refrigerator in the kitchen. I don't know if we have any of his type.

"What type is he?" Steven asked as his brows dipped even lower.

"I'm AB Negatives." Trent whispered.

"Go look Miss Abby, if there isn't any, we'll have to find someone here with the same type." He continued stitching the worst of the wounds.

Abby rushed to find the blood with little hope they had that type. It was one of the rarest and if they didn't have any, she would have to be the donor.

With a deep breath, she opened the door and found one pint and hoped it would be enough. Somehow she knew it wouldn't.

She handed the bottle to Steven and told him that was the only pint.

"We need to find someone with the same type because this won't be enough." He hooked it up to the rest of the I.V. fluids he pumped into him.

"Don't bother, that's my blood type. You can have all you need." Abby said cringing at the thought of needles.

"Okay, let's get him up to his room and be careful." Steven ordered as the men moved to pick him up. "If there's a comfortable chair for Abby to sit in, I'll get her hooked up to an I.V. and get the blood we'll need."

Soon after Steven had her hooked up to the I.V. and was checking Trent's vitals again. She wondered how much Trent was paying him, whatever it was she was sure it wasn't enough.

"Will he recover?" She couldn't help but ask.

"Between Billy's quick action and your blood, I believe so. If he doesn't get an infection he'll be fine." Steven assured her. "I'm going to take your grandmother down for dinner. I'll be back soon with some juice and dinner for you."

Abby could barely keep her eyes open. Between the I.V. draining her blood and the stressful day she experienced her strength waned more by the second. Still, she couldn't help but notice how pale Trent had become.

Despite her anger and the constant memory of Milly's words, she still liked him, God help her she liked the arrogant, handsome man. Since her conversation with Barbara, a strong empathy for the man formed in her heart.

When the men carried him upstairs, she noticed the familiar scars on his back. She cringed remembering how she received those same scars on her back. Yet there were scars no one else could see in her heart. There was no doubt Trent carried those as well.

Abby's eyes closed in a light sleep when she heard Trent move. She looked at him happy to see his color was a little better since Steven had given him the pint of emergency blood.

"You'll do anything for attention won't you?" She tease moving to stand up.

"The only attention I want is yours." He said weakly.

"Just don't make a habit of nearly getting yourself killed for it." She swayed on her feet.

"Miss Abby, you should sit back down." He said as she reached for the bed and passed out.

"Steven!" He yelled wishing he weren't tethered to the I.V. in his arm. "Help!"

After hearing the call for help Steven appeared with Gina helping Grandmother Abigail into the room. He set the food for Abby on the nightstand and asked Trent what happened to her. He rushed to pick her up and put her on the bed next to Trent.

She stood up and passed out after a few steps." Trent winced.

After checking to make sure her I.V. was intact, he was about to get some smelling salts to wake her when she opened her eyes.

"Why did you get up?" Steven asked frustrated by her stubbornness.

"I wanted to sit on the bed to talk to Trent." She answered sheepishly.

Well now you're going to stay put on that bed until I tell you otherwise." He growled.

Gina stood by the chair she seated Grandmother Abigail in. When she was sure Steven had everything under control she left the room.

Abby couldn't hide the concern in her eyes while watching Steven check to see if Trent pulled any stitches.

"I'm gonna be fine Miss Abby. Steven is taking good care of me." Trent winced when a particularly stubborn bandage pulled as Steven removed it.

"I'm doing my best." Steven said switching the empty I.V. fluids and blood bags for new ones as Trent fell asleep again.

Grandmother Abigail stood and shuffled to the bed. Taking her hand, she said with tears in her eyes. "Child you're such a wonderful young lady. Even after that parasite screamed that Trent was using you, you still offered your blood to save him."

"Is it true grandmother? What she said?" Abby asked tearfully.

"I don't believe a word of it. Trent has always been an honorable man." She dabbed her eyes with an embroidered hanky. "However, I have no knowledge of his plans or feelings concerning you. That's for you to find out on your own. I can't interfere, although it would give me great pleasure to help you child."

"It's okay, grandmother, things will work out the way they're meant to be." Abby squeezed her hand. "Good or bad, you have to accept the outcome and move on."

"So young, yet so wise. My son raised and intelligent, compassionate, and stubborn woman." Her face beamed with pride though sadness peeked from her eyes. "Steven told me what that Boudreau woman said to you. He didn't mean to eavesdrop, but he felt it necessary to look out for you. Frankly, I'm quite proud of you.

They conversed until Steven insisted Grandmother Abigail retire for the evening. Despite her protests, she gave in, and he helped her from the room.

Per Steven's orders, Abby remained in the bed. The opportunity to study Trent as he slept was too good to pass up. His dark hair fell over his forehead as his long lashes rested under his closed eyes.

Milly's harsh words shredded her heart again, while ringing in her ears. Tears stung the back of her eyes. *Life is so unfair! I just found him and he's out of my reach!*

"Your face will freeze like that if you keep frowning." Trent whispered.

"Who would notice?' Her face fell.

"I will. You're too beautiful to hide behind that wall around you." He mumbled sleepily. "If I were in better shape, I'd show you how beautiful you really are."

Heat rushed to her cheeks, even though she suspected the drugs did the talking, it didn't prevent her from dreaming.

"Be careful Mister, you might say something you'll regret." She warned him.

"I'd never regret loving such a beautiful woman." He yawned.

"That's the drugs talking, Mr. Winthrop." She said sadly.

"Just wait until I'm back on my feet." His voice faded into a whisper. "I love you Abby O'Malley."

Abby fell into stunned silence. *"How can he be in love with me? We only met four days ago!"* The tension between them was strong and she thought he hated her. Even so, her heart yearned for his declaration to be true.

Steven broke her train of thought when he stepped into the room grumbling about Grandmother Abigail being downright unreasonable at times.

Abby smiled remembering her mother saying the same about her father.

"It's a good thing you were here to give your blood." He smiled down at her. "It saved his life."

"I really didn't have a choice did I?" She shrugged. "The look on Lance's face said no one else had the same blood type."

"I wouldn't have done it if I suspected what that Boudreau woman said was true. Why risk it? With him out of the way there wouldn't be a Milly Boudreau or the problem she's become." He replied.

"Can I go to my room now?" She changed the subject.

"No. I want you to stay here until morning so I can keep an eye on both of you. If I'm checking on your grandmother, and he wakes up, he might pull some of those stitches." He insisted.

"We'll just have to make sure he doesn't move around too much won't we?" She sighed.

"If I had someone as beautiful as you next to me, you can bet I'd be moving around." Steven's tone became serious.

Abby's cheeks flamed almost purple with embarrassment. Oh, Steven was good looking, but there was something about Trent that made her feel safe.

"I'll keep him sedated, that way the risk is much lower. I'll be back in an hour so I can eat and check on your grandmother. If you need anything just yell." He grinned.

"Yeah, I'm so loud, lucky me." She frowned thankful he was leaving.

He dropped a light kiss on her forehead and left the room. Unsure of his intentions, there was no doubt who she wanted between the two men. However, the danger to her heart where Trent was concerned scared her.

Chapter Thirteen

Abby was anxious to get out of Trent's bed and go to her own room as Steven returned to check on Trent.

"I'd appreciate it if you'd stay and watch over Trent for me. Caring for your grandmother is a full-time job and I sleep whenever I get a chance to." He said his tone just shy of it being an order. "I'll go downstairs and get you something to eat if you're hungry."

Abby wanted to yell at him, but knew it was useless to argue. "Yes, I'm hungry, thanks. I'll stay here but under protest."

She didn't see the smile on his face as he left. It felt good to be in charge of more than her grandmother and with Trent sedated, he had more time to talk with Abby.

When he returned she sat up leaning against the headboard to eat. She enjoyed the leftovers mostly because she didn't have to make the food herself. When she finished Steven took the tray and set it aside on a bedside table.

"Now, lie down and get some sleep." He smiled down at her. The moment their eyes met after she settled in, His expression changed, and he gently kissed her lips. "I'll check on you after a few hours of sleep."

Heat rushed to her cheeks as he picked up the tray and left the room. She was flattered, but there was no feeling like when Trent touched her. The first time Trent kissed her, she lost all sense of reality. No, Steven would never hold a candle to Trent Winthrop.

Steven stopped in to check on Trent once more before going to bed. His eyes fell on Abby's beautiful face in slumber. In that moment, he decided to win her heart. No matter what the high and mighty Trent Winthrop said.

When she didn't push him away when he kissed her encouraged him. Maybe he had a shot after all. The competition with Trent most certainly be rigorous. Trent would be a formidable opponent.

Not only did the man have a massive bank account, property, and power, but he was devilishly handsome. He wasn't completely blind to the fact that women threw themselves at him constantly.

Still, there is more to love than money and power. Even though it would take a miracle to win her over, the reward would be worth it. A small sliver of hope that what the Boudreau woman said to Abby would sway her to think Trent wasn't worth the trouble.

Trent moaned drawing his attention off Abby. While checking his sutures and vitals he felt proud. Regardless of being an RN, he had done an excellent job of patching him up.

Lance had required a couple of stitches, a dose of strong antibiotics and a mild pain medication. Billy helped Gina take him back to their cottage where he would stay to keep watch over him just in case something went wrong.

"I'm doing a fantastic job if I do say so myself," He grinned.

A yawn snuck up on Steven as he finished checking Trent over and he left to grab some sleep while he could.

Not long after Steven left, Trent began dreaming of the wolf attacking him. Because of the medications Steven gave him, the entire dream twisted into something more sinister.

Abby jumped when his moan became louder. She scooted closer to him and carefully draped her arm over him. The small contact seemed to calm him, so she relaxed into a light slumber.

Trent searched for Abby in the forest. Someone had taken her, and the entire staff had searched for days, but couldn't find her. He sent them back to the compound to rest and replenish their supplies while he continued to search alone.

He stopped and dismounted to stretch his legs. The forest remained eerily silent until a terrified scream split the air. He jumped onto his horse and galloped toward the sound.

His heart nearly stopped when he broke into a small clearing to find Abby bound hand and foot lying on the ground. Carefully looking around, he determined they were alone.

He jumped from his horse and began freeing her from the ropes binding her. Lance's words, *"He's back!"* ran through his mind as a gruff voice growled behind him turning his blood to ice.

Abby woke up when she felt his body go ridged and he shouted, "Abby! Run!"

Abby struggled to restrain his arms as he thrashed around yelling, *"Don't let him catch you!"*

Abby screamed, "Steven! I need your help! He's having a nightmare!"

Steven burst into the room and quickly filled a hypo. A few minutes later the sedation calmed him, yet he still moaned and talked in his sleep.

Steven's face turned grim as he checked his handiwork. Trent pulled several stitches, the more serious injuries to his shoulder began hemorrhaging. He looked at Abby, "I need you to call Billy. I'm gonna need his help." He instructed her while applying pressure on the shoulder. "Tell him to hurry!"

She ran as fast as she could to the study hoping the phone number was by the phone. With each step, fear threatened to overcome her. *"Who was he fighting? Could it have been the face in the shadows? Had he seen him too? Did he know who he was and why he was haunting her?"*

When she entered the study, she found the number for Lance and called. After telling Gina what happened, the woman told her Billy would be there shortly.

Relieved Billy was on his way, she hung up and turned to go back upstairs. Fear started at her toes and crawled to her head in an instant. Her entire body broke out into a cold sweat. There by the fireplace her worst nightmare glared at her with a sadistic grin on his disfigured face. Now she knew without a doubt that he had followed her to the island. Unable to move, her throat constricted and kept the scream she tried to force from her lips from escaping.

The disembodied head drifted closer to her as his grin turned into a grotesque smile. The pain of her racing heart trying to escape her chest drowned out all other sound in her ears. Her breathing became more erratic, as she stood petrified unable to escape. The face drifted ever closer, as inky blackness slowly covered her eyes then she fell limply to the floor.

Abby began to regain consciousness with the feeling of being lifted from the floor. It took only a second for her to begin fighting her captor. A scream ripped from deep in her chest as she fought for her life.

"Miss Abby! Calm down!" Billy barked at her. "I've got you, you're safe now."

Realizing who was carrying her, she dissolved into hysterical sobs. Her tears soaked his shirt as her body trembled with relief that she was safe.

Steven looked up when Billy stepped into the room with the hysterical woman in his arms. "What happened to Miss Abby?"

"She must have passed out." Billy growled, hiding the fear sending chills down his spine. "I found her on the floor int the study."

"Put her on that side of the bed and help me get him sewn back together." He ordered noting Abby looked as though she'd seen a ghost.

From where she was on the bed, she watched them work on Trent. Still terrified she calmed somewhat knowing the two men would protect her from the apparition. One thing she couldn't figure out was why he was following her.

She caught Billy discretely glancing at her occasionally. It wasn't out of concern, but she saw genuine fear in his eyes.

Did he witness what happened to her in the study? Does he know the face in the shadows?

Steven misread the fearful look in her eyes, "He's going to be fine. He didn't bleed as much this time." All the while jealousy jabbed his heart. He would give anything to have her look at him like she did Trent.

Billy knew that being an outsider, Steven had no clue about what was going on. His concern for Miss Abby had grown exponentially by the minute. He wondered why he had shown up now and why it had gone after Miss Abby?

The complete terror Abby experienced drained her far more than any other encounter with him. Before long she was fast asleep.

A solid hour of working on Trent exhausted Steven more than he already was. When the last bandage was in place, Billy turned to make a hasty exit.

"I need you to stay and help me. I can't work twenty-four seven. I need to rest too." Steven stopped him from leaving.

"I ain't no nurse or doctor." Billy protested eager to get out of the mansion. "First aid is all I know from helping patch up rodeo riders and clowns until they could be moved to the hospital if needed."

"Don't worry, Abby's asleep, and Trent is sedated. I'll check on Grandmother Abigail before I turn in. Steven insisted stifling a yawn. "If something happens you can wake me. Just keep an eye on them."

Billy did not want to stay another minute in this mansion, and even though he was mad, he stayed. It angered him that Steven was right. If he were too tired he could make a mistake that could cost someone their life.

He sat quietly in the chair next to Abby's side of the bed, studying her young innocent face. He had witnessed what happened in the study. Just like he knew they weren't chasing a feral animal or native, they were hunting *him*.

There were a few on this side of the island who feared someday he would return. They'd all heard the stories how he'd fallen off a cliff on the north side of the island. There were also rumors that he was attacked by a pack of feral wolves. The main cause of the rumors came about because they never found a body.

He had just signed on when the awful things began to happen. The young woman that claimed Trent was the father of her child was haunted by the phantom.

A few nights after the baby arrived, the child disappeared without a trace. They searched for weeks but found nothing. Billy wondered at the time why Trent wasn't more upset by the loss of his child.

There were a plethora of question that remained unanswered to this day. Over the years, he got to know Trent quite well. He knew the man to be compassionate and fiercely protective of those he cared for.

Now that it had returned, some of the stories began to consume his thoughts. No one knew the entire story and until now he believed them to be fables and ghost stories.

Lance and Gina had the same attitude that night seven years ago. Oh, Trent insisted he was dead, but Lance's demeanor told him otherwise.

Billy closed his eyes and forced himself to forget the day he arrived in the garden of Eden, complete with the serpent tormenting the O'Malley family and anyone close to them.

Abby shivered in the darkness so thick she couldn't see her hand in front of her face. Trepidation started at her toes winding its cold claws in and around her until it reached her heart. It was beating so fast that she thought it would explode when the sound of someone breathing in the darkness reached her ears.

Closer and closer the interloper came with only a whisper of sound. Just when she thought to escape, a small flicker of light illuminated the twisted smile on his scarred face. Hands closed around her neck and slowly, deliberately squeezed increasing the pressure.

Billy jumped when Abby's scream disturbed the silence. He quickly prevented her from hurting Trent. That scream told him all he needed to know. She fought the very thing he wanted absolutely no part of.

Abby's eyes flew open with complete terror spilling from them along with tears. In that moment, he knew there was no turning away from her. His heart broke for her when he realized whether he liked it or not, he would do what it took to protect her.

Steven ran into the room wide awake afraid of what he would find. The scream he heard would have awakened the dead.

Billy eased Abby back onto the pillows as she cried hysterically. While Steven sedated her, Billy watched in total silence. Uneasiness shrouded him for what lie on the horizon. "*It was supposed to be over. Seven long years with nothing and now...*" Billy moved toward the door anxious to be anywhere but here.

"Are you all right?" Steven asked curious about his silence.

"I'm just peachy!" He answered sarcastically.

"What's going on around here? Trent and Abby having terrifying nightmares, and everyone sharing secret glances that would qualify for a horror movie. When I ask about it they clam up. I need to know if we're in danger of something." Steven insisted.

"If Mr. Winthrop wants you to know, he'll tell you. I'm not and will not speak for him. You'll have to ask him. Furthermore, I'd like some shut eye of my own."

Steven stood with his mouth open wondering what just happened as Billy's back disappeared into the dark hallway.

Chapter Fourteen

Gina rushed to the door when Billy pounded on it. Dread filled her when she caught a look she had seen before and hoped never to see again.

"Billy? What's happened?" She stepped back to allow him inside.

"I need to talk to Lance!" Billy demanded. "Now!"

Gina knew enough about this young wrangler not to argue or ask questions. "He's in the den, I'll make you a cup of coffee."

"Make it strong." He grunted a response as he disappeared into the den.

Gina took her time so Billy could relax a little. She prepared a coffee tray to set on the coffee table.

Lance looked up from his newspaper when Billy plopped heavily into the chair opposite of him. Noting the frown on his face, he asked, "So, Billy, why are you so surly this morning?"

"I'll give you one guess!" The young wrangler worked hard to control his emotions. "He's back Lance!"

"I knew there was a strong possibility of that when we searched the forest. But you know how stubborn Trent is. He's convinced the man is dead. What happened last night?"

Gina put the tray on the table and handed Billy his coffee then sat on the sofa to listen to his story.

Billy winced from gulping the too hot coffee, then told them almost everything he had seen and heard.

Gina shivered in the fear that blanketed her. "Is he really back?"

"Until we have evidence he's returned we can only speculate. However, I believe he is." Lance said.

"If you would've heard Abby scream in terror, you'd be positive. I had to get outta there." Billy shuddered. "What if he goes after Grandmother Abigail or Trent? What about Miss Abby?"

"If the legend is true, how did Jake escape the curse? Miss Abby was born in America, so how does he know about her?" Lance's eyebrows furrowed.

"Don't forget, Trent was the father of the baby he took, and he's not even an O'Malley." Billy commented.

"I believe he left the island somehow since we didn't find either of them. What better way to torture someone than not knowing what happened to your child?" Lance shook his head.

"All I know is he's back and I don't want any part of it." Billy said vehemently.

"There's a silver lining here, there aren't any O'Malley babies on the island. According to the legend, that's all he wants, the first-born child of the O'Malley family. That's why old man O'Malley disapproved of Jake's marriage forcing him to leave the island. In so doing, his firstborn grandchild would be safe."

"What's to stop him from taking her now?' All he cares about is torturing the O'Malley family and Grandmother Abigail is still alive. Now that Abby's here I fear for both of them." Gina spoke up. "Another thing, why did he take Trent's child? His parents were born in Greece."

Silence filled the room as the trio mulled over their discussion until Lance slammed his fist on the arm of his chair. "With Trent out of commission, it's up to us to watch over them. I've come to think of Trent as my son, and I've already come to think of Abby as a daughter. I won't stand by and let him destroy them!"

"How do you catch a ghost? The only way I knew it was him..." Billy stopped realizing he said too much.

"What are you hiding Billy? Tell me!" Lance ordered angrily.

Billy squirmed under Lance's glare, "I started upstairs and happened to glance into the study. Abby stood by the desk frozen in fear looking toward the fireplace. I hurried to the door and stopped dead in my tracks. Lance, I saw him! For a split second I took my eyes away from him to check on Abby. When I looked back, he was gone!"

"How did he get past you? There's no way outta there without being seen!" Lance exclaimed.

"I don't know!" Billy fought the cold chill racing down his back. "I know this is gonna sound crazy, but it was only his head! He moved toward Abby with a twisted smile. My blood turned to ice, and I heard Abby fall to the floor."

"Have we stepped into an alternate universe or something?" Lance's thin eyebrows shot up to his balding head. "I'll say it again, I won't stand by while my family is tortured! I won't do it!"

"Lance honey, calm down! We love them too, and you won't be any help if you have a stroke being so angry." Gina interrupted.

"I don't think I can go through this again." Billy said for the first-time showing emotion.

"I'm gonna get to the bottom of this or die trying." Lance said glancing up at his wife. "The O'Malley's and Trent have suffered enough!"

"I guess if you're determined to do this, I'm in." Billy sighed. "Where do we start?"

"At the beginning, where else?" Gina went to the bookshelf. "I'm with you too, and no arguments."

She carefully retrieved a vintage leather-bound book. Even the pages were yellowed and cracked with age.

"Mr. O'Malley gave this to me the day before he died." She sat on the sofa. "He said I would need the information in it someday soon. All we've had are rumors and folk tales. At any rate, we may discover more about the O'Malley family."

"I should go back to the mansion and keep an eye on things." Billy stood up. "Let me know what you find out."

"Lance's eyes twinkled with mischief, "It might be a good idea if you keep your rifle handy, not that a ghost can be shot, but you'll have a sense of security."

Gina quickly covered her smile when Billy growled over his shoulder. "That ain't funny!"

The door slammed behind him while they laughed.

FACE IN THE SHADOWS

ABBY AWAKENED WITH a head full of cotton and an upset stomach.

"Good afternoon, Miss Abby." Steven said while taking her pulse.

"Thank God you're okay, child!" Her grandmother shoved Steven out of the way.

"Don't try to get up, that sedative I gave you hasn't completely worn off." He said over her grandmother's shoulder.

"It's okay, child. I'm here to take care of you now." Grandmother Abigail said squeezing her hand.

"Thank you, grandmother." She smiled up at the old woman.

Billy appeared at the door to get Steven's attention. When he saw him, Billy jerked his chin toward the hall and indicated he should follow.

When they were out of earshot of the other, Steven asked, "Wanna tell me what's going on?"

"Before I tell you anything, you cannot ask any questions. Capiche?" Billy asked.

"Okay." Steven answered thoroughly confused.

"As of now, there will be armed guards inside the mansion under my orders. We already have some posted outside on the grounds. You keep your eyes open for anything unusual." Billy informed him. "There will be someone at the door to Grandmother Abigail's room and one at Trent's room. When Miss Abby is able to return to her room, someone will be posted there as well during the night."

"I don't understand, why?" Steven asked.

"That's a question." Billy glared at him. "Just follow orders for now. If you even feel something isn't right, you tell one of us. You got it?"

"Yeah I got it, but I have the right to know if we're in danger." He insisted defiantly.

"Yes." Billy replied. "Keep your eyes and ears open and not a word to anyone. Now let's get back before they suspect anything."

Abby sensed something was wrong the minute they entered the room. For the moment she dismissed it, but there would be questions when her grandmother went to lunch.

Billy sat in a chair next to the window brooding, watching over everyone in the room.

Finally, Steven took her grandmother to eat lunch. He ordered Abby to stay in the bed a little while longer.

Her gaze landed on Billy, and she knew he was hiding something big. "What's going on that's got you so moody?"

"Nothing I wanna talk about." He grumbled.

"It might make you feel better to talk about it." She tried to coax it out of him.

"No." He grunted and moved his chair into the hall by the door.

Abby watched him with her mouth hanging open wondering what his problem was.

Trent stirred slightly, diverting her attention from Billy. She looked and met his dark eyes.

"Am I dreaming or are you still here?" He asked weakly.

"You're dreaming." She smiled.

"Then don't wake me up." He coughed wincing in pain. "I appreciate what you've done for me."

"Do you need Steven?" She asked worried about his cough.

"I'm okay for now." He brought her hand to his lips.

"I'm relieved you're recovering. But do me a favor, don't do this again." She insisted. "I don't know how much more blood I can spare."

"Trust me, I don't enjoy being in pain." He coughed again.

"I'm getting Steven." She moved to get up. "He needs to check you over."

"Please, just stay with me. He'll be along soon." He whispered. "I don't want to be alone. I want to make sure you're safe."

"What are you talking about?" She asked wondering if it had something to do with his nightmare.

"I'd just feel better if I knew you were here with me." He coughed again.

"I'll stay. Rest for now." She agreed. "I'll be right here."

He drifted off to sleep still holding her hand as a sense of unease enveloped her. *"What is going on around here?"*

GINA STRUGGLED TO READ some of the journal to her husband because the writing had faded over the years. So far, they learned Miles O'Malley gave gifts to the natives when they arrived on the island.

The chief of the tribe granted him ownership of the east side of the island. Together with his brother Shawn, and those who traveled with him, they settled happy to be free of the tyranny of the families of old Ireland.

Curious about the white skinned people with fiery hair, some of the younger natives slipped away from their village and watched from the trees as they began building wooden huts. The chief sent the older tribal members to bring them home, but they had been seen.

Miles, being a gentle soul made friends with them in hopes they could live peacefully with them. What he didn't know was his brother Shawn had a cruel streak that he kept hidden from everyone for years.

Nearly a year later, the settlers barely survived the winter, and spring brought with it food and the ability to finish their settlement.

Several weeks into the summer months, the natives attacked with no warning. Miles couldn't understand why but joined the settlers in the battle. For days they fought for their lives. No one noticed Shawn and his undesirable friends weren't around.

They snuck into the village, killed the old men, and took the more beautiful young women as slaves. In the end, many of the natives had been killed or wounded along with several settlers.

Miles was furious with his brother when he found out what he had done. Seizing the opportunity while his brother and friends were drunk, the settlers imprisoned them. Miles freed the women and took them back to the village.

The few remaining braves captured and tortured Miles for the massacre of the natives. Then the medicine man cursed the O'Malley family. The ghost of their most powerful ancestor would take every firstborn male child of the O'Malley family as long as they were on the island.

As payment for bringing their women home, the chief stopped short of killing him. A young brave was ordered to help him return to the settlement as a warning to stay on the east side of the island.

The journey back Miles listened to the young brave tell the story of how he alone survived the massacre of his blood brothers on the hunt.

Outraged with his brother, Miles had him beaten in front of the entire settlement for his crime.

As soon as Miles could travel, he took his family and left the island with a broken heart. He would never forget the pain of his brother's betrayal.

Gina sat back unable to read any longer.

"Well, we now know why and where the curse began. The question is how do we stop it?" Lance sighed.

"One thing caught my attention was the curse was the first-born male child would be taken. Trent's baby was a girl not to mention she wasn't in the O'Malley line, and Abby is a girl. Why would the curse pertain to her?" Gina asked thoughtfully.

Chapter Fifteen

Abby nearly jumped for joy when Steven released her with the stipulation she didn't over exert herself.

Propped up on pillows frowning at Steven, Trent had been ordered to stay in bed. Apparently, he would be stationary for another few days before he would allow him to walk in the hallway.

After breakfast, Grandmother Abigail and Abby sat in the room with Trent chatting quietly about her father while he slept.

"My Jake couldn't sit still and was always into something. No matter the situation, he had a smile for everyone. I truly believe the softer side of him came from his great-great-grandfather Miles O'Malley." She dabbed tears from her eyes.

Abby hung on every word her grandmother spoke hoping to learn why her parents never spoke of them or the island.

"Your grandfather also had a softer side, but he battled depression. You see this island has a dark secret..." She continued when Billy appeared in the doorway.

"Grandmother Abigail, would you like some tea?" He asked. "Abby would you go ask Barbara to bring some for the two of you?"

Confused and a touch angry with him, she didn't make a fuss unwilling to upset her grandmother. Something was going on and no one wanted her to know what it was.

When he was sure Abby was out of earshot, he turned to Grandmother Abigail, "Mrs. O'Malley, please don't tell Miss Abby anything about the family history."

"Why ever not child?" She frowned in confusion.

"You know why. It's for everyone's safety, especially hers." Billy answered.

"You mean..." Her eyes filled with tears.

"That's exactly what I mean. You can't tell her. I'm sure Trent will explain it all to her when he feels the time is right." Billy explained.

Grandmother Abigail agreed to keep quiet as tear spilled down her weathered cheeks. "I can't believe he's returned. Why now? There haven't been any children since Trent's child was taken. Unless... Oh dear Lord, don't let him take my grandchild."

"That's why I'm here Mrs. O'Malley. Lance and Gina are working to put a stop to this nightmare. Lance is determined to end this once and for all." Billy assured her.

She turned fearful eyes on the young wrangler, "Can it be stopped after all this time? Many have tried and failed."

"I truly believe Lance has the determination to stop it. You've gotta have hope Mrs. O'Malley." Billy said putting a hand on her shoulder.

STEVEN HAD NO IDEA what was about to happen when he tossed the empty bottle of water in the trash. He looked up just as Abby stomped into the kitchen ready for a fight.

"Are you feeling all right?" He asked noting her flushed cheeks.

"I'm just peachy!" She hissed. "I want to know what's going on around here! You've been distance since you disappeared down the hall with Billy. Now he's interrupted my grandmother in the middle of telling me about my family." Her voice rose with each word. "You know something so tell me!"

"I don't know what's going on. Billy just told me to help keep an eye on the three of you. He wouldn't tell me why though."

Clearly unsatisfied with his answer, she turned to Barbara, "Bring some hot tea upstairs! I'm going to get to the bottom of this right now!"

The two employees watched her storm from the room with surprised looks on their faces.

Beyond furious, she would find out why Billy was keeping secrets. She was his boss, and he would danged well tell her what she wanted to know, or else.

The minute he saw Abby, Billy knew she was spoiling for a fight. No matter, he could be just as stubborn, especially since he had orders to keep his mouth closed.

"Billy! You've been keeping something from me, and I want to know what it is!" She insisted angrily.

"It isn't my place to tell you anything. You'll have to wait for Trent to decide what he wants you to know. Please know that we're on top of the situation for now." He tried to calm her down.

"What situation?" She asked stomping her foot.

Trent had a coughing fit, and Abby rushed to his bedside forgetting everything for the moment. She would get the answers she wanted later.

"Let me talk to her Billy." He wheezed.

Steven arrived and Trent asked Grandmother Abigail to excuse them. They passed Billy who sat in the hall brooding over the situation he found himself in once again.

Abby sat on the edge of the bed while Trent shifted to a better position for the conversation he had to have with her.

"Miss Abby, can you do something for me?" He winced.

"I'll try." She said with a sinking feeling she wouldn't get the answers she wanted.

"Do you think you could trust me?" He asked with hope in his eyes.

"Again, I'll try." She fought to remain calm.

"Until I've fully recovered will you quit asking about your family?" He requested.

Once again her hopes were dashed against an invisible stone. She wanted answers but everyone was against her getting them.

"Only if you get better soon and tell me what everyone is hiding from me." She sighed with frustration.

"I promise when the time is right, I'll tell you everything." He crossed his heart.

He reached for her hand and froze in fear looking over her shoulder. Abby turned to see what he was staring at, and the hand of terror squeezed the air from her lungs.

Hovering in the shadow of the corner was the face of the man terrifying her. His twisted smile and angry red eyes robbed her of all speech.

Billy knew something was wrong when the room went deathly quiet. He appeared in the doorway when the vile creature disappeared into thin air.

Desperately trying to keep her from falling, Trent was grateful when Billy caught her as she slid from the bed.

"Steven! Get in here now!" Trent bellowed wincing from the strain.

Billy gently laid her on the bed as her eye's fluttered open with terror shining through her tears. "Did you see? It was right there! Did you see?"

"It's alright Abby, you aren't crazy. Billy and I saw it too." Trent took her hand to soothe her.

A mixture of fear and relief raced through her as Trent put his good arm around her while she sobbed.

"What the devil is going on in here?" Milly's furious voice barked from the doorway. "What is she doing in bed with my fiancé?"

Anger flashed through Abby as she sat up wiping her tears. *"Why does this woman keep showing up unannounced?"*

"Billy, hand me your rifle!" She ordered beyond furious.

"Wait! I..." Milly sputtered backing out of the room.

"I told you what would happen if you ever showed your face on my island again! The last time I checked, my word is law here since I own it, so if I shoot you there won't be any repercussions." Abby scooted off the bed. "Billy, I said hand me your rifle!"

Billy complied biting back a smile. The moment Abby's hand closed around the barrel; Milly screamed running down the hallway. Her feet hit the stairs and shortly the front door slammed, and the mansion fell silent.

"Well done, Miss O'Malley." Trent chuckled. "However, did I miss something? When did you tell her you'd shoot her?"

"It's a long story, which I'm sure Steven would enjoy telling you. He's been teasing me ever since it happened." She scowled.

From the flash of anger in her eyes, he truly believed she meant what she said. That thought sobered him a little. "That was most entertaining, what do you do for an encore?" He teased to lighten the mood.

"Nothing you can handle I'm sure, especially in your condition." She smirked with the earlier terror forgotten.

Billy took his gun and escaped into the hall having no desire to see what might happen next.

GINA CONTINUED TO READ the O'Malley family history finding most of the settlers left with Miles and his family.

Shawn eventually fell in love and married. His wife died in childbirth with their first child. Shawn was left with the little boy to raise alone. That night, a monstrous storm raged against the island, and the curse claimed its first child.

Out of desperation, Shawn went to the village elders to beg forgiveness hoping the medicine man would end the curse and return his child. His effort was useless, and no forgiveness came from the tribe.

In the dark days after the visit to the village, Shawn grew despondent and eventually threw himself off the high cliffs on the north end of the island.

Though they searched, his body was never recovered, effectively ending the line of Shawn O'Malley.

Gina gently closed the book with tears in her eyes while Lance sat in shock silence. The memory of Trent's daughter being taken. He refused to marry Barbara's daughter but took excellent care of her during her pregnancy. A few weeks before his daughter was born, she began seeing the apparition that eventually stole the child shortly after it graced the world with its presence.

After weeks of searching, they found no trace of the child or the thing that took her. One year later, the young woman took her own life unable to bear her loss any longer.

DARK SINISTER STORM clouds gathered on the horizon sending shivers of apprehension through Abby. Under different circumstances, the lightning flashing through the clouds would have been an amazing light display.

Charlie sat in the hall outside of Trent's room settling in for the night. Deep down he hoped for a quiet night.

Abby opted to sleep in the chair next to Trent's bed under a plush throw. Finally comfortable, she discretely looked at Trent only to meet his teasing smile.

Heat flooded her cheeks as she said, "Go ahead and say it. I know it's killing you."

"And ruin that glow on your beautiful face?" He chuckled.

"You're becoming quite sassy, Mr. Winthrop." She teased. "It appears my blood did more than save your life."

"Maybe I was waiting for the right moment to turn on the charm." He grinned.

Unaware of Milly's tirade, his words cut deeply, and the mixed signals he kept giving her brought tears to her eyes. Burrowing under the throw into the soft oversized chair, she couldn't respond.

Confused, Trent wondered what had upset her. Clearly sharing her thoughts was out of the question.

Despite his best efforts, he fell in love with her. If he couldn't keep his promise to find a way to end the O'Malley curse, he would have to force her to leave the island. He wondered how he could do it feeling that way about her.

Chapter Sixteen

Trent insisted Charlie find Steven after she fell asleep.

Clearly Steven had been asleep when Charlie knocked on his door. With a yawn he stepped into Trent's room, "What's wrong? Are you in pain?"

"No, I want you to tell me what happened between Abby, and Miss Boudreau." He demanded.

"I don't know everything because I didn't hear their entire conversation." Steven felt uncomfortable. "The day you went into the forest, Milly showed up unannounced, which I'm beginning to wonder about how she does it, I was with Grandmother Abigail when I heard Milly screaming.

I came to investigate, and the study door was ajar."

"Well, go on, what did you hear?" Trent persisted.

"Maybe you should ask Miss Abby about this." Steven hoped he would drop it.

"If I wanted to ask her I would have, but I'm asking you so spill it!" He growled impatiently.

"Okay, I didn't hear much but Miss Abby told Miss Boudreau if she returned to the island, she'd put a bullet between her eyes." Steven gave in.

"I can see there's more." He persisted.

"Just remember, I didn't hear the entire conversation. Miss Abby told her she could have you with her blessing. That's when Miss Boudreau left. Then Miss Abby burst into tears."

Trent silently absorbed what Steven told him with rising anger.

"Um, there's more but, as I said, I didn't hear everything." Steven said squirming.

"Thanks, you can go now." He dismissed him.

Steven left feeling guilty for sharing what he heard with Trent. Yes, he left out most of it, but he felt it wasn't his place to divulged what he did. Now he worried that his shot with Abby was in jeopardy.

BILLY DROPPED IN ON the Elliot's before relieving Sam from his late-night watch.

Gina handed him a super strong cup of coffee as he went through to the den to talk.

"So, where do we go from here?" He asked sitting in a chair.

"Slow down." Lance raised a brow. "Don't you wanna know what we've discovered first?"

"Will it make any difference if you tell me?" He asked.

"No, but we have the factual story about the O'Malley family." Gina spoke up. "If you know their history, we can all make informed decisions about where to go from here."

"Make it quick, Sam's due to be relieved in an hour." He grumbled.

Gina relayed the important parts of the story to him.

"Wow, that's just... Wow!" He spoke after a long pause.

"We knew about the war, but not why it started." Gina said.

"But we still don't know how to stop it." He looked for direction.

"That's the mystery we'll have to solve." Lance told him. "Don't say a word to anybody, especially Trent or Abby. Trent would blow his stack if he knew we're looking into this. Who knows how Miss Abby will react."

"If you want to keep Miss Abby in the dark, you better talk to the old lady. She almost spilled the beans yesterday." He grumbled. "That's when that ghoul showed up in Trent's room. Yes, Trent, Abby and I saw it."

"I'll handle Grandmother Abigail." Gina stood to remove the empty cups.

Lance arose from his recliner and said, "I have to do Trent's work since he's laid up. I'll take the opportunity to poke around for more information."

"He'd be up doing the work himself, but Steven is adamant he stay in bed for now." Billy stood, "I'd better get up there and relieve Sam."

"We'll be up later." Lance said then closed the door behind him. "I'm gonna make sure everyone hears Trent give me permission to work in the study so no one will be suspicious."

"After I talk with Grandmother Abigail, I'll join you to help." Gina hugged her husband of nearly forty years.

TRENT HADN'T SLEPT a wink all night long, going over the conversation he had with Steven. He suspicioned the man hadn't told him everything. *"What had Milly said to Abby? Why had she told Milly he was hers for the taking with Abby's blessing?"*

One major flaw in Abby's thinking was he had no desire to be with Milly since he caught her cheating on him after high school. They were nineteen and any feelings he had for her died that night.

"Did she tell Abby about the baby everyone thought was his"? No one knew he was covering for the old man. Barbara and O'Malley knew the truth about the old man's indiscretion.

Barbara's daughter wanted to be rich and powerful, much like Milly Boudreau. She had tried to seduce him, but he rejected her, so she slipped into O'Malley's room one night and she became pregnant.

Mr. O'Malley instructed him to pay Barbara and her daughter a handsome settlement to keep them quiet.

He shook himself from his musings, anxious to get back to his normal routine. It was time to work on the second promise he had sworn to. O'Malley was adamant about him finding a way to break the curse on his family.

Deep down he felt there was something in the family's past that would solve the mystery of how it began. That would be the key to putting an end to the reign of terror the face in the shadows forced upon the family.

Depending on the outcome of his research, maybe...

Abby stirred in the oversized chair ending his train of thought. She'd slept through the storm even though it buffeted the island most of the night. He hoped she'd felt safe because she was in his room.

He longed to touch her red hair and stare into her emerald eyes. His heart ached with love, and he couldn't do a thing about it.

"Good morning, sleepyhead." He smiled at her.

"Good morning." She answered softly.

As sleepy as she was, the way Trent looked at her made her wonder if Milly was wrong. That look was so familiar to her because her father looked at her mother the same way.

"What's going on in that beautiful brain of yours?" He asked forcing his feelings into a tight box.

"Nothing I want to share with you." She stood and folded the throw blanket.

"Running away are we?" He raised a challenging brow.

"You wish." She giggled.

Steven stepped into the doorway when Abby barreled into him.

"Oh! I'm so sorry Steven. I didn't mean to..." She stopped with a pretty pink flush on her cheeks.

Trent didn't miss the happy look Steven displayed when his arms went around her.

"It's quite all right Miss Abby. You may run into me anytime you wish." He smiled down at her flushed face.

He reached up to brush a stray lock of hair behind her ear letting his fingers linger on her cheek.

The green monster of jealousy hit Trent right between the eyes. Somehow he would have to keep those two apart.

BILLY STEPPED ONTO the landing as Abby slipped into her room. He waved at Sam and took up watch by her door.

Lance and Gina showed up a short time later to begin their covert operation. Gina went to find Grandmother Abigail, while Lance stopped to visit with Trent.

"Good morning! It's nice to see you're back among the living." Lance smiled when Trent sent a scowl his way.

"How's the arm?" Steven moved to look at it.

"Fine thanks, Gina's taking good care of me." Lance stepped around him to talk with Trent. "Are you ready to talk business?"

"No, he's not! He still needs a few more days bed rest. You'll have to take care of any business that comes up yourself, Mr. Elliot." Steven insisted.

"I can conduct my business from here." Trent's voice contained a warning.

"No, you won't. You're still healing inside from some traumatic injuries. You'll stay in that bed, or I'll sedate you." Steven crossed his arms glaring at Trent. "I'll have Miss Abby sit with her grandmother if necessary."

"Lance, I believe you'll have to handle the business for a few days. It seems I'm under bed arrest." Trent growled angrily. "If there's an emergency, just deal with it."

Lance laughed at the look on his face. It was obvious Trent lost this round and he wasn't used to losing.

"I'll get started. Enjoy your vacation." Lance laughed leaving the room.

He sat behind the large desk and took care of the more pressing business and began his search starting with the filing cabinet. He went through every folder reading each scrap of paper he found.

GINA SAT ON THE BALCONY off Grandmother Abigail's room with the old woman.

"Grandmother, I know you wish to share your entire life with Miss Abby, but you must let Trent handle things." Gina spoke kindly to her.

"I understand, and you're right. I don't believe she would understand what happened between Jake and his father." She agreed.

"I have to go help Lance get caught up on the paperwork since Trent is down. You have a good day with your granddaughter." Gina hugged the old woman and left.

By the time she made it downstairs, Lance slammed the last drawer on the file cabinet closed.

"You haven't found anything have you?" She asked.

"No. I think this is gonna take a lot longer than I thought." He shook his head.

"Well let's get started on the books. You start on that side, and I'll start here." She pulled three books from the shelf and began skimming through the first one.

And the search began in earnest to find something to break the curse.

Chapter Seventeen

Abby took time to enjoy a hot bubble bath praying it would ease the terror and anguish plaguing her since she arrived. Leaning back with her eyes closed, the bubbles slowly faded taking her cares away. Her mind focused on Trent holding her in his arms and gently kissing her.

She swore when Milly's words returned to haunt her again. The memory of the look of horror on her face when Billy handed her his rifle was oddly satisfying. The thought struck her of how the woman entered the mansion without anyone's knowledge. Where did she go when she left? If memory served, there was no sound of a boat motor from the docks.

Trent would know and she would ask him after she grabbed some coffee she decided while slipping into an emerald-green wraparound dress. Finishing everything off with a touch of red lipstick and a spritz of light perfume. For the first time in days, she felt happy again.

Billy leaned against the wall lost in thought. How had they wound up in this supposed curse again? He sent a short prayer toward Heaven that no one would disappear again.

Abby opened the door startling him from his dark thoughts.

"How are you on this beautiful day Billy?" She smiled at him.

"I don't see what's so wonderful about it, but I have to say you wear that smile well Miss Abby." He grinned.

"You know smiles are contagious." She giggled. "Would you like some coffee? I'm headed down for some."

"I've already had some, thanks but I'll accompany you downstairs." He fell in step beside her.

TRENT SLAMMED HIS FIST on the bed wincing from the sudden movement. He was going stir crazy. No radio, no books, no magazines and worse he was all alone. Where was Abby anyhow?

He was used to being alone, free to do as he pleased. Since a certain red head with green eyes stumbled over the threshold of his life, he'd come to realize how lonely he really was. Now it threatened to drive him mad.

At this point he would almost welcome a visit from Milly. He shook his head, *Dang! I must be getting desperate if I want to see that parasite.*

Abby caught his attention when she appeared in the doorway with a tray loaded with tea, sandwiches, and magazines. The more important thing to him at the moment was the angel carrying the tray.

She set the tray over him so he could eat, then crossed the room. Sunlight chased the gloomy shadows gripping his heart away when she opened the curtains and doors to his balcony.

She turned toward him, and the sunlight engulfed her in a brilliant aura of light. Abby was his angel coming to rescue him from the deep waters of loneliness.

Abby sat on the edge of his bed with something on her mind but didn't know how to ask.

"What's on your mind beautiful?" He asked before taking a bite of his sandwich.

"I've been thinking about Milly." She replied with a slight blush.

"Why?" Trent almost choked. "She means nothing to me not to mention she's been nothing but trouble since you arrived."

"True, but how is it that she seems to show up without a sound. And when she leaves I never hear a sound from a boat motor."

"She doesn't live on the mainland, her family lives on an island about an hour from here. You don't hear the sound of a motor because the dock is too far away to hear a good motor start." He explained.

"Okay, but that doesn't explain how she gets into the mansion without being seen or heard." She accepted his reasoning.

"I'm sure the doors are left unlocked because we know everyone here so there's no reason to secure the mansion from intruders. Although since Milly has caused so much trouble of late, we should change that." He said.

"But…" She tried to push the issue.

"She'll think twice about coming back unannounced after you tried to shoot her." He teased.

"Don't forget, I warned her." She felt her face heat.

"Abby, What did she say to make you so angry?" He couldn't contain his curiosity.

"Just showing up was enough. If you remember I was nursing a hangover that you caused." She hedged.

"You know you can trust me, right?" He said with a grin that melted her heart. "Besides, who am I going to tell?"

"I have an idea, let's talk about something a little more cheerful." She didn't want to allow the harsh words to ruin the rest of her day. "Surely there's something better to talk about other than the ravings of a lunatic."

"Oh, so now I'm a lunatic? You can't possibly be talking about little old me. If you are I will definitely take offence to it." Milly startled them from the doorway.

Billy jumped in front of her demanding, "How did you get in here?"

"You shouldn't sleep on the job you overgrown washed up cowboy." Milly glared at him turning her attention back to Trent, she continued. "Would you really like to know what I said? Maybe it would help you with your little promises that old man insisted you make."

"Enough! You have no idea what you're talking about. I suggest you leave before Abby makes good on her threat." Trent shouted with an icy glare at the woman.

"She won't hurt me, because I know all about the secrets you're hiding from her, and if you want them to be kept secret you'll keep your father's promise of marrying me." She snapped.

"What are you talking about?" Abby asked looking between the two.

"Oh, he hasn't told you everything yet has he?" She smirked.

"Miss Boudreau, I will never marry you. EVER! Get that through that stone cold heart of yours. My so-called father is dead! Any and all promises he made to anyone, especially you died with him." Trent growled furiously. "I would die a lonely old man before I'd marry the likes of a two-timing bimbo."

"I'm no bimbo! You'll change your mind." She hissed before addressing Abby again with a devilish look in her eyes. "Be careful, Miss O'Malley, there are dark forces at work on this island that have plagued your family for generations. They'll eventually come after you and I'd hate to see anything happen to you. Oh, wait, that would get you out of the way wouldn't it?"

"That's enough Milly! You have no idea what's going on here so just drop it!" Trent bellowed.

"Why on earth would I do that? Abby deserves to know the truth doesn't she?" Milly shot at him.

Abby was completely lost in their conversation. What was Milly talking about?

"They won't tell you will they?" She said smugly.

"Billy! Get her outta here now!" Trent blew up.

Billy didn't hesitate, in fact he would enjoy following this particular order.

"Go ahead! Ask Trent to tell you the whole story! I'll bet he won't do it! I'll bet no one on this island will! When you want the facts, I'll be happy to give them to you!" She screamed as Billy pulled her from the room and down the hall. After he shoved her through the front door, he slammed it shut locking it with a grin.

Abby sat in stunned silence unsure of what to say or do. Now she was afraid of the secret everyone kept from her.

Trent took a moment to calm himself, wishing he could tell her. From the fear in her eyes, the one thing he dreaded was that she may leave. Above all that was the very thing that couldn't happen. Now that he had found her if she left there was no way to protect her.

Abby finally broke the tense silence, "Trent? What is everyone keeping from me? Should I be afraid of my family's past?"

Her words sent a knife into his heart. He couldn't bring himself to tell her, not if she were to ever have a normal future. Those secrets would haunt her for the rest of her life. In his mind, she was too fragile to handle the horrors of her ancestors past.

He took her hand and kissed her knuckles then spoke, "Remember I asked for your trust, and you agreed?"

"I didn't know how serious it was, at least that's the feeling I got when you and Milly argued. If I'm in danger, you should tell me." She insisted.

"I promise when the time is right, I'll tell you." He crossed his heart.

"Everything?" She asked relenting.

"Yes, everything. I promise you'll be happy you waited." He insisted before kissing her.

Abby knew in that moment; it made no difference whether what Milly said was true or not. If she left the island it would be with a broken heart.

This time Trent didn't pull away, losing himself in her innocent kisses. No matter his intentions, when he made the promises to her grandfather, he didn't realize she would be the one he fell in love with. Somehow he would end the stupid curse on her family and marry her.

Chapter Eighteen

Lance and Gina searched most of the day but found nothing helpful. Gina pulled three more books from the shelf she worked on, and another book slid into the opening left behind and onto the floor.

Carefully retrieving it, she could see it was as old as the one in her possession. "Lance, I think I've found something." She said over her shoulder. She took it to the desk where Lance set aside the book he perused.

Gina opened it and knew they'd hit pay dirt. It was the diary of Shawn O'Malley.

Lance grinned and said, "I think you've found what we've been looking for."

"We should take it home, that way we won't be disturbed while we read it." Gina quickly slipped it into her bag.

Barbara stepped into the room startling them. "Will you be dining with us this evening?"

"No thanks, I believe we're done for today." Lance gathered the books on the desk and replaced them on the proper shelf.

"I have some chores to finish before bedtime." Gina said.

"Okay." Barbara left the room suspicious of the couple.

Shortly they were heading down the path to their cottage, anxious to find a way to end the curse.

SEVERAL WEEKS WENT by and the winter chill had set in. Snow fell gently to the ground covering everything in a soft white blanket.

Abby sat in the cozy chair next to the ceiling to floor windows remembering her childhood adventures in the snow. While the snow fell she recalled how quiet the animals were. It was as though everything went to sleep for the winter.

A soft sigh slipped from her lips as she watched the winter wonderland forming before her eyes. The wood in the fireplace crackled under the dancing flames. For the first time since she arrived on the island, she felt happy and at peace.

Trent and some of the wranglers had found and cut down the huge Christmas tree in the corner of the room for her to decorate with Grandmother Abigail overseeing the task.

"Look at this one!" Grandmother Abigail held up a homemade Styrofoam ball hollowed out with a picture of her father in the middle of it. A pipe cleaner served as the hook for hanging. "Jake made this in the third grade for me."

The two spent hours decorating the huge tree, until finally Grandmother Abigail had grown too tired to go on. Abby would never forget the memories she made that day. Each of the ornaments left carried memories she would never discover now that her only living relative was in the twilight of her life.

Trent watched from afar helping only when needed. He enjoyed the childlike joy she unknowingly let him see. Sympathy for Abby hit him when he witnessed the sadness she carried for her deceased parents.

Finally finished, she stood back with her hands fisted on her hips elated it had turned out so beautiful.

The soft glow of the twinkling lights and the fireplace were the only lights in the room. Abby sat in the overstuffed chair wrapped in a soft throw nursing a cup of hot chocolate with tiny marshmallows, warming her small hands.

Leaning back in the chair she felt so content and happy she didn't want the moment to end.

The ghoul stalking her was all but a forgotten memory. It hadn't shown up in weeks, which was a relief to everyone. Even Milly had all but disappeared after her last unannounced visit.

Abby had no choice but to trust Trent's decision to keep the secrets everyone except her and Steven knew about. The sweet nurse asked her if she knew why everyone was so secretive? Since she had no clue she assured him that it was nothing to worry about.

She decided to take things one day at a time, and she'd make every second count. Trent had stopped pulling away from her and would sit for hours holding her while they watched the logs in the fireplace reduce to glowing embers.

"Yes, I'm happy for now." She thought.

Christmas arrived and Abby's heart nearly burst with excitement. This was her favorite holiday, and this year would be extra special.

Growing up, even though her parents didn't have a lot of money, they made each one special.

When they died, Christmas wasn't the same. She felt like it died with them. Still in honor of her beloved parents, she celebrated. Tree or not, presents are not it made no difference. Deep down she felt they were with her in spirit celebrating with her.

Trent turned from the fireplace when she quite literally bounced into the room. The excitement in her eyes, and the smile on her flushed face drew him into the spirit of the holiday.

Abby stopped in the doorway enchanted by the scene set before her. It reminded her of the old postcards of a cozy Christmas evening. The only thing missing was a cat curled up on the rug in front of the fireplace and stocking full of goodies hung on the mantle of the fireplace. In a quick mental note, she committed the scene to her memory for when...

Trent startled her from her thoughts when he touched her arm. Smiling he pointed up where a sprig of mistletoe hung above them.

Abby willingly allowed him to pull her into his arms and kiss her passionately. A kiss of promise, and of love.

When she smiled up at him his heart nearly burst with happiness. He led her to the sofa and retrieved his gift for her and placed it in her hands. "Go ahead, open it."

In her excitement, she ripped the paper off the tiny box. When she opened it a gorgeous teardrop emerald, green pendant surrounded by diamonds on a delicate silver chain winked in the light.

Trent took it from her and clasped it behind her neck. Whispering in her ear, he said, "A token of my appreciation for trusting me. Merry Christmas sweetheart."

Abby jumped to her feet and grabbed the present she'd made for him.

He opened it to find a ring made from a woven red string. Puzzled, he looked to her for an explanation.

"That's to remind you I am trusting you to keep your promise to me." She smiled.

"I have to say you surprised me." He smiled slipping it on his finger to find it fit perfectly. "How did you know how big to make it?"

"Easy, we've held hands enough recently I figured it out." She giggled. "And I might have slipped into your room and measured one of your other rings."

"You're a sneaky little vixen." He said and kissed her again.

Steven led Grandmother Abigail into the room. A happy smile graced her face seeing the two of them acting like little kids caught doing something wrong.

During the last few weeks, she watched the love between them grow. Her heart filled with joy to see love shining in their eyes. She only hoped she would be around to at least see them wed. So many things could happen to interfere, she thought sadly. She knew of the curse that rested on the family but didn't know how to stop it.

Trent appeared in front of her and stopped her under the mistletoe. He quickly kissed her wrinkled cheek and stepped back when she laughed and punched his arm. The red of her cheeks gave her a healthy glow.

"Behave yourself Master Trent! Miss Abby will get jealous!" She grumbled cheerfully.

Grandmother settled into her favorite chair watching Trent hand out the Christmas gifts.

Abby's heart soared watching her gleefully ripping the paper to see what was inside. Trent gave her a nice shawl. Abby gifted her with a nice plush lap blanket to keep her warm.

Each in turn opened their gifts enjoying the banter and sweet moments that ensued. The most touching gift came from Grandmother Abigail to both Abby and Trent.

"It has been a joy to watch the love blossom between you these last few weeks. I know it will be a long time before you are free to marry, but I want to give you my blessing with these." She said with tears spilling from her eyes as she handed them each a ring box.

They opened them to find a wedding set. His was a platinum band with teardrop emeralds on either side of a round diamond. Hers was a platinum wedding band with diamond and emerald chips alternating the circumference of the ring and the engagement ring a one ct. round diamond with two half ct. teardrop emeralds on either side matching Trent's only daintier.

Abby choked back the pain in her heart. Even though she hoped, she felt deep down Trent would never be hers. Tears flowed as she hugged her grandmother and kissed her cheek. "Thank you Grandmother Abigail, it's perfect."

"I wanted to give them to you in case I wasn't around when the time came. Maybe they'll bring you the happiness I lost so long ago." She gave them a sad lonely smile.

"Come on. Let's sing some Christmas carols!" Abby hurried to the baby grand piano.

This Christmas would be one to remember. Grandmother Abigail hadn't had a happy Christmas in years, and Abby was just as joyful. This year she had family of her blood to enjoy it with.

Trent was proud of himself for bringing the two most important women in his life together one last time. He could tell Grandmother Abigail wasn't long for this world. Abby would be devastated when it happened.

Shortly, Grandmother Abigail asked Steven to take her upstairs. She said she wasn't feeling well and wanted to lay down.

Abby kissed her goodnight and for the first time since she'd met her, Abby told her she loved her.

The old woman kissed her with tears in her eyes and said, "My dear child, I've loved you from the moment I laid eyes on you. You've made these old bones happier than I've been in years."

Trent's heart tugged a little seeing the old lady so happy. He had a strong feeling that when Grandmother Abigail died, Abby would leave the island. Fear of the curse ultimately destroying her was the only thing that eclipsed how devastated he would be if that happened. Somehow he had to prevent her from leaving.

Chapter Nineteen

Gina poured over Shawn O'Malley's diary for two weeks, leaving Lance to keep Billy informed.

Shawn wrote in detail about his childhood and the abuse his mother, he, and his brothers, suffered at the hands of their father.

Miles had his mother's kind heart and often would take beatings meant for one of his brothers, and on a rare occasion for his mother. He would take the blame for their irresponsibility and foolishness. In doing so his brothers became even more careless. Miles didn't realize in protecting them, their hearts became dark and cruel. By the time he understood the harm he did, it was too late.

After their mother died, two of the brothers escaped one night and joined a crew of sailors bound for America.

Miles, his wife, son, and Shawn, the youngest, set out to find a place of safety far away from their father. Several other families joined them looking to Miles, who was a natural born leader, for guidance.

Upon their arrival, the settlers built several homes on the east end of the island. The natives on the west came to see the white skinned people with the fiery hair.

Miles formed a friendship with them, and they helped them survive their first winter in exchange for blankets.

Several weeks into spring, Shawn and his friends went hunting one morning and came upon several young braves on their own hunt. Shawn gathered the young men together at gun point and took their weapons. Then he and the men turned them loose to hunt them down like animals.

Only one brave escaped but he was wounded. When he crawled into the village, the chief became outraged. In that moment, he declared war against the settlement.

Shawn and his friends had returned to their homes with meat they'd stolen from the natives they murdered. In celebration the hunting party became quite inebriated to the point of unconsciousness.

While the settlers turned in for the night, the natives attacked. They fought for several days until Shawn and his friends slipped into the village and killed almost all of the men and took several of the younger women as slaves.

Miles waited until Shawn and his friends were too drunk to fight them and imprisoned them. While they waited for their punishment, Miles took the women back to their village.

When it came time to free the men, all but Shawn showed remorse for their actions. Shawn laughed in his brother's face, having given himself over to the darkness residing in his heart. In his anger, he lashed out at Miles and his friends.

In that moment, Miles heart hardened toward his brother. "You have brought a curse upon our family by the hand of the native's ancestor. The firstborn male child of our family will be taken from us if we stay on the island."

Soon after Miles, his small family and several of the settlers left the island, never to return. In doing so, Shawn and the vile men he led were left to live their lives as they saw fit.

Gina sat back in her chair to control the sickening feeling that threatened to overpower her when Lance came in for dinner.

"Have you been reading all afternoon?" Lance asked.

"After I put dinner in the oven, I sat down to read, and time got away from me." She replied sheepishly.

"Well, did you find anything to help Miss Abby?" He asked hopefully.

"Because of Shawn O'Malley's lawlessness and black heart, the first-born male child of the O'Malley family would be taken if they didn't leave the island." She explained praying that somehow the answer to eliminating the curse was in this sick twisted diary.

Gina wished she could just get to the end of the story without reading the details of his evil misdeeds. There were times Lance had to stop her from reading. In all his fifty years he'd witnessed some sickening things, but what Shawn O'Malley wrote made him queasy.

Gina continued after a short break. Eventually Shawn grew tired of the life he'd chosen and took a wife from the mainland. He brought her home to the island where everyone feared him. A few months later she became pregnant with their first child.

Shawn hadn't given the curse his brother mentioned another thought after Miles left. In her eighth month of pregnancy, she began seeing a ghost hiding in the shadow of several rooms of their home. The closer her time came to be delivered; the ghoul appeared to Shawn reminding him of his brother's warning.

The night the baby was born, a monstrous thunderstorm raged against the island. Shawn took his little boy to the study cradling him, while railing against God for his wife's death during childbirth. The child in his arms was the only connection to the love of his life.

Deep into his sorrow, the apparition appeared again and took the child from its father who couldn't move in his paralyzing fear. He watched helplessly as the fiend disappeared with his child.

Shawn formed a search party, and they searched for weeks but found nary a sign of the child or his captor. He eventually went to the village begging them to give his child back and end the curse.

That was the last entry in the diary.

Silence filled the room as Lance absorbed what they had learned.

"How could anyone be so horrible?" Gina asked trying to forget the pictures the diary painted in her mind.

"I don't know, but I do know that since that time no one lost a child until..." Lance's eyes lit up.

"Until Trent's child disappeared." Gina finished the sentence. "But Trent isn't related to the O'Malley's at all. He was born in Greece and his parents were full blood Greeks too. That means..."

"That means the baby had to have been O'Malley's and Trent covered for him. But why?" Lance asked bewildered. "And why wasn't Abby's dad taken, he was O'Malley's son?"

"Barbara's daughter sure paid a lot of attention to Trent when she first arrived, but Milly began coming around about the same time." Gina spoke up feeling sick again. "You don't think O'Malley took advantage of her do you?

"I don't know, but I'd be willing to bet Trent does. If he was covering it up he must have had a good reason for it." Lance swore.

ABBY SAT BY THE WINDOW watching more snow blanket the already white landscape. For the first time since her parents deaths, she had found peace. *"For now."* She thought while praying things might turn out differently. *"I'll make the most of every moment I have with Grandmother and Trent. If and when I leave here I have no doubt what Milly said will be true."*

Trent stood quietly in the shadow of the foyer watching her. *"God she is beautiful."* He thought resolving in that moment to make sure she remained here with him.

Abby felt Trent's eyes on her and turned to face him with tears glistening in her eyes.

Panic spread through is chest as he rushed to her side. Kneeling beside her chair he picked up her hand and asked, "What's wrong Miss Abby?"

"I was thinking about Grandmother. She's getting weaker and I know someday soon she'll no longer be with us." She whispered through a tight throat.

"Yes, Abby. She'll eventually die, but she's with us now." He agreed. "But that's not the only thing that's bothering you is it?"

"Trent, you, and I both know someday I'll leave here without you. I'm sure in your loneliness you'll find Milly to be a suitable mate." She confessed. "My heart is already breaking when I think of you being with her instead of me."

Trent knew from looking into her shining eyes her heart was truly breaking. Cupping her cheek in his hand, he wiped away a fresh tear and said, "Abby give me the time I need to get some things worked out. I told you before, you'll never regret waiting for me."

With tears sparkling in her eyes, she tried to speak, "I will but..." She couldn't get the words past the lump in her throat.

He pulled her into his arms, cradling her as he gently kissed away her tears. Whispering softly, "My sweet Abby, please trust me to make things right. I love you. Everything I'm doing is for you. The promises I have to keep are for your happiness. You'll never have to leave unless you want to."

Trent kissed her then looked into eyes fill with love, probably more than she would admit. He also saw the fear of losing him hiding in their depths. He walked her to her room stopping to open her door. Abby stood on her tiptoes to kiss him goodnight when Steven bellowed for help.

They ran into Grandmother Abigail's room where they found Steven giving her CPR.

"Abby, breathe for her! Trent take over so I can get her hooked up to the oxygen!" Steven ordered.

Steven worked on her for over an hour, but she had already passed on.

Abby sat quietly holding her lifeless hand with tears streaming down her flushed cheeks. It was a miracle she had found her, and she enjoyed three months with her. That was three months she never dreamed of having. If Trent hadn't introduced them, they wouldn't have ever met.

In that moment, she realized Trent had brought them together. Glancing up she found herself alone. Steven and Trent stepped into the hall to give her time alone to tell her grandmother goodbye. The one thing she hadn't been allowed to do when her parents died.

Leaning toward her grandmother, Abby's tears fell onto her lifeless cheek. She kissed her forehead and noticed the slight smile on the old woman's face as she pulled away one last time.

Trent stepped inside the room to check on her. Sensing him, she ran into his arms sobbing hysterically.

Steven stood back ready to help if needed. He had long since given up his quest to win her heart. Witnessing the tender way Trent soothed her, he knew he didn't have a prayer.

Trent swept her into his arms and carried her to her room while her hot tears soaked into his shirt. With Steven's help, they changed her clothes and put her to bed. Steven left to prepare Grandmother Abigail's body for burial.

Trent held her as deep sobs coursed through her tiny body. He sighed while gently stroking her silky red hair until she fell asleep.

Slowly going downstairs to the study to get a drink, his mind reflected on the days since he had first met Grandmother Abigail. His heart splintered from the death of the only woman who had ever treated him like a son.

After he finished the drink, he poured another one. Placing the glass on the desk, he stepped to the bookshelf where he had hidden the Diary of Shawn O'Malley.

The night Mr. O'Malley died, he gave it to him, insisting the answer to the curse might be in the yellowed pages. When he saw the book, he knew the mystery of the island would be put to rest.

Trent pulled the books away from the shelf he hid the book behind. Reaching behind them, he found it missing. Panic ripped through him as he flung books to the floor frantically searching for it.

"Where could it have gone? I know that's where I hid it." He thought when fear wrapped its claws around his heart, *"What if Abby has found it? Surely she would've said something if she had, Wouldn't she?"*

Billy chose that moment to knock on the study door before stepping inside, observing Trent replacing books on the shelf.

"What happened?" He asked warily.

"I'm looking for something. You haven't seen Abby in here looking around have you?" Trent asked barely keeping the panic out of his voice.

"No sir, but I ain't always in the mansion. Did you lose something?" He asked as a knot formed in his stomach.

"Yes, I'll find it." Trent mumbled. "Is there something you wanted?"

"I came to tell you Lance and Gina want to talk to you tomorrow when you're free." He replied guessing he was looking for the diary.

"Around nine. I'll meet them here." Trent said. "Tell them Grandmother Abigail passed away about an hour ago."

"I'll let them know. Sorry." Billy said wasting no time in leaving.

"Well, I guess I should go to bed. I can search tomorrow." Trent sighed after downing the glass of liquor on the desk.

As he passed by Abby's room, he heard her muffled cry. Looking in on her, he saw her thrashing in her bed. He crossed the room and gently shook her.

Frightened, Abby sat up fighting as though her life depended on it.

"Abby, wake up." He shook her a little harder.

She stopped struggling and opened her eyes. "Trent? Oh, Trent!"

The terror in her eyes made his blood run cold as he wondered what had happened to her?

Chapter Twenty

Abby took precedence over everything the next morning. Trent forgot about the diary while he made the arrangements for her grandmother's coffin to be built and digging the grave next to Mr. O'Malley.

Lance and Gina showed up at nine to offer their condolences to Abby and Trent. They insisted that what they wanted to speak with him about could wait.

Steven had dressed the old woman in a pretty pink dress that Abby chose from her wardrobe, sobbing hysterically. He sedated her after Gina and Lance left to help Trent with the arrangements. It broke his heart to see her in such grief. What made it worse is that Trent was the only one who could comfort her.

Gina returned to sit with her while Steven went to help Trent and the men put Grandmother Abigail into the coffin and ready it over the grave.

At four p.m. they held a small graveside service for her. Trent told of how she made him feel like he had had a mother for the first time in his life.

Lance remembered how she would slap his hands away from her fresh blueberry pies, and the older hands shared their good memories of the matriarch of the island.

Abby's heart hurt wishing she had more memories of her grandmother. At least she had a very special one that she held dear. Christmas night she told her grandmother she loved her, and her reply filled the empty place in her heart where family resides. That memory would be locked away in her heart for the rest of her life.

Tears streamed from Abby's eyes and dripped onto her coat forming tiny beads of ice as she watched them lower the coffin into the ground.

Everyone returned to the mansion while Trent stood a short distance away allowing her to say goodbye. Tiny flakes of snow slowly drifted from the sky covering the grave in a soft white blanket.

Trent went to her and put his arm around her shivering shoulders.

"It's time to go inside. You can visit when the snow stops falling sweetheart." He said quietly.

She turned her tear-filled eyes with tiny icicles covering her lashes and said, "Thank you, Trent.

"For what?' He asked completely surprised.

"For helping me find her and allowing us time together before she..." She sniffed.

"I only wish I could've done it sooner. Had I known about you before, you would've been brought here long ago." He said softly.

"You'll never know the joy you gave both of us. I only wish..." She hiccupped.

Trent understood what she tried to say and silently picked her up to carry her inside. Everyone had gathered in the living room to mourn their loss in quiet conversation.

Abby sat in her favorite chair by the window watching the snowfall come down heavier and faster. The voices in the room faded into nothingness as numbness overtook her heart. Shock and grief bore down on her, and her mind couldn't cope.

Trent talked with several of the guests, but his eyes were ever watchful over Abby. She didn't look too well, and he worried about her since he had awakened her from the nightmare she had. The look of terror in her eyes made his blood run cold. He had to find out what terrified her so.

Lance caught his attention, and he reluctantly followed him into the study. "What's so all fired important that it can't wait until tomorrow?"

Billy told us you were looking for something last night." Lance cleared his throat.

Trent stiffened, "You know what I was looking for don't you?"

"Yes. Mr. O'Malley gave Gina the history of their family and we found the diary. So, we've been trying to find a way to fight that curse."

"Why? Nobody asked you to stick your nose in it!" Trent growled.

"Hear us out Trent." Gina said calmly.

"I've come to think of you and Abby as my children. I know you're not babies, however you both are dear to my heart. I can see the love growing between you and I'll not stand by and let the same sadness ruin your lives." Lance explained.

"We'll discuss this in the morning. Bring both books back with you. Tonight, I have an obligation to Abby." He growled. "I don't want to leave her alone for very long."

When he entered the living room, he immediately noticed she was gone.

He told Lance and Billy to check the upper floors while he checked the dining room and kitchen.

When he saw Barbara he asked, "Have you seen Abby?"

"Yes, she went outside about ten minutes ago." She told him.

Trent threw his coat on and ran into the cold snowy night praying he could find her.

The wind picked up causing the snow to sting his face. Thankfully, he thought to grab a flashlight and soon found her prints quickly disappearing in the falling snow.

Lance had all the hands out looking for her toward the forest, the barns, and the docks.

Trent continued in the direction of her fast-fading footprints and knew where she was. He yelled for Lance and rushed to Grandmother Abigail's grave.

By the time he reached her, Abby was nearly buried beneath the snow. Lance followed in his footsteps, so he wasn't far behind with a blanket to wrap her in.

Trent brushed the snow from her and bundled her in the blanket with Lance's aid. He picked her up and with Lance's help they trudged through the deepening snow.

When they made it back, Trent took her upstairs where Gina and Steven met them in her room.

Gina shooed them from the bedroom while she changed her out of the wet clothes. Then she opened the door to allow them inside.

Steven checked her vitals and asked Gina for more blankets and to have Trent start a fire in the fireplace across the room.

Trent paced the hallway unable to control the emotions building inside him. Fear of what could happen to her wrapped its cold clammy fingers around his heart. She had to be okay, he couldn't take it if...

Barbara picked the wrong moment to ask if she could help.

"Why didn't you stop her from going out in this?" He turned his angst on her.

"I...I thought you knew. She walked out of the door without a word." Barbara defended herself.

Steven stepped into the hall just before he unloaded on the housekeeper. "You found her before frostbite set in. I'll have to watch her closely in case her temperature spikes too high. You can see her if you want."

Barbara made herself scarce the moment his attention turned toward the nurse.

Trent crossed the room with his emotions raging inside him. He was angry, scared, relieved, and confused all at once.

Unable to deal with anything or anyone, Abby watched the snow hit the window and slowly slide down the glass as it melted. Her heart filled with such grief she felt as though she were drowning in a pit of darkness. Even when her parents died, the grief was minimal. She supposed it was her age that saved her from this kind of soul crushing pain.

Maybe it hurt so much worse now because she knew now she was totally alone in this world. With no family to call her own, a black hole formed where her heart used to be.

Trent sat on the edge of her bed and took her hand only to have her pull away without looking at him.

"Abby?" He whispered from his constricted throat.

When she failed to answer, unable to allow the sadness of leaving the man she loved one day to mingle with the sorrow already squeezing the life from her.

Everyone she loved in life either died or went away. Right now, protecting her heart from further disappointment and misery was all she could bear.

Trent called her name once again holding his breath hoping for an answer.

She closed her eyes as tears formed again and turned away from him without a sound.

Rejection cut deep into his heart as he stood and left the room in silence.

Deep sobs erupted from the bottomless well of despair when Abby lost the battle to keep them at bay.

The knife lodged in Trent's heart twisted deeper when her cries reached his ears on his way downstairs.

He went to the study, poured himself a glass of scotch, and took two more bottles with him to the sofa. Determined to drink himself stupid, he hoped it would numb the pain in his heart.

Lance and Gina stood in the foyer at a loss watching him knock back glass after glass of the liquor.

Gina left her husband to deal with Trent while she returned upstairs to help with Abby. Steven held Abby while she cried but knew deep down the young woman would much rather be in Trent's arms.

It bothered him that she hadn't allowed Trent to comfort her. Even though it was torture for him, Steven offered the comfort she wouldn't allow Trent to give.

※

LANCE SAT DOWN QUIETLY waiting for Trent to speak.

"Wanna drink?" He offered before downing another glass.

"Nah, you're drinking enough for both of us. Wanna talk about it?" Lance asked wisely turning down the drink.

"What good would it do? Abby's already pulling away from me. She's gonna leave me, can't say as I blame her." Trent slurred his words.

"Good Heavens Trent! That poor girl just lost the last living relative she has on earth. You gave them the most precious gift anyone could give another person. Because of you they had almost three months of joy together." Lance tried to reason with him. "Abby knew her grandmother was old and feeble, she's not stupid. She knew one day Abigail would pass on."

"Whoopee! So, I did a good deed. Look at what it got me! I save her life and she wouldn't even look at me!" Trent lashed out hurt and angry. "For pity's sake she wouldn't even look at me!"

"It'll all be better in the morning." Lance said gathering the empty bottles.

"Lance, I love her. I want to stop that stupid curse. Somewhere in this mansion there's got to be an answer." Trent said before downing the last of the scotch.

"Gina, Billy, and I will help you Trent. You aren't alone in this. Abby as gone through so much in her young life, she deserves to be happy, and I mean to make that happened." Lance grumbled.

"So did Barbara's daughter. She deserved to be happy too. Old man O'Malley couldn't help himself when she slipped into his bed that night. The rest is history." Trent tried to stand. "I need another bottle."

"Why did you say the baby was yours Trent?" Lance asked with keen interest.

"Old man O'Malley thought if I said it was mine the curse wouldn't come true. I only did it because of Grandmother Abigail." He muttered.

"You were protecting the baby and Abigail?" Lance asked as the truth dawned in his eyes.

"Yes, Grandmother didn't know the baby was O'Malley's. Barbara did though, she's the one who put her up to it. He wouldn't have anything to do with Barbara, so she brought her daughter here for me. When I wouldn't have anything to do with her she concocted the scheme to trap O'Malley." He rubbed his eyes.

"Why didn't you fire her?" Lance asked confused.

"O'Malley paid them off." He yawned. "After the baby disappeared, he made me promise to end the curse. That's when he told me about Abby. He made me swear to keep her from getting married on the island if she chose to live here."

"When did he find out about her?" Lance absorbed all the information.

"His son wrote him letters from the day she was born. When they stopped, he searched for her. After he found her, he hired that attorney to keep an eye on her. Somehow he found this Walter character and helped him become her legal guardian. The attorney had his will with instructions to give to her when he died." He laid his head back against the sofa. "I never dreamed I'd be so foolish and fall in love with her. I tried not to, but she's so beautiful. I feel like I'm drowning when she looks at me. When she touches me…"

"I think you've had enough scotch tonight." Lance grabbed the last bottle from his hand.

"I ain't even started yet." Trent laughed.

"At any rate, you are not alone in this. Let us help you." Lance insisted. "Besides, that ghoul hasn't shown up in the last two months. Maybe it's over."

"You don't get it! It will never be over until we find a way to break it!" He grabbed at the bottle when Lance snuck it away from him. "Lance I can't lose her. I had hoped to have it figured out by now. Not that it does me any good, I've probably already lost her."

"Let's get you to bed, Trent." Lance signaled Billy who stood in the foyer in case he was needed.

Trent tried to fight, but soon gave in. In his condition, he knew it was useless as the two men hoisted him to his feet and half carried him upstairs. After they dumped him on his bed, they left him to sleep it off.

GINA SAT IN ABBY'S room keeping watch over her when Lance knocked on the open door.

He stepped inside and dropped a kiss on her temple. She looked up at him and said, "I think we should stay here tonight."

Lance agreed and kissed her goodnight before going down the hall to the room next to Trent's. Gina stayed until Steven relieved her, then she found the room Lance was in and went to bed ignoring the snores coming from her husband.

What little Abby slept was filled with nightmares of losing her parents and her life in the system as an orphan. Then a miracle happened when Walter and his wife stepped in and became her legal guardians.

The day they met, he told her he knew her father. Soon after, she was free to live in their home. Abby drifted in her sleep again and the hall appeared as she ran but seemingly couldn't get to the end of it.

When she finally reached for the door handle, the door flew open and the face in the shadows glared at her while claw-like hands reached for her. Screaming she tried to dodge the hands, but they gripped her shoulders and began pulling her into the inky darkness.

Steven yelled for help as he worked to hold her down. When he touched her he felt like he'd grabbed a hot coal.

Gina and Lance rushed in and between them they managed to hold her down enough for Steven to sedate her.

Soon after the one thing they feared happened. Abby's fever spiked to one hundred four. Steven quickly gave her medicine to bring her fever down, he turned to Gina.

"You and Lance stay with her for a few minutes. I'm calling my friend Dr. Marcus. She's gonna need better care than what I can give her. I don't have the supplies" He said leaving the room.

Chapter Twenty-one

Trent woke up with the worst hangover ever. Even during his college days, he had never felt this bad. His head felt like someone had put it in a vice and gradually tightened it.

Someone knocked on the door as he slowly sat up on the side of the bed. "Come in." He moaned.

When the door opened he looked up to find Lance standing in the doorway shaking his head.

"Don't even go there. I ain't in no mood for a lecture." He growled.

"Wasn't gonna. I thought you might wanna know Abby's taken a turn for the worse. Steven and a Dr. Marcus have been working to get her fever down most of the night." Lance told him. Dr. Marcus just left. He gave Steven instructions for her care. We're supposed to call him if she doesn't improve in a day or so."

"Does she want to see me?" Trent asked feeling guilty for her condition.

"She's been calling for you all night, but she's outta her head with the fever." Lance replied. "After what I saw last night, she's gotta be outta her mind."

"I said no lectures!" He grumbled.

"No lecture, just an observation." Lance grinned mischievously. "You might wanna get cleaned up before you see her. She might have a relapse if she regains her senses."

The look Trent shot him made Lance laugh as he went down the hall. When he stopped by Abby's room, he found Steven changing out the empty I.V. bag.

Steven, you might wanna give Trent something to clear his head when he shows up. He's got a killer hangover this morning." Lance grinned.

"That's all I need! By the time spring arrives, I'll be a certified doctor!" He grumbled from lack of sleep. "We need more supplies since y'all are going through what I have like water."

"He'll be here in a few minutes. Gina and I will be busy with our normal routines. Trent can take over for you now."

TRENT STOOD IN HIS shower letting the hot water work through the fog and fatigue from the hangover. *Trent you're such an idiot! A stupid selfish idiot! Abby wasn't in her right mind. The poor woman was devastated and grieving the loss of her last living relative, and you throw a tantrum instead of staying with her!*

The pity party had to stop, he decided when he stepped from the shower. If he wanted her, he would have to fight for her.

When he neared the door to her room, he could hear her calling out for him. When he stepped into the room, Steven handed him a couple of pills and a glass of water.

"I don't need those." He growled angrily.

"Take them! It'll help your head, though it won't change your mood any." Steven snapped a little testy himself. "Now, I'm gonna get some rest. I do need to sleep at least once a week."

Trent took the pills as ordered and sat down in the chair by the bed when Steven continued.

"If she becomes restless in her sleep, just hold her down until she stops. I can't give her any more sedatives until later. We're running low and she's had enough for eight hours. I'll dose her when I return if she needs it."

Trent watched him stomp from the room feeling like a scumbag. Because of his tantrum, that he was now paying dearly for, everyone else had to care for her.

His attention turned to Abby while she slept. Her silky red hair enhanced the delicate features of her innocent face.

He leaned back in the chair and closed his eyes for just a moment hoping the pills would help soon. He vowed never to throw such a tantrum again.

Abby's fever caused her to hallucinate. She stood in total darkness praying the apparition wouldn't find her. Her heart thundered in her chest as she strained to hear any sound or movement around her. Trembling inside, she dare not move or make a sound. If it weren't so dark, she could at least see him.

The urge to run arose inside as a scream formed in her throat when she felt the hot breath of the fiend from behind her. The moment his hands touched her shoulders, she began to fight with everything in her.

Trent grabbed her arms to keep her from pulling the I.V. port from her arm. Gathering her in his arms he managed to hold her while she fought to be free. He began speaking softly to her hoping to calm her down.

Abby felt the arms go around her and the feeling of safety encompassed her. For a brief moment, she opened her eyes and realized Trent had rescued her. Tears fell from her eyes as she begged him to keep her safe.

Trent's heart soared when he realized she wanted him to stay with her. Then reality set in when the heat from her feverish body bit into him meant she most likely had no idea what she was saying.

This rollercoaster of emotions strengthened his resolve to get to the bottom of the mystery that followed her. However, it would have to wait until she recovered. It made no difference whether she wanted him or demanded he leave; he would solve it to free her of any more heartache. He loved her enough that he would let her go if it made her happy, no matter how much it would break his heart.

THREE DAYS LATER, ABBY'S fever had broken in the middle of the night. She opened her eyes and focused on Trent snoozing in the chair beside her bed. Confusion filled her thoughts wondering why he was there unshaven with mussed hair and wrinkled clothes.

With no idea she'd been ill, she wondered if he had been sick.

Trent jumped when his head fell forward. He looked up and met Abby's eyes studying him intently.

"Welcome back." He smiled at her.

"What do you mean, welcome back?" She asked with furrowed brows.

"You don't know? Abby, you've been ill for close to five days now." He informed her. "Thanks to Steven you didn't die."

"How did I get so sick?" She blinked searching her memories for anything from the last few days.

"I'll let Steven tell you what happened. I'm glad you're okay now." He stood and stretched.

"Trent, is something wrong?" She asked confused by his aloofness.

"No, I'll have Steven come check you over. I have some work to catch up on." Trent moved toward the door. "I'm glad you're feeling better."

Abby watched him leave with no clue to what was going on and why Trent seemed so distant.

Steven appeared a few minutes later to check her over.

"The worst is over now. You'll need to stay in bed a couple of days to get some strength back, but you'll be fine now." He told her.

"What's going on with Trent?" She asked hoping he knew something.

"My guess is, he's nearing exhaustion. The morning you became ill, he came in and never left your side." He explained.

The thought of him staying by her side warmed her heart, but she needed to know how she became ill and why he was so distant."

Steven explained everything to her except for why Trent was acting so strange.

Abby had no recollection of what happened. Listening to Steven tell her about how high her fever was and how she hallucinated, she worried if she had said something wrong.

CLEAN SHAVEN AND SHOWERED, Trent buttoned up the shirt he put on when Lance knocked on his door.

"Come in." He called out feeling only somewhat better.

Lance opened the door and entered the room looking at him.

"Well? What do you want?" He barked getting annoyed.

"I just stopped in to see Abby. She's a bit confused by your attitude." Lance bristled.

"I'm just tired that's all." He made an excuse.

"I seem to remember something you told me the night of your tantrum..." Lance's temper began to rise.

"I don't remember and really don't want to know." He shot him an icy glare.

"For your own good I'm going to ignore that." Lance bit out, then reminded him how he cried over Abby's perceived rejection. Then he followed through with the whole evening's conversation.

Trent sat on the bed with his head in his hands listening to his drunken words and Lance showed no signs of stopping.

"One more thing, you can't blame Abby for her feelings that night. The poor girl was in a state of shock and grief. I doubt she even remembers any of it. So, if you love her like you said, you need to get in there and tell her so. Then you need to meet me and Gina downstairs and end this curse so you two can be happy. Whether or not it's together or separate depends on you Trent. If you want to be with her then prove it and fight for her. Isn't she worth that much to you? If not, well, we'll just be wasting our time." Lance scolded him.

Trent cleared his throat. He knew Lance was right. Looking at the floor like a schoolboy in trouble, he wasn't ready for another knife twisting in his heart and his pride made it worse.

"What if she rejects me again? I can't and won't be able to take that again." He said quietly.

"If she does, she didn't love you to begin with and you'll know." Lance said patting his shoulder.

Trent finally nodded his head. "I'll wait until this evening, meet me in the study after you get the books."

Trent headed down the hall after he finished dressing and met Barbara halfway downstairs.

"I'm gonna need coffee and scones in the study. Lance, Gina and possibly Billy will be in a meeting with me. No one is to disturb us unless Abby takes a turn for the worse." He ordered.

The tone in his voice she recognized all too well. "Yes sir, what would you like for lunch?"

"I'll have Gina let you know." He replied continuing downstairs.

He was putting the last of the business in order when Lance, Gina, and Billy entered the study.

"Lock the doors, I don't want anyone hearing what we're talking about." Trent insisted sitting on the sofa like a small boy who had lost his first real fight.

Gina's heart went out to him when she caught the torment in his eyes.

"So, tell me what you know so far." Trent said already weary of the task ahead.

Gina answered, "We know that until the event involving Barbara's daughter, no other children had disappeared since Shawn O'Malley's child.

The memory of the night Mr. O'Malley called him to the study flooded Trent's thoughts. Guilt still plagued him over the horrific end Barbara's daughter suffered.

I was a fool! How could anyone resist a beautiful girl crawling in bed with them? Trent, I couldn't help it! He'd said with tears in his eyes with fear marring his weathered face of what may come.

I'll tell everyone the baby is mine. I'm sure we can buy her and Barbara off. She and her mother are nothing but gold diggers anyhow. Trent offered.

I knew I could count on you Trent my boy. Someday I'll reward you handsomely for your loyalty to me. The old man sighed in relief.

"Trent?" Gina called out gaining his attention.

"Yes?" He responded pushing the memory away.

"Why did you say that baby was yours?" She asked again.

"I'm sure Lance told you all about it, since I spilled my guts to him the other night." He growled.

"I want to hear it from you. Lance may have left something out, or you didn't tell him everything." Gina insisted.

Trent drew a deep breath as guilt assailed him again and told them everything.

Chapter Twenty-two

Abby did a little happy dance when Steven determined she was well enough to get out of bed. Now she could see something besides the four walls of her room.

Trent and the others hatched a plan to keep Abby occupied. Gina offered to help her clean her grandparents room out. Meanwhile, Lance and Trent would search every nook and cranny for any clue to break the curse. Billy was promoted to assistant head wrangler for the time being. He would keep the workers and laborers on task.

Trent had gone through almost everything in Mr. O'Malley's bedroom, but all he had found was a few old letters of nothing consequential.

THE SUN BROKE THROUGH the clouds bringing out the sparkling fairy dust on the snow. Cardinals and various other birds searched for food while smaller animals scrambled away from their natural predators.

Abby watched them without seeing. Memories of the last three months brought tears to her eyes. They were the happiest times she had experienced since before her parents died.

Trent quietly watched her from the doorway. The yearning to hold her again intensified when he saw her wipe tears away from her cheek.

"Abby? Is everything okay?" Trent asked startling her.

"Oh! Um, yeah. I'm just thinking." She sighed wiping more tears away.

The one thing he hated since meeting her was seeing her cry. Desperation to comfort her, to show her how much he loves her nearly took him to his knees. Shoving those feelings aside, he had already made up his mind to keep his distance. Late last night he and Lance found some ancient documents. Hopefully, they would contain something when they reviewed them.

"Don't cry Abby. I'm keeping my promise. I just need a little more time." He spoke quietly then turned to leave. "I'll see you later."

He left before she responded afraid he wouldn't have the resolve to leave.

Lance was already busy looking through the mountain of old papers when he stepped into the room.

"Is Gina coming to help Abby?" He asked pouring himself a drink.

"Yes, she had something to do before coming over. She won't be too long." Lance replied. "It's kind of early for that ain't it?"

"I'm a big boy, I can handle my own business thank you very much." He snapped.

"Turning yourself into an alcoholic ain't the answer." Lance held his hands in the air. "I'm just saying."

"I said, I can handle it." He grabbed a stack of papers and sat down to review them.

"Okay, but the next time you get drunk, you're on your own. I'll leave you where you lay." Lance growled.

Trent refrained from answering him because he knew his friend was right.

<hr />

LOST IN HER THOUGHTS, Abby didn't hear Gina arrived. "How are you this morning Miss Abby?" She asked cheerfully.

"Okay. I need something to do." Abby admitted leaving her thoughts behind.

"I have the perfect solution. We can go through your grandparents room now. Trent wouldn't allow anyone to go in there because of your grandmother. It's time to clean it out now." Gina smiled at her.

Abby graced Gina with an excited smile. *Maybe I can find some answers.*

<hr />

"SHAWN O'MALLEY DIED over a hundred and fifty years ago. He only sired one child before committing suicide. By all accounts, no other O'Malley child was taken until seven years ago." Lance commented.

"Something else is bothering me. Why has that wraith only shown himself to Abby, Billy, and me?" Trent said. "Abby said it appeared to her on the one-year anniversary of her parents death. Then it showed up every time it stormed."

"I told you he was back, but you wouldn't hear of it. It wouldn't surprise me in the least to find he's working for Miles O'Malley hisself." Lance shook his head.

"Miles O'Malley died a long time ago. And just because we never found my father's body doesn't mean he's the face in the shadows. He wasn't disfigured in any way like that fiend we saw." Trent disagreed. "All we have is more questions and no answers!"

"If we find out who that fiend is, maybe that will give us the answer to ending the curse." Lance said, "We've only scratched the surface, let's keep digging."

ABBY PAUSED BEFORE stepping into her grandparents room. Her grandmother had so enjoyed being home, yet occasionally she would catch sadness in her eyes. She knew her grandmother missed her grandfather and son. They were her whole world until her grandfather and father had a disagreement about her mother. No matter how many times she asked, her grandmother refused to tell her.

Her grandmother finally left when she found the letters from her father. When she confronted him about it, grandfather forbade her from contacting Abby in any way.

Thanks to Trent, she managed to secure the cottage on the mainland that Abby met her in.

"Abby?" Gina asked, "What's wrong?"

"I'm just remembering my time with my Grandmother." She sighed pushing open the door.

Gina was so easy to talk to before long she told her all about her visits with her grandmother.

Gina listened while she helped Abby go through her inheritance. Abby had little to say that gave her any information to help them in their search.

They continued to pack things as Abby carefully touched each item wondering how it came to be in her grandparents possession. In her head she imagined her grandfather presenting a special piece of jewelry to her grandmother. Or the pressed flowers in the family bible she imagined her father with a dirty face handing over the flowers to his mother with a big smile on his face.

Gina found Abby filled the missing piece of her heart. After losing her own little girl from Tay-Sachs disease, together they decided not to have any more children. Something died inside her that day. Even as much as she loved Lance, for a time she couldn't live with the disappointment of being unable to fulfill their dreams of having a house full of children. She left Lance and traveled home to her mother. Many times, she thanked God they had finally worked things out and were happy.

The day she met Abby O'Malley it was as though God smiled on her allowing this young orphan to be in her life. Trent had become the son Lance had dreamed of, but she was finding Abby filled the place where her daughter had been.

TRENT GREW MORE FRUSTRATED the longer they searched. "I feel like we're just spinning our wheels here. It could take months, even years to go through all the hiding places in this mansion. I'm tired, let's call it a day." He flopped into the chair by the fireplace.

"Okay, but we're learning all sorts of things about this island. In my book our time isn't wasted." Lance said putting the books he was going through back on the shelves.

"Lance..." Trent began.

"Yeah?" Lance answered.

"Nothin... You want a drink?" He asked.

"No and you shouldn't either." Lance growled.

"Okay papa. I'll be a good little boy." He grinned.

"What?" Lance looked up innocently.

"Yeah, I love you too. The truth is, you've been more of a father to me than my own dad. O'Malley liked to think of me as his son, but to me he was only my boss. Grandmother Abigail treated me more like a son than he did." Trent said.

"Since we're having a moment," Lance grinned, "I think of you as my son too. I saw how you reacted when you were told your father was looking for you. The day of the wolf attack, everyone in the room saw the scars. I had no idea how badly he abused you. It broke my heart." Lance said with tears glistening in his eyes. "Despite all that, you've turned out well and I don't want you to make a mistake and ruin what you've found in Abby."

"That will have to wait. I vowed to solve the mystery for her well-being." He shook his head. "I was stupid to fall for her."

"Trent, take some advice if you don't do something soon, she's gonna leave here. I can see the handwriting on the wall." Lance said.

"I don't know what to do. She's nothing like Milly who's been around the block way more than a time or two. Abby's innocent and I won't take that from her. That should be given to her husband on their wedding night."

"I agree, and it should be yours on your wedding night. Forget what old man O'Malley made you promise. He was nothing but a puppet master manipulating everyone around him, especially you." Lance growled.

"I'll take care of it, I promise." Trent sighed in defeat.

Lance and Gina left for their cottage leaving Trent and Abby alone in the mansion. Barbara had the evening off, and Steven ate with the wranglers tending to one who got tangled in some barbed wire.

They ate the meal Barbara had left for them in total silence. Abby felt as though she'd just met him. When they were finished, he helped her from her chair and led her to the living room where Barbara left refreshments for them.

Trent offered her some tea before pouring himself a glass of scotch.

Confused and nervous by his politeness, she wondered what he was up to. Especially since he had barely spoken to her since she recovered.

Now he sat across from her watching every move she made. So much so, she felt like she was under a magnifying glass. She took a sip of her drink and moved to set it down spilling it in the process.

"Perhaps you would prefer what I'm drinking." He offered.

"Yes, thank you." She agreed in need of something to calm her nerves.

To her surprise he sat next to her after she accepted the drink from him.

Forgetting how potent the scotch was, she took a big gulp and coughed. Embarrassed, she set it on the table and stood to leave.

"Going somewhere? You should finish your drink and enjoy the fire." He spoke softly.

"What do you want?" She asked suspiciously. "You've made it quite clear that you want nothing to do with me. You've barely spoken to me since I recovered."

"I'd like to rectify that if you'll permit me to." He said.

"Are you trying to get close to me so you can steal my inheritance, or use me for some sick sense of satisfaction? Maybe you want to use me to keep Milly Boudreau away?" She hissed. "I'm sorry, but I'd rather sit alone in my room, away from you!"

Trent caught her before she knew he'd moved stopping her from leaving the room. She turned to slap him as he prevented her from hitting him and jerked her against his hard chest while glaring into her eyes.

"Let me go!" She struggled against him.

Anger filled his eyes, "I think not Miss Abby O'Malley, you have no idea what I'm doing. I don't know who gave you those ideas, but you are dead wrong. I don't need your fortune or this island. I have everything I need except for a woman."

Chapter Twenty-three

Abby stared wide eyed at him feeling like he'd slapped her. She watched the anger in his eyes turn to desire.

Trent's tight rein on his emotions broke as he looked into her eyes. He captured her lips in a punishing kiss. Lost in his desires and wants he backed her against the door.

Abby's heart raced in fear as his kisses became more passionate and demanding. Desperation filled her as she struggled to get free of his painful grip. Her nails scraped his cheeks as she clawed to get away from him.

Enraged, he ripped her dress before her pleas filtered through the fog clouding his mind. Realizing what he had done, he released her, "I'm so sorry Abby. I didn't mean to... my God what have I done?"

Abby seized the opportunity to escape him, running upstairs to her room and locking the door behind her. She fell across her bed sobbing hysterically.

Trent threw on his coat and stomped outside desperate to get away from the guilt and shame of his actions. He berated himself for losing control of his desires. The reality of his actions driving her away from him left an empty dark chasm in his heart. *Why did I have to fall in love with her? Why does she have to be so beautiful?*

The anguish in his soul drove him forward without realizing where he was going. Finally stopping he looked around to find he was alone in the forest without a rifle. He turned to retrace his steps when he heard something. Holding his breath, he stopped to look around, but saw nothing. Shaking his head, he continued to retrace his steps thinking no one would be out here at this time of night. Not unless they had a death wish or was an idiot like him.

The feeling of eyes watching him sent a cold shiver down his spine. Occasionally, he'd stop to look around, then continue his trek toward home.

Once he closed the door to the mansion behind him, he took a deep breath and released the tension that had built up inside his chest.

Using the last bit of energy he had, he climbed the stairs to his bedroom. As he passed Abby's door, he could hear her still crying. His heart fell with the knowledge he was the cause of her tears.

Even though he was the last person she wanted to see, he knocked on her door.

"Who is it?" Abby called out fearfully.

"It's Trent, can I come in?" He asked holding his breath.

"Why? To hurt me again?" She cried.

When she unlocked the door, he opened it, he watched her sit back on the bed, eyes wide with fear and tears escaping down her cheeks.

"Are you hurt?' He asked feeling lower than dirt.

"I'll be alright. What do you want?" She grabbed a pillow and hugged it defensively.

"I'm so sorry. It's so hard to control myself around you. I can only stay away for so long before..." He said clearly miserable.

"Why have you stayed away?" She asked with such hurt in her eyes it clawed at his heart.

"When you refused to talk to me or even look at me after I found you. I thought you didn't care. So, I backed off." He explained with angst in his face.

I don't remember anything about that entire week. After Grandmother died, I couldn't function. She was the only family I had left. If it weren't for you, I never would have known her. It made me love you more." She told him.

"But... I thought... Oh Abby, I'm so sorry." He said crossing the room. When she recoiled as he approached her and knelt on his knees beside the bed, he put his arms around her and cried begging her to forgive him.

Gently running her fingers through his dark hair, she whispered. "Trent I love you more than I can convey to you. Despite how badly I want to hate you right now, I can't help but forgive you."

He looked into her smiling face and let go of the grief and condemnation he harbored in his heart.

She gently brushed away his tears and kissed his forehead. In that one simple action, the emotional turmoil he harbored for most of his life exploded from the box he hid them in.

Abby sank to her knees and held him until he cried the last tear from his eyes. Scrubbing his face, he looked into the face of the most wonderful and beautiful woman in the world. He pulled her in for a long kiss. She hesitated, but soon relaxed into his arms. He knew she understood some of what he went through, but the secrets he carried came with a cost. Now he wasn't sure he wanted to carry them anymore.

To add to his mortification, he had been taught it was a sign of weakness to cry, but to do it in front of a woman was beyond all that was holy. Abby O'Malley changed all that. Since meeting her everything he'd ever been taught flew out of the window.

Abby watched his eyes fill with torture and she kissed him again. When she held him in her arms, his pain miraculously turned into peace.

"Trent, whatever your carrying, won't you let me help?" She asked hopefully.

"I can't Abby. I made a promise to your grandfather, several promises in fact, before he died. I have to honor my words, or you'll never have a happy life. Nor will I." He said with such angst tears gathered in Abby's eyes.

LANCE LISTENED TO GINA tell him about why Grandmother Abigail moved to the mainland. Old man O'Malley knew about Abby almost from the day she was born. Grandmother Abigail found the letters and her husband forbade her from contacting them. She begged him to bring her only child and his family back to the island. When he refused she left with Trent's help.

Lance told her of what they'd discovered, reasoning it out as he spoke.

"Something else is going on here. I don't know how or why, but I will figure it out. If I'm any judge of character, Trent will put a stop to it, and whoever is behind it." He said.

"I'm tired, let's go to bed." Gina yawned and kissed him on top of his balding head.

"I'll be up in a minute love." He said giving her a peck on the lips.

He just locked the door when he saw a figure step into the forest. Quickly donning his coat, he grabbed his rifle and slipped out of the door. Keeping his distance, he quietly followed and realized it was Trent. Worry and shock warred in his mind as he wondered, *What the devil is he doing out here this time of night and why is he going into the forest unarmed?*

Managing to keep out of sight, he remained quiet when Trent turned to go back. Lance waited to follow. He observed Trent stopping several times and look around before trudging on. Lance wondered if he was waiting for someone. It concerned him because this was so out of character for him.

When Trent disappeared into the mansion, Lance shrugged his shoulders and went back home baffled. He'd get to the bottom of it tomorrow. After he explained himself to Gina, he took her in his arms and fell asleep holding her.

Abby snuggled into the warmth surrounding her, as she felt the soft steady beat of a heart against her back. The memory of the torment in his eyes broke her heart again.

The conversation they had crawled through her memory.

Trent, stay with me. Let me comfort you tonight. She pleaded with him.
He pulled away from her, I don't trust myself to keep my hands off you.
I trust you. We'll only sleep, nothing more. She assured him.

Unable to refuse her, he crawled in the bed behind her gently pulling her close. In no time, he slipped into a deep sleep.

Trent moved tightening his arm around her, feeling his warm steady breath as he nuzzled her neck in his sleep.

Enjoying the feeling of comfort, she realized he must have been exhausted since this was the first time he'd moved all night.

True to her word, she didn't give him any reason to try anything with her.

Considering how quickly he fell asleep, she figured he needed the rest. Contented, she dozed lightly never wanting him to leave.

Barbara came to let her know breakfast was ready and found the door slightly open. Anger grew into rage when she peek to see Trent in Abby's bed.

She closed the door and stomped downstairs muttering, *How could he, after rejecting her daughter and telling everyone the baby she carried was his, even though it was O'Malley's?*

Now this slip of a girl, Abby swept in and captured Trent's heart, when he wouldn't give her Susan the time of day while she was alive.

In her heart, she resolved to make Trent and Abby O'Malley pay for their sins.

When she reached the kitchen, she grabbed the dough she had rising and punched it down. She always found it therapeutic to take her aggression out on the dough. With each punch, she envisioned Trent or Abby. She didn't know how to do it, but Millie would. When spring finally comes around, things would get extremely interesting. A wicked smile formed on her lips as she formed the dough into rolls.

TRENT SLOWLY OPENED his eyes a little confused by his surroundings, and why Abby was asleep next to him.

The soft aroma of her hair, the feel of her in his arms felt so right. If he weren't careful, she could be as addictive as any drug.

Abby snuggled closer as she felt his arms tighten feeling the quickening pace of his heartbeat. He nuzzled her neck with light kisses.

"Abby, my sweet Abby." He whispered.

"Did you sleep well?" She asked enjoying his tender attention.

"Mm, yes." He mumbled against her hair.

"We should get up, It's nearly noon." She wiggled against his grip.

"Uh huh." He nibbled her ear.

"You need to stop... What if someone comes looking for us?" She asked.

"Ok." He continued teasing her.

"Trent you promised." She reminded him trying to get free. "Someone will find us."

"Let them. I'm perfectly content right where I am." He informed her.

"But Trent..." She began when he flipped her on her back and kissed her.

Unable to resist him, she returned his kisses with the eagerness of an innocent.

"I'll stop and go away. I'll see you downstairs." He slid away and moved toward the door.

"That's not fair!" She grabbed a pillow and launched it at him.

He ducked out of the door just at the pillow sailed into the hall. He slammed the door shut and turned to find Lance glaring at him. "I came up to find out if you were okay when you didn't meet us downstairs. Apparently you're really okay."

"Nothing happened, well, almost nothing, Papa. I'll be downstairs in ten." Trent grinned turning toward his room.

"I'll be waiting!" Lance grumbled stomping toward the stairs.

Wondering what made Lance so grumpy, Trent quickly dressed and in no time shut the study door behind him. *Time to face the music.* He thought.

Chapter Twenty-four

Ignoring Lance's glare, Trent grabbed several books off the shelf of one of five massive floor to ceiling bookshelves. He sat on the couch and looked up to see Lance flipping through the pages of the book he had picked up. Quietly, he opened the book he took from the top of his pile.

After a long loud silence, Lance almost exploded, "You gonna tell me what happened last night? From the look of your face, you had a fight with a bobcat."

"What's got your tailfeathers in a ruffle this morning?" Trent smiled for the first time in a long while.

"I can see what's got you in a good mood." He snapped. "She was an innocent for God's sake."

"Don't worry Papa, she still is." Trent's voice clouded. "I almost lost her last night."

"Wha... I don't understand. And why did you take a walk in the forest last night, alone with no weapon?" His eyebrows furrowed in confusion.

Despite the repercussions, Trent told him the whole story of what happened last night.

Lance quietly listened as his anger grew, until he told him Abby had forgiven him and helped him get over some of his issues. That seemed to calm him somewhat, but he was still angry.

"That's the reason you caught me coming out of her room this morning. I didn't do anything to spoil her. Although I could get used to sleeping next to her, I haven't slept that good in a long time." Trent said with a smile.

"You should be horsewhipped attacking her like that! You're danged lucky she forgave you. Although it appears she helped you get rid of a lot of grief last night. If you don't marry her when this is over, you're a fool." He grumbled.

"I plan on it, so let's find something so we can move on with our lives." Trent agreed.

"Okay, but I'm warning you Trenton Dale Winthrop, if you hurt Abby again, you'll answer to me!" Lance glared at him with a promise of retribution in his steel gray eyes.

"Okay Papa, I promise I'll never harm a hair on her beautiful head." He teased. "Feel any better now?"

"You know sometimes you can be a real jerk!" Lance laughed.

They resumed their search hoping it wouldn't take long to end the curse that started over one-hundred years ago.

GINA AND ABBY LAUGHED and talked as they boxed everything up. Their relationship was cemented while Abby went through her grandmother's jewelry. Most were vintage pieces she figured were older than her great-great-grandmother, and priceless. Gently touching each piece, she felt a connection to her ancestors bringing tears to her eyes.

Gina put her arm around Abby and suggested, "I think we need a break."

When Abby agreed, they went downstairs. Gina excused herself to check on her boys and insisted they take a break in the dining room as well.

When they stepped into the foyer, Abby threw herself into Trent's arms with love shining in her eyes.

"How are things going in your grandparents room?" Trent asked.

Lance and Gina slipped into the dining room to give them a moment.

"We're almost finished. It's hard to decide what to keep or throw out." She sighed leaning against his chest listening to his heartbeat. "I don't know what their favorite or cherished treasures were."

Holding her tightly he said, "Pack up all the clothes and this spring we'll take it to the village on the other side of the island. The rest you can keep or throw away. It's all yours anyhow. Now, I have to get back to business."

She touched the scratches on his face and said, "I'm glad we worked everything out. I'm much happier and from your mood so are you."

"One of these days…" He growled before stealing a kiss.

"Okay, you two lovebirds, it's time to finish our work." Gina glared at Trent.

It was obvious Lance had spilled the beans to her. Smiling at her he said, "Yes, momma."

As he passed her, he swooped her into his arms with a bear hug teasing her.

"Put me down!" She hit his shoulder laughing.

Dodging another swat, he hurried into the study thinking Abby was correct about his mood.

Gina had wondered about the scratches on Trent's face, but Abby seemed no worse for the wear. She was angry at Trent for terrorizing Abby, in her book he needed a good spanking.

Her respect for Abby grew the more she got to know her. The young woman's ability to forgive was astonishing. If it had been her, she would have left and never looked back, much like Grandmother Abigail did.

Abby started singing softly, as she folded the clothes and packed them away.

Gina wiped a tear from her eye. "That was beautiful Abby. Where did you learn it?"

"I made it up in the first foster home I was sent to. I found if I held onto it, I could overcome the many trials thrown at me." Abby shrugged with embarrassment. She'd never sang it to anyone.

When they were finished, Abby wondered what she would occupy herself with now.

Sensing her worry, Gina said, "Tomorrow we can start in any room except Trent's, yours, and the one Steven is using. It should keep us busy until spring, then you can start redecorating those rooms."

Abby stopped looking at Gina with uncertainty in her eyes.

"What's wrong?" She asked concerned.

"I've never decorated anything in my life. I wouldn't know the first thing about it." Abby confessed quietly.

"Don't worry, I'll teach you everything you need to know. I never had the opportunity to instruct my own daughter. It would be my honor to teach you." She managed blinking back tears.

"Thank you Gina. I can't think of anyone else I'd enjoy having to teach me than you." Abby hugged her.

Lance and Gina stayed for dinner enjoying the light hearted atmosphere. The only thing marring that was Trent noticed Barbara's attitude toward Abby had changed. Until today, she had been respectful to her leaving him no choice but to correct her, which would happen after dinner.

Gina, Lance, and Abby went to the living room while Trent reprimanded Barbara concerning her attitude. He joined them in the study sitting next to Abby.

Abby giggled and wiped her eyes while listening to Lance and Gina tell stories about Trent when he first arrived on the island. She tried to keep a straight face when he sat next to her and failed miserably. Gina found it equally funny when Trent shot her a mischievous look.

"Go ahead Gina. Get it all out of your system. I have a few stories of my own to tell." He warned her.

"Okay, it's just... the look on your face when you fell off that horse was priceless." She giggled.

"Why don't we talk about your attempt to make gooseberry jelly?" Trent asked with a wicked grin on his lips.

"I'm shutting up!" Gina sobered giving him a cold stare.

Lance stood claiming he was ready for bed and helped Gina to her feet. Abby hugged her and watched Trent walk them from the room.

Trent watched as they disappeared into the darkness thanking God for the blessing of having them in his life. He closed the door and went back to the living room. Nearing the door, he heard the most beautiful singing coming from the room. He stopped in the shadow of the foyer and listened. Her lovely voice touched a part of him he never imagined anyone would ever reach.

Feeling eyes on her she apprehensively turned and relaxed when she saw Trent enter the room.

He sat next to her, and she leaned against him with her head on his shoulder.

"Abby, will you sing for me?" He asked holding her closely.

"Promise not to laugh?" She asked.

"I promise." He swore.

Abby began singing softly. He closed his eyes allowing her voice to wash over him calming his weary mind. He drifted away to a peaceful place he never wanted to leave.

Abby fell silent and looked up to find him relaxed with a look of serenity resting on his face.

"That was beautiful." He whispered quietly.

"I think it's time for bed. Gina and I have a lot to do tomorrow." She said.

"That's probably for the best. I don't want a repeat of last night. Ever." He sighed.

"Good night." She kissed his stubbled cheek.

"Good night my sweet Abby." He pulled her in for a kiss.

Climbing the stairs did nothing to stop the ache in her heart. She didn't understand the feelings growing inside her. Maybe when she felt more comfortable around Gina she might explain them to her.

Chapter Twenty-five

Crocus and day lilies were peeking through the last remnants of snow. Birds fluttered and hopped searching for food and materials for their nests. The unmistakable sign that spring was nearly upon them.

Valentines Day would arrived in ten days and Abby wanted to give Trent something but had no clue what that would be. A smile graced her face when she thought of how their love had blossomed since Christmas.

Whatever he and Lance were working on kept him locked in the study for hours on end, leaving her anticipating his presence when they emerged at the end of the day.

Most days, Gina kept her occupied and she was grateful for their budding friendship, although Abby began thinking of her as a mother. Oh, she couldn't ever replace her own mother, but Abby now felt close enough to confide in her.

Barbara had been courteous to her since the night Trent tore into her about her attitude. She still didn't know what she did to offend the woman.

Their evenings were fill with unsatisfied love, Trent made himself a promise to slow down with her. No matter how bad they wanted each other, he pulled away. He was determined to wait until their wedding night.

Trent and Lance continued their search for answers and found many stories about the island. Some were well known, others were new to them. Still, they were no closer to the answers they sought.

"These are all just stories from people. How do we know which ones are fact or just somebody's imagination?" Lance asked.

"There are so many, I have to wonder if we'll ever find anything." Trent blew out a breath. "I want to get this over with so I can be with Abby. It's tough being down the hall from her knowing she feels the same way."

"I'm proud of you Trent. I know it hasn't been easy for either of you but trust me it'll be worth the wait on your wedding night." Lance reassured him.

"I want to give her a wedding fit for a queen." Trent said. "Everyone we know will be invited."

"I can almost see Milly Boudreau's face when she finds out." Lance chuckled. "You're gonna have a big battle on your hands with her."

"I'm surprised she hasn't made an appearance yet. The snow is nearly gone." Trent said even as a sense of foreboding teased the back of his mind.

"We can thank our lucky stars she hasn't been around to upset the apple cart between you and Abby." Lance grinned.

"You might as well know, I have a special gift for Abby on Valentine's Day." Trent looked at Lance sheepishly.

"Don't tell me, an expensive bottle of perfume?" Lance rolled his eyes.

"This." Trent held out a ring box with a one carat diamond ring nestled between the velvet folds.

"Wow! You're going to propose?" Lance asked in surprise.

"Yes, but we'll have to keep it quiet until this is over." Trent frowned.

"Don't worry, now we have more of an incentive to end this." Lance slapped his shoulder.

ABBY AWOKE WITH AN air of excitement wondering what the day would bring. This year Valentine's Day would be special. Since the death of her parents, she hadn't observed the day since she had no one to celebrate it with her.

She grabbed her prettiest dress and slipped into it, taking a long look in the mirror, pleased with the fit. When she finished carefully applying her make up and styling her hair she felt special. With a final spritz of the most expensive perfume she owned, she knew Trent wouldn't be able to resist her. She purposely delayed going down to breakfast so she could make a dramatic entrance.

Trent became worried about Abby since breakfast was nearly over. He was halfway upstairs when Abby appeared on the landing. Caught by surprise, he stumbled up the next step.

Abby's heart leapt for joy when she caught the look on his face. *Yup, it was so worth the time and effort.*

"Good morning, Master Trent!" She flashed perfect white teeth framed with ruby red lips curved into a smile.

"Um, good morning, Miss Abby." He said after clearing his throat.

"Are you feeling okay?" She smiled innocently.

"You little vixen! Come here!" He growled pulling her into his arms.

The soft scent of her perfume fogged Trent's senses pulling him into a dream-like state. The dress, her perfectly styled hair, and flawless makeup made her the most beautiful woman he'd ever seen.

Passionately kissing her, he held her tightly in his arms as his ability for thought was lost to him. He could feel her fingers running through his hair and became lost in her innocence.

"What do you think you're doing, Abby O'Malley?' The familiar angry voice barked.

Trent turned to see Milly standing in the foyer with fury glaring from her eyes.

"What are you doing here?" Trent growled.

"I came to wish you a happy Valentine's Day, but I see someone beat me to it." Milly snapped.

"I dare say, I'm the best gift he's ever gotten." Abby smile triumphantly.

"I feel sorry for you. Remember what I said would happen. You wait and see!" Milly yelled.

"Get it through that thick skull of yours Milly, He doesn't love you and he never will!" Abby put her arms around Trent's neck and kissed him deeply. The poor man couldn't help but respond to her.

"It's going to be quite a spectacle when he comes to his senses. I'll be here laughing when it happens!" Milly stormed out of the mansion.

"Well, that was fun." Abby grumbled angrily.

"Uh huh." Trent kissed her neck.

"Trent?" Abby whispered.

"What have you done to me woman?" He groaned placing his forehead against hers.

"I gave you me for Valentine's Day." She giggled.

"I can hardly wait for our wedding night." He muttered.

Abby froze and looked at him wide eyed, "What did you say?"

Trent took the ring box from his pocket and said, Abby Jane O'Malley, will you marry me?"

Stunned into silence, she wondered if he had found what kept them apart.

"Abby?" Trent stepped down a step his heart beating wildly with apprehension.

"Yes! I'll marry you Trenton Dale Winthrop!" She answered throwing her arms around his neck and kissing him as tears fell freely from her eyes.

"You scared me for a second there." He slipped the ring on her finger. "There's one condition, we can't let anyone know until I finish what I've started. It would be dangerous if anyone knew."

Although she was confused, Abby trusted him, so she agreed. "I'll wear it on a chain around my neck until further notice." She promised.

THE DAY CAME WHEN COATS were no longer needed, and she could sit in the gazebo again.

Settling back in the chair, she drank her hot tea and listened to the nature sounds around her. A sense of contentment shrouded her like a warm blanket. The face in the shadows was a long-forgotten memory.

Trent talked with her about returning to the main land to clear out Grandmother Abigail's cottage. He left the decision to keep it or sell it up to her.

She thought long and hard about it, and decided to keep it as a place to stay when they were on the main land. They would keep it closed when not in use.

Gina's shadow shook her from her thoughts, and she jumped to her feet.

"It's nice to see you so happy about planting flowers." She giggled.

"Yes, let's go." Abby's energy rubbed off on Gina.

Barbara caught sight of them from the window seething in anger. She grumbled under her breath, "It should be my Susan out there not Abby."

Milly kept in touch with her over the winter months and had plans for Abby O'Malley. Trent would either marry Milly or she would kill him if he refused.

A twisted smile formed on Barbara's lips as she wondered what kind of sadistic fun Milly had planned for Abby. Milly was as ruthless as she was beautiful. Once she set her sights on something she would get it or die trying.

As far as Trent was concerned, she hoped Milly snagged him, they deserved one another.

"Yes, I'll get my revenge on the O'Malley family and on Trent Winthrop." She thought happily while making their evening meal once again resisting the urge to poison them.

It was better that Milly be blamed if something happened to them.

ABBY HAD DIRT ON HER nose and cheeks, in her hair, under her nails and a smile on her face when Gina declared the flower bed finished.

They had just stepped from the dining room when Trent and Lance came from the study.

Trent's eyes danced with mischief when he saw Abby. "Have you been making mud pies?"

"Be careful Mister or you'll be having one for lunch." She teased.

"What if I'm allergic to worms." He chuckled.

"More protein for you, and I'm sure Steven will have something to relieve your itch." She countered. "Come on Gina before he makes me mad."

She turned toward the stairs, but he caught her and kissed her thoroughly. Sputtering a bit, he said, "I think I'll pass on the pie."

Abby slipped from his grasp and ran upstairs with Gina and Lance looking on like proud parents."

It took Abby longer than anticipated, she hoped they weren't waiting for her before eating.

Hurrying down the hall, she came to an abrupt halt when a familiar voice called her name. Turning to see the woman in her mansion again, uninvited caused her temper to flare.

"How did you get in here?" Abby asked angrily. "One would think you'd get the hint we don't want you here. Especially since we run you off every time you show up."

"And here I was worried you missed me." Milly feigned hurt.

"You don't miss a splinter in your hand when it's gone." Abby said with anger flashing in her eyes.

"So, no happy reunion then? I've missed talking with you, especially after walking in on you and Trent. We should compare notes." Milly taunted.

"I can assure you no one has missed you at all." Abby spat. "Besides, if you were that good, I wouldn't have been the one he was kissing."

"Why you little…" Milly hissed.

"Little what? Anyone could tell he was and is completely under my spell." Abby provoked her.

"You let him didn't you!" Milly flew into a rage. "I told you when you leave you'll be heartbroken and alone. You'll see when you leave knowing I am to be his wife. It will be me he holds in his arms at night instead of you!"

"No, you will never be my wife, Milly!" Trent said coming up the stairs startling her. "I didn't hear the bell on the door ring, how are you slipping in so easily?"

"My little secret, just know this isn't over by a long shot Trent!" Milly yelled. "You'll dump her before this is over, if…"

"If what Milly?" Trent growled. "What are you planning."

"That's for me to know and you to find out." She sneered.

"I believe it's time you left Milly. I'll show you to the door." Trent grabbed her arm and jerked her downstairs.

He opened the door and pushed her toward it when she grabbed him and kissed him. Shoving her away, he wiped his mouth and said, "Goodbye Milly, don't come back!"

Trent locked the door behind her and turned when Abby ran into his arms sobbing. Seeing that horrid woman kissing him broke her heart. The fact she knew Trent didn't initiate it and pushed her away took a tiny bit of the sting out, but it still hurt.

Holding her close, he whispered softly, "Abby, I'm yours, no matter how long it takes, or what happens. My heart and soul have been imprisoned by the depth of love you've shown me. No way will Milly have any part of me, ever."

Abby nodded her head against his chest listening to his strong steady heartbeat. Closing her eyes, she felt the tension slowly fade away as he held her.

"Did you see her come in?" Trent asked.

"No. She was hiding upstairs out of sight. I was almost to the stairs when she scared me." Abby trembled.

"Well, she's gone now. We'll have to make sure the doors are locked from now on." Trent said hugging her tightly. "By the way, what's this about me being under your spell?"

"Whatever do you mean Mr. Winthrop?" She looked up batting her eyes.

"You little witch! I'm completely under your spell and you know it. One day you'll be my wife and I can assure you there will be no contest with Milly Boudreau without having bedded you yet."

Arm in arm, they joined Lance and Gina in the dining room where they waited for them.

"I take it Milly's back again." Lance grumbled. "How is she sneaking in? I know she didn't come through here, and she couldn't have gotten in through the front door it was locked. I checked it this morning."

"Let's figure that out later, I'm hungry." Trent said wanting the whole thing to go away, knowing in his heart it wouldn't. At least until he did something about it.

After an uninterrupted lunch, Trent decided to get away from the mansion and enjoy the spring weather. Lance had Princess and Midnight ready for them. Abby had gained enough confidence around the horses she felt comfortable in the saddle.

They set out enjoying the fresh air and the soft breeze keeping the air cool. When they came upon a field of wildflowers, Trent stopped and helped Abby off her horse then tied them to a sturdy tree with plenty of grass to munch on surrounding it.

Abby took off running with him chasing her. They played, then lay on the grass watching clouds talking and teasing each other, until the shadows of night began to creep across the field. Abby picked up the huge bundle of wildflowers and held Trent's hand as they went back to where they left the horses.

Trent dropped her hand and trotted to the tree where the horses had been tied up. They'd somehow gotten loose and were, hopefully, at the stable by now.

Abby caught up to him worried when she noticed the horses were gone.

"Where are they?" She asked.

"They must've gotten loose. Lance will come looking for us when they get back to the stables without us. In the meantime, we need to start walking." He said putting his arm around her.

Slipping her arm around his waist, they started down the trail for the barn with the armload of wildflowers.

Frogs began singing in the distance as crickets joined in the symphony. A chill settled in causing a slight fog to form on the trail. The moon rose shining on them lighting their path. Millions of stars twinkled like tiny diamonds against the dark velvet night sky.

So engrossed in their peaceful stroll, Trent forgot how close to the forest they were. A twig snapped behind them, causing icy cold fingers to run down Trent's spine. He turned to see what made the sound and quickly pushed Abby behind him as a feral wolf advanced on them snarling with sharp looking teeth.

Just as it lunged at them, Trent shielded Abby from the attack. A lone shot rang out and the animal fell at their feet. Relief flooded them when they saw Lance and Billy leading their horses. Trent was never so glad to see anyone in his life.

"Thought you might need some help." Billy said handing the reins to Trent.

"I figured you might, I guess I didn't tie them up very well." Trent smiled catching the look Lance shot Billy.

He helped Abby onto her horse, then hopped in his saddle and led the way back to the stables. While riding he discretely looked at the ends of the reins and could tell they'd been cut. Now, he began to worry. Whatever had started in the fall was beginning all over again.

Stopping at the mansion, he helped Abby dismount, kissed her, and said he'd be back in a few minutes. Oblivious to the danger Trent new loomed on the horizon she skipped into the mansion calling for Barbara to find a vase.

Chapter Twenty-six

Lance pounced on Trent as soon as they got to the stables wanting to know what happened.

"I tied them up good, they couldn't have gotten loose on their own. When we got back to the tree I discovered they were gone." Trent said with an uneasy feeling swirling in his stomach.

"Mr. Winthrop they was cut loose and scared off. I like to never caught em." Billy drawled.

"Who would do such a thing?" Lance asked scratching his head.

"I'll give you two guesses. I think we need to go back to stricter security measures again." Trent turned to Billy with a weary sigh. "Well, Billy? Are you ready for some double duty again?"

"Whatever you need boss." Billy nodded clearly unhappy. "And here I just got rested up from the fall."

"I can't believe this is happening again." Trent growled. "Any ideas?"

Lance and Billy shrugged their shoulders as bewildered as Trent.

"Billy have someone take first watch, two-hour shifts so no one is too tired for their other duties. See you in the morning." Trent said walking away.

Lance stood in silence for a few minutes as Billy began unsaddling the horses.

"I wish it were still winter. I hate having this double duty." Billy grumbled handing the horses to a couple of stable boys.

Lance's eyes lit up when an idea formed in his mind. He'd have to talk to Trent about it in the morning.

Abby teased Trent unmercifully about eating mud pies after dinner as they walked into the living room. Settling on the sofa, Abby leaned against his shoulder. The cozy fire burning cast a soft glow in the room surrounding them with a feeling of serenity.

"Sing for me Abby?" Trent asked putting his arm around her.

The world seemed to disappear as Abby sang and old Irish lullaby to him. Her voice softly weaving a spell of warmth around him. The tension from the danger they were in slowly faded away leaving him free and happy inside.

Abby O'Malley had become his dream lover, that one perfect woman that all men dream of, and he would stop at nothing to marry her.

Abby changed into her summer pajamas and slowly combed her long silky hair before slipping between the cool sheets of her bed. She stared at her ring until she fell asleep dreaming of her wedding day.

Bolting up in bed from a sound sleep, Abby scanned the dark room. Was she dreaming? There it was again, the slight sound of someone breathing. Her gaze was drawn to the fireplace. There in the moonlit room was the hideous face staring at her from the shadows.

Fear tingled in her toes and quickly raced to the top of her head. Unable to move, the scream that formed in her throat wouldn't come until she forced it out. The moment she screamed everything went black.

Billy and Trent burst into the room in time to see her fall back onto the pillows.

"Go get Steven!" Trent ordered Billy as he pulled Abby into his arms.

He pushed her hair away from her face gently patting her cheek.

Abby slowly opened her eyes in confusion until she saw Trent. She latched onto him as if he were a lifeline. Her tiny body trembled with such fear her stomach hurt.

Trent held her tightly while rocking her whispering, "I'm here sweetheart, it's okay, I'm here."

Steven arrived with Billy close behind a few moments later. Trent pried her hands from him to allow Steven to check her over. He gave her a light sedative to calm her.

Then he turned to Trent with an angry cold stare, "What did you do to her?" He demanded. "She's in shock! Was she attacked again?"

"You know as much as we do. I was asleep and he was on watch." Trent said turning to Billy. "Did you see anything?"

"Nobody came in here from the hall. I was watching." Billy shook his head.

"Then whoever scared her must've been in here already." Trent said angrily.

Abby began sobbing hysterically again. Trent sat down beside her and held her close gently rocking her.

"Trent... he... he... was... here! He's... coming to... get me!" She cried. "How did..."

"It's okay Abby, I don't know how he got in, but he's gone now. I won't leave you alone again." Trent promised soothing her. "Billy, stay with her while I talk with Steven in the hall."

Steven turned on him the second they were out of earshot. "You attacked her again didn't you?"

"What are you talking about?" I'd never hurt Abby!" Trent asked barely keeping his temper in check.

"I heard her begging you to stop in the living room after she recovered. When she ran to her room, I stood outside her door to make sure she was okay. When you took off to the forest, I returned to the bunkhouse." He snapped.

"Why were you in the mansion after you were told to stay in the bunkhouse?" Trent demanded.

"Convenient that no one was in the mansion leaving you alone with her!" He shouted.

"I asked you a question and I expect and answer!" Trent demanded.

"I needed more supplies and took the opportunity to get them. I was about to step into the hall when Abby started screaming and I saw her run upstairs into her room. Any man who would terrorize a woman like that is... is..." The words died in his throat when the anger in Trent's eyes silenced him.

"Take care what you say Steven, I've apologized for that mistake, and we are on very good terms, if you get my meaning." Trent growled. "I don't have a clue why this is happening, but I'll figure it out. God help whoever's behind it."

Steven cleared his throat, "I hope it's soon. She could've had a heart attack. I've never witnessed the level of fear she exhibited. Sorry about before, I just assumed... well you know."

"Go on back to the bunkhouse. We'll discuss what to do about this situation tomorrow." Trent dismissed him and returned to Abby's room.

When he stepped into the room he told Billy to keep watch in the hall. He closed the door behind him and crossed the room to her bed.

The moment she was in his arms she seemed to calm slightly. "I'm here darling, I'll take care of you." He soothed her.

He put her back under the covers on the bed and lay down beside her using a throw to keep himself warm. Abby snuggled into him as his arms encircled her tightly allowing her to fall asleep crying.

Trent stroked her silky hair filled with anger. Someone was terrifying the love of his life. He would get to the bottom of it one way or another.

Suspicions rolled through his mind, but without proof it was useless to say anything. Deep down, he felt something else was going on here. Abby hadn't had a child and the curse was for the firstborn male child if he remembered right. So, Abby would be safe since she was female even though she was Jacob's first born.

Trent comforted her each time she awoke afraid of the ghoul terrorizing her. He finally gave into the exhaustion and fell asleep.

"Trent?" Abby whispered trembling.

"I'm here sweetheart, you're safe." He muttered tightening his hold on her.

"I'm scared. He's coming for me!" She cried. "He's coming to take me! I know it!"

"Why do you think he's going to take you?" He asked fully awake now.

"I found a book about the island in grandfather's things and read some of it." She confessed. "I'm sorry."

"You should have told me. I wouldn't have let you read it." He fought to control his anger.

"I wanted to know about my family. Grandmother Abigail said she couldn't tell me anything. When I found the book…" She sniffed. "After what I read, I don't think I want to know any more. I didn't even finish it."

"Let's not discuss it any longer. You can give it to me later today." He insisted hoping she wouldn't ask him anything he couldn't answer.

"I'll go get ready for the day. Billy is outside the door if you need anything, just yell. I'll be here in a flash." He said watching fear cross her face.

"I…" She didn't finish because she knew he couldn't stay.

"I'll be back shortly. You should get ready too. We need to go to Lance and Gina's and figure out how to protect you from this ghost." He kissed her on top of her head.

By the time Trent returned, Abby had showered and dressed. When she opened the door he was clean shaven and smelling delicious. Her pesky stomach felt funny again.

After breakfast, they strolled down the path to Lance and Gina's home. Gina opened the door smiling happily until she saw the look on Trent's face. Something was wrong and she had the feeling she knew what it was.

Chapter Twenty-seven

Trent and Lance left Abby with Gina before going to supervise the men working in the fields.

"Trent, something dawned on me last night. All the trouble stopped when winter came. Milly quit showing up unannounced and that ghoul even stopped appearing out of nowhere. Could they be connected?" Lance asked when they were halfway to the field the men were baling hay in.

Trent mulled over what Lance told him and replied, "You're right. What I need to find out is how they're getting in without anyone seeing."

"Dollars to donuts, she's the key to solving this mystery." Lance said.

"Keep this under your hat. We'll figure it out later." Trent insisted. "Right now, we've got work to do."

GINA TAUGHT ABBY HOW to cook a chicken and rice casserole and the vegetables to compliment the dish. They had a good time talking about their lives. Everything went well until Gina asked what happened the night before.

Abby told her about the face hiding in the shadow of her room and in the study. Chill bumps rose on her arms as she felt the fear all over again. "It started showing up on the one-year anniversary of my parents death. After that, every time it stormed at night it terrified me. But since I've come here it just shows up when it wants to."

"I'm so sorry you've gone through so much in your life. Thank God your guardians found you." Gina hugged her. "It's time to take the cake out of the oven and put the rolls in. When the rolls are done the casserole will be ready to eat."

While they waited on the rolls, Gina suggested they move into the house with them. There were two unoccupied rooms upstairs. They would have to share the bathroom, but other than that they had their own privacy.

Abby was thrilled with the idea and couldn't wait to tell Trent about it.

By the time the table was set, the two working men brushed hay off their clothes and stepped into the kitchen.

While they washed up, Abby put the food on the table while Gina poured their wine.

After dinner, and clean up, they settled in the den with an after-dinner drink.

Abby sprung the idea she and Gina came up with. "Gina and I were talking, and we think it would be a good idea for us to stay here until this is over. There are fewer rooms to hide in and we'll have our own rooms here."

Trent mulled the idea over in his mind and said, "Steven is already staying in the bunkhouse and I'm sure it's going to ruffle his tail feathers some. I will also make Barbara take a long vacation. We can pack our things up tomorrow and move in here. The day after we'll make the trip to the mainland and close up Grandmother Abigail's cottage. We'll take Steven so he can replenish his supplies, and Barbara can go do whatever on her vacation. While we're there we'll replenish our supplies and have a few days of our own to relax."

"Wow! I'm impressed!" Abby exclaimed laughing. "You had a plan all figured out in what? Five minutes? But there's a flaw in your thinking. I want to stay here tonight. We have plenty of time to pack what we need and make the trip to the mainland tomorrow. Gina can help me while you take care of Barbara and Steven.

Shaking his head he said, "Gina, you're having a bad influence on my bride to be."

Gina and Abby laughed as they followed Trent and Lance toward the mansion. They disappeared upstairs to avoid his inevitable confrontation with Barbara. Still, they heard them arguing from Abby's room.

"What's the deal with Barbara?" Abby couldn't contain her curiosity any longer.

"All I know is, she's mad a Trent for something." Gina sighed.

Trent met them downstairs to help carry Abby's luggage after talking to Steven about their plans of leaving early for the mainland.

In no time at all they were settled into their rooms at the Elliot home. Gina and Lance turned in leaving the lovebirds sitting on the sofa watching the fire dancing on the logs in the fireplace.

Gina and Lance wanted a lot of children, but it didn't happen. The house was built twenty years before to raise a passel of kids, even though they married later in life. After a couple of years, Gina found out she was pregnant, and they were deliriously happy.

Their happiness was short lived when the doctors discovered a rare genetic disorder. If Gina carried the baby to term the child wouldn't live more than a few years.

Lance, just as devastated as Gina, made a point to make as many memories with their child as they could. They treasured every moment of every day with little Grace after she was born.

When little Grace passed on, Trent thought Lance would lose his mind. Gina made the decision to have herself sterilized so they wouldn't have any more children. She couldn't bear to lose another. Unable to cope with the grief, she left Lance and went home to her mother's.

Those were dark days for his friends and being apart nearly killed Lance. Gina was the love of his life and after a few days, he brought her home kicking and screaming. Many months passed with agonizing strife between them. In a last-ditch effort to save his marriage, Lance made a trip to the mainland and bought a new diamond wedding set for her. He returned armed with expensive wine, gourmet chocolates and an extra-large bouquet of red roses.

Gina was speechless and agreed that working together they could overcome the grief tearing them apart.

From that moment on Gina knew she'd never love anyone like she did Lance. Their love brought them through and made them stronger.

While Trent remembered the situation he realized he wanted that kind of love with Abby.

Abby quietly observed the emotions crossing Trent's face and asked, "What are you thinking about?"

"Us." He smiled pulling her across his lap. She rested her head on his shoulder. "Sing for me Abby."

The soft melody from her lips soothed the ache deep within his wounded soul. The ache his abusive father had instilled in him at an early age. Until Abby, nothing or no one could touch that part of him.

This had become a ritual for them every evening. She kissed him when she was through, and he held her contentedly while they watched the fire slowly turn to glowing embers in the ash.

Trent became so content, he fell asleep while she ran her fingers through his hair.

"Come on sleepy head, it's your bedtime." She shook him giggling.

Half asleep, he allowed her to pull him upstairs by his hand. She stopped in front of her door and said, "Goodnight."

He took her face in his hands and looked into her eyes, the innocence he saw there shone brightly with love. His heart overflowed with love for her as he gently caressed her lips with his.

"Keep that up and you won't get any sleep tonight." She whispered against his lips.

"I won't anyhow. You've captured my heart and soul since the day you crossed the threshold of my life. I don't think I've had a goodnight's sleep in forever." He replied huskily. "Goodnight my sweet Abby."

When he slipped between the sheets he tossed and turned dreaming about his lovely bride to be.

EXCITEMENT FILLED ABBY when she awakened and jumped out of bed full of energy. Deep down she hoped by going through her grandmother's things she would find some clue about what everyone was intent on hiding from her.

The task before her would be joyless because of the finality she had no family left. Maybe Trent would find what he was searching for.

Trent was poised to knock on her door when it flew open, and Abby barreled into him. Before she had time to breathe, he kissed her.

"Are you ready?" He asked gruffly.

"More than you know." She said with her eyes glittering like perfect emeralds.

Walking hand in hand downstairs, Abby hoped they would finally get to be together forever without hiding the joy she felt in her heart.

Lance and Gina were already eating when they entered the kitchen. Abby busied herself making plates and pouring coffee for her and Trent.

While enjoying the delicious food Gina prepared, they discussed their plans for the day. Although most of it would be on the boat, Trent felt they could make an itinerary for clearing out Grandmother Abigail's cottage and replenishing their supplies.

Before leaving, Trent checked the weather report and found a small thunderstorm between them and the island. According to the report it wouldn't amount to much. Trent knew the weather could be unpredictable and prepared for the worst. Abby would be anxious, but he still wanted to save her any embarrassment.

The small yacht moved away from the island as they enjoyed the fresh sea air. While Steven pestered the captain with a million questions about navigating the boat, Barbara sat in the middle section avoiding everyone. She seemed almost angry Trent had ordered her to go on vacation.

The rest of the passengers sat at the stern of the ship laughing and relaxing. For a time, the dark cloud that hung over the lovebirds had been forgotten.

Trent's feeling about the weather report were correct. The approaching storm had intensified and looked ominous on the horizon.

He had every confidence in Captain MacDonald the best captain in the area.

Abby was already looking anxiously at the approaching storm. Trent suggested they move below deck to avoid getting wet. Steven opted to stay topside with the Captain.

Barbara sat as far away from them as she could refusing to look at them. Abby noticed the subtle looks of hatred the woman shot her when no one else was looking.

When the storm hit, Abby trembled against Trent. Gina tried to lighten the atmosphere by teasing Lance. Thankfully, the storm didn't last long, and Abby relaxed.

Steven stopped halfway down the steps to check on everyone and returned topside when he noticed the look Trent shot him. His perspective of

Trent had changed since their confrontation. Nothing would ever make him cross the man again, he was a frightening opponent.

The rest of the trip was spent enjoying the sun after the storm passed as quickly as it came. The few dark clouds remaining gave the appearance of a silver lining as the sun shone behind them.

Trent watched the light bring out the copper highlights of her red hair. Her smile outshone the sun while happiness danced in her mesmerizing eyes. He realized what a blessed man he was to have found her.

The mainland appeared on the horizon seemingly from nowhere. In a short period of time, they were in the limo heading back to Grandmother Abigail's cottage.

Abby's eyes sparkled with unshed tears as the limo stopped in front of the small home. She would always treasure the memory of the day Trent brought her here. She had been so angry with him for springing her grandmother on her without warning.

The memory of her grandmother's joy when she realized Abby was her grandchild tore open the scar in her heart as grief gripped her again.

The simple request from her grandmother for a hug resurfaced and she couldn't control the flood of tears bursting from her eyes.

Trent held her until she quieted, then helped her from the car. Pride rushed through him when she bravely stepped into the cottage to face packing away the last of her family. Abby was now the last in the Miles O'Malley line.

Chapter Twenty-eight

Dust covered everything since no one had been in the cottage since fall. Gina and Abby immediately dove into cleaning while the men went to get supplies and food for their stay.

After dinner, they settled on the old furniture in the small living room with a fire burning in the little fireplace. They relaxed in the cozy atmosphere before making plans for the next day.

"I think we should start in the attic so if there's anything down here you want to keep, we can store it there until you decide if you want to sell or keep the cottage." Trent suggested.

"Maybe there is something you'd like to keep Trent." Abby smiled at him.

"Why would you think I'd want anything?" He asked shocked.

"You spent more time with my grandmother than any of us. I'd like you to have anything that was special to you. Something to remember her by." Abby said softly.

"I'll think about it, if I decide on anything I'll let you know." He replied visibly shaken by her generosity.

"I'm ready for bed." Lance grumbled.

"Okay, Mr. Grumpy." Gina giggled. "Goodnight you two."

After everyone said goodnight, Abby fixed Trent a drink. She sat on his lap, and he laid his head on her shoulder. Abby let out a small sigh.

"What's bothering you?" He asked running his fingers through her hair.

"I wish we were married. I love you so much." She whispered.

"I know sweetheart. The feeling is mutual. Maybe we'll find what I've been looking for here." He said with regret in his voice.

"What promise did you make that's keeping us apart Trent?" She asked with tears glistening in her eyes.

"How much of that book did you read?" He asked.

Something about a war with the natives and how one of my ancestors killed almost the whole village. I quit reading it and put it away." She said.

"That's all you read?" He asked hoping she knew more.

"Yes. I opened it in the middle and read a few pages and was afraid to read anymore." She shook her head.

"What else have you discovered since you came to the island?" Trent asked.

"Only what Barbara told me about you, but that's all." She shrugged.

"What'd she tell you?" Trent stopped playing with her hair.

"That your mother died when you were born, and your father took it out on you." She said sadly. "I saw the marks on your back, so I know it's the truth. I have some of the same scars on my back too."

"I can't tell you what I'm looking for until it's over. Please believe me when I say I'm doing everything in my power to end this quickly. Please trust me." He pleaded.

In answer to his question, she lay her head on his shoulder and began singing softly to him.

The soft lyrics combined with the serene melody of her song took him away from the tension he suffered while running her estate and searching for information.

Her sweet voice drowned out the voices from the past that haunted him. He hated it when she finished the song and announced it was time for bed.

In answer he said, "Goodnight Princess."

"I'll see you in the morning." She said going upstairs to her room.

He had another drink as his thoughts began to plague him. *"I don't know how long I can keep this up."*

He put the glass in the sink and went upstairs. Nearing her room, he could hear her singing softly as the alluring scent of her perfume assaulted his senses. A desperate prayer slipped from his lips, *"God help me solve this mystery so I can marry her."*

He shut the door to his room, kicked off his boots, and crawled into bed fully clothed. Sleep would evade him like it has since the first night he met her.

ABBY CLOSED HER EYES while singing Trent's favorite song. She let her mind go back to his sweet kisses and how safe she felt in his arms. In frustration, she looked toward Heaven and prayed, *"Lord, please help him find what he's looking for so I can become his wife."*

Sleep came off and on for her until she finally gave in and got up. Glad the cottage was silent, she began making breakfast like Gina had taught her. She just put the cinnamon rolls in the oven when Trent dragged himself into the kitchen looking for coffee.

Abby grabbed a cup and filled it to the brim. She set the cup before him noting he still wore the same clothes as the day before. They looked slept in. He was unshaven and looked as though he hadn't slept at all. Slouching in the chair, he rubbed his face.

She kissed him while he fought to keep his hands off of her. The beast inside him was proving to be difficult to keep at bay.

Sensing the battle within him, she pulled away and sat quietly sipping her coffee. "No sleep last night?"

"Do I look that bad?" He grumbled.

"You do look a little rough around the edges this morning." She said feeling sorry for him.

"It's your fault, you little vixen, when you look at me I feel like I'm the luckiest man in the world. When you kiss me, the beast in me comes alive threatening to overtake me. Every touch sends shards of carnal passion through me. Your perfume assaults my senses and the moment I look into your eyes, I'm lost to your bewitching power. Never have I met anyone who does to me what you do." He told her with agony and desire flashing in his eyes as he spoke.

"I may not have been with a man before, but you do the same to me." She confessed. "I'm sorry I affect you the way I do, but I have no idea what the desires you have feels like."

Trent moved to pounce on her when the timer on the oven went off.

Abby hurried to take them from the oven when he said, "I'm gonna get cleaned up."

Abby pulled the rolls out and put the casserole in, she sat back down sipping on her coffee thinking about what he said.

Gina and Lance emerged from their room to the wonderful smells of fresh coffee and breakfast drifting upstairs. They passed Trent in the hall as he made his way back to his room.

Lance smile discretely at his wife. He knew the battle Trent was fighting. Only a man would completely understand.

Abby had just put the finishing touches on breakfast when they entered the kitchen. Gina noticed the faint dark circles Abby tried to cover with makeup. Her heart went out to them. Whatever Mr. O'Malley made Trent promise him kept them apart.

Lance remembered the torment he'd gone through when he met Gina. Yeah it was bad, but he'd never seen anyone in as much torment as Trent.

Trent returned just before everyone dug into the food. He looked much better, but his mood was still surly.

Abby outdid herself with the cinnamon rolls that nearly floated off the plate, and a casserole that melted in their mouths.

Lance and Gina finished and went upstairs to organize the attic where the work would begin.

Trent began to feel some energy after eating and helped Abby clear the table. Together in silence they washed and put away the dishes.

Abby turned to go upstairs when Trent grabbed her and kissed her.

"That's for the wonderful breakfast." He whispered above her ear. "And this is for understanding what I'm going through."

Abby returned his kisses and then pulled back. "We should get upstairs before they wonder what we're up to."

"Okay, you little enchantress, let's go." He grinned realizing what she was doing, and it made him love her a little more.

Clutching her hand, they went upstairs to begin their task while Gina and Lance were moving trunks and building boxes to sort things into.

Abby took her time with each item she picked up. Any normal person would have just chucked some of the stuff in a box, but she examined everything. These treasures were the artist's paintings of her family's lives.

Abby had only a small glimpse of her grandmother's life and her things were more precious than gold.

Two hours later, they ran across a box of letters and other papers that Trent took downstairs to go through later with Lance.

Gina and Abby continued sorting clothes and various knick-knacks. The clothes were going to charity along with the other items she didn't want. Abby told Gina if there was anything she wanted she was more than welcome to it.

Trent pulled another heavy trunk in front of her to go through.

Abby opened it and realized it was full of her father's things from his youth. Pictures, paintings, old school papers her father had done in school along with special awards, ribbons and some toys were packed carefully away. Halfway through the trunk she found letters tied with a red ribbon, wrapped in a baby blanket. Opening the first one, Abby found they were from her father while he was away at college.

He wrote about how he'd met the most wonderful woman in the world. How he'd proposed to her, and that he would bring her home for Christmas.

Tears fell from Abby's eyes as the dark fingers of grief gripped her heart. They dragged her into the depths of despair once again.

Gina put an arm around her gently squeezing her shoulders in sympathy, but it was too late, as tormenting grief incased her in its cold embrace.

Trent pulled the letters from her hands and packed them back into the trunk and moved it to the other side of the attic. "You can go through those when you're in a better frame of mind."

They continued until late in the evening and the attic was neatly organized.

Chapter Twenty-nine

Abby awoke with puffy red eyes and an awful headache. She'd cried most of the night from the renewed grief that had found her the day before. In her desire to be alone, she had skipped dinner and went to bed early.

Trent stopped on his way to bed to check on her. Even though she knew he could hear her crying, she couldn't answer his knock. All she wanted was for the pain in her heart to go away.

Throughout the night she relived the deaths of her parents and grandmother over and over again. She suffered in silence praying that the flood of emotions would go away like her tears that eventually came to an end.

Abby received no answers when she asked God what she had done to deserve the grief and misery she had experience since the age of eight. This was a battle she had and always would fight alone.

Involving her new family she had come to love sent new daggers to her heart seeing them at a loss in how to help her.

The clock chimed and she forced herself to get out of bed. It was already nine a.m., and the others would be waiting to start working on the second floor of the cottage.

Extra makeup barely hid her red rimmed eyes. She made a valiant effort to seem normal and almost succeeded until she saw Trent in the hall as she left her room.

When he opened his arms she sank against him as she soaked his shirt with more tears.

"I think we need a day off. Let's go shopping okay?" He asked holding her trembling body close.

Abby nodded her agreement numbly against his chest. The soft beat of his heart comforted her somehow. Maybe it was the deep tone of his voice or maybe being safe in his arms, at the moment she didn't care.

"Let's tell the others." He said calmly leading her downstairs.

Hand in hand, she followed obediently too withdrawn to care about anything at the moment.

Gina jumped up from her chair and asked, "Would you like some breakfast or coffee?"

"No thanks, I'm not hungry." Abby said with a weak smile.

"We're calling a day off, anyone for shopping?" Trent asked.

Gina discretely shook her head no at Lance, as she told Trent they'd stay and go through some of the papers they'd found. She knew being alone with Trent was the best thing for her.

"If you're sure." Trent gave Gina a grateful look as he guided Abby toward the door.

Rain clouds hid the sun mirroring her mood as they strolled down the street toward the quaint little town that remained untouched by progress. They passed a plethora of shops that sold everything from fine wines and chocolate to grocery and feed stores.

Trent purchased anything she seemed interested in hoping to lift her spirit.

At lunch time he took her to his favorite restaurant on the edge of town. When they were seated he asked her what she would like to eat.

Even though she wasn't hungry, at his insistence she ordered a small sandwich. Despite his best efforts nothing helped her, and he was quickly running out of ideas.

Abby could see how hard Trent was trying to cheer her up and her heart went out to him. In an effort to make him feel better, she choked down some of the sandwich even though it churned in her stomach. Oh, how she wished she could crawl out of the darkness of grief and back into the joy of light.

Everything in her young life had conditions and complications to it. Even her love for this wonderful man in front of her. But there was something holding him back from her and that knowledge loomed like a thick dark cloud over her. He had begged her to trust him, to let him figure out something. Yes, they were engaged, but yet another condition was it had to remain secret.

"Why was her life riddled with secrecy, conditions and grief?" She wondered sadly.

"What do we have here?" A familiar voice broke through her thoughts. "They'll let anyone in this place."

Trent visibly cringed thinking, *"Great, Milly is the last person I need to deal with today."*

"Are you two having a quarrel? You've hardly said a word to each other since you came in." She taunted.

"Milly, we're in no mood for your shenanigans today, so leave us in peace." Trent growled.

"So tell me Abby, having fun on the island yet? See anything weird going on?" Milly asked cruelly.

"That's enough Milly, why don't you skip along home and torture someone there?" Trent bit out.

Milly ignored him and sneered, "What's the matter Abby? Cat got your tongue, or maybe you've finally come to see that I'm right."

The longer Milly taunted her, Abby's grief turned into anger. The bottle she kept her feelings in since the age of eight was quivering under the pressure ready to explode.

Abby stood to her feet facing Milly with her hands fisted at her sides.

"Are you going to run away now like a good little girl? Like I told you, you'd leave brokenhearted and alone pining for a man who took you for everything you've got." Milly provoked her fiercely. "I warned you what would happen, but don't worry, I'll take good care of him for you. Trent is much too good for a ragamuffin like you. He really shouldn't marry beneath his station."

"Listen you bimbo, you have no idea who you're dealing with or what's going on here." Abby desperately tried to reel in the rage building with in her.

"If I don't what? What can a pathetic little orphan like you do to me?" Milly laughed wickedly.

No one saw Abby's fist as she hit Milly on the end of her nose so hard it knocked her off her feet. Before Trent could grab her, Abby was on top of Milly pounding her face and body. Milly grabbed hair and scratched at Abby's face enraging her further.

Trent had a hard time separating the two women. When he had a good hold on Abby, she struggled out of her mind with rage, as the restaurant owner pulled Milly to her feet and escorted her to the door still screaming at Abby. The few patrons cheered and whistled enjoying the sight of Milly Boudreau's comeuppance.

Trent finally made Abby snap out of her unconscious rage after receiving a few hard punches and kicks himself.

"Abby! Stop it!" Trent growled. "Milly's gone."

Abby seemed to run out of steam and came back to her senses. Trent kept a tight hold on her to keep her from going after Milly.

"It's okay Abby, calm down sweetheart." He whispered softly as she began trembling.

"What just happened?" She asked in wide-eyed confusion as the scratches on her face began to sting.

"I'll just say, I don't want to make you mad at me, ever!" He chuckled.

"What did I do?" She asked with panic in her voice.

"I don't think Milly will bother us for a while after the beating you gave her." Trent chuckled with pride in his eyes.

Abby had been in fights before, but always received the worst end of them because she cowered from the bullies. Everyone picked on the loner, the outcast.

"Have you had enough excitement for one day?" Trent asked pulling out his handkerchief.

"Yes, let's get out of here." She hung her head.

"We need to get you cleaned up first. You've got some pretty deep scratches on your face." He put his handkerchief on her cheek.

Still in a state of shock, Abby numbly followed him into the pharmacy for supplies to doctor her wounds.

Word had already spread, and the pharmacist was more than happy to fix Abby up. Laughter ensued when he found out it was Abby that had beaten the daylights out of Milly Boudreau. He took great delight in the fact that someone so petite had finally taught Milly a long overdue lesson.

The sun had broken through the clouds by the time they left the pharmacy. Trent seated her on a bench in front of the florist shop while he slipped in to buy her some flowers.

Abby closed her eyes feeling the sun warming her skin, even though the scratches were stinging a little more, she actually began to feel as though a weight had been lifted from her small shoulders. It scared her to think she lost control like that, but maybe that's what she needed all along.

When Trent return she opened her eyes to a dozen red roses nestled in baby's breath. Looking up at him her eyes filled with tears, no one had ever bought her flowers before.

They walked arm in arm back to the cottage until they reached the front door.

Trent pulled her into his arms and kissed her. "Welcome back, my sweet Abby."

He opened the door and allowed her to enter first.

Gina and Lance looked up at the same time and were shocked by Abby's appearance.

"What happened?" Lance glowered at Trent.

"I didn't do anything! I swear!" Trent laughed backing away with his hands raised in surrender.

"Well? What happened?" Lance demanded angrily.

"Abby got into a little skirmish with Milly Boudreau." Trent said grinning.

"Are you okay dear?" Gina asked concerned.

"I'll be fine, it's only a few scratches. They'll heal okay." She said as her cheeks heated.

"I'm sick of that Boudreau woman! Always popping in unannounced, spewing out poison, and now physically attacking Abby! Someone needs to put a stop to it Trent!" Lance lost his temper.

"I have a feeling Milly won't be able to pop in for a long while. She smarted off as usual and Abby attacked her." Trent chuckled.

Lance shook his head in disbelief as his words sank in. "Abby attacked her?"

"Yes I did." Abby looked down in shame.

"From what I saw, Milly got the worst end of it. She probably has two black eyes, a busted nose and a couple of loose teeth, and maybe a broken jaw and a few cracked ribs." Trent stated proudly. "Not to mention a few good hits to my ribs while pulling her off of Milly."

"I sure wish I could've been there to see that!" Lance chuckled. "I'll bet it was a sight to see."

"Oh, it was. The entire restaurant was clapping and cheering when the owner threw Milly out." Trent laughed.

"I'm not proud of what I did." Abby muttered defensively.

"It's been a long-time coming dear. Someone was bound to pound some respect into her one day. You just happened to be the lucky one to do it." Gina squeezed her shoulder.

Gina took the roses from Abby to put in a vase while she went upstairs to change.

Abby looked at her reflection in the mirror. Blood drops had ruined her blouse and the bandages on her face troubled her. *"Why did I do that? I've never hit anyone in anger before. Although, I have to admit it felt kind of good now that it's over."*

Trent had also purchased a good bottle of wine for their dinner which Gina had on the table in no time.

The tantalizing aroma of Gina's cooking reached Abby's room. Her stomach growled reminding her how little she had eaten since yesterday.

Trent seated her at the table a short time later as Lance begged him to tell the story again.

Abby listened quietly realizing that she didn't remember much of what happened.

"You should've seen Milly's face as she hit the ground. Then when Abby jumped on top of her, Milly tried to fight back, but Abby's fists were flying so fast, she barely had time to defend herself." Trent told them.

Gina and Abby cleaned up, while Lance and Trent went into the living room.

"We haven't found anything important in that box. We're trying to organize them, but I don't think there's any clues there." Lance said.

Trent's emotions churned deep inside him.

"What's wrong?" Lance asked.

"I'm tired of this whole thing. I've had enough of the situation my father put me in with Milly and her family, and the promises, O'Malley forced me to make, which I'm regretting daily." He confessed. "I want to marry Abby and being around her is driving me crazy."

"I'm sure we're on the verge of finding something. I feel it in my bones." Lance tried to be positive.

"I was so angry with Milly when I heard what she told Abby, the day she and Gina worked in the garden. I almost told her we're engaged. It wouldn't do for anyone, especially Milly to find out about us." He growled. "I'm to the point I want to run away with her and start a new life somewhere away from all of this."

"Maybe you should, Trent. God knows you two love each other. Take her away to someplace where no one knows the O'Malley or Winthrop name. Settle down and start a family." Lance told him.

"I can't, not with those promises and secrets hanging over us. If I don't do this, it will haunt me the rest of my life." Trent hung his head in defeat.

Chapter Thirty

Several grueling days later, the cottage had been cleaned, sorted, and rearranged. The local charities loved them for their huge donations.

They made a trip to the neighboring city to order several new pieces of furniture which gave Abby a much-needed diversion. Gina kidnapped her from Trent's side to go shopping for clothes and such, while he and Lance ordered supplies for the island. Steven went with them to order supplies for a small clinic area in the main mansion until a small building could be built.

They returned to the cottage weary from the work and shopping. Steven went to the marina to stay on the yacht to wait for deliveries that weren't being shipped to the island.

Lance and Gina turned in early leaving Abby alone with Trent for the first time in more than a week. They managed to put their relationship on hold avoiding the inevitable disappointment that plagued him when they went their separate ways for the night.

Trent handed Abby a glass of wine and sat next to her with his usual glass of scotch. Peace washed over them as they watched the sparks from the dying fire float up the chimney. Abby leaned into him when he put his arm around her.

"Will you sing to me Abby?" He asked.

Her voice wrapped around him like the warm summer sunshine, lulling him into a deep pool of peace.

When her voice fell silent, he looked into her eyes. His fingers lightly touched her cheek where Milly's scratched her. The marks were nearly healed and fading.

Unable to resist, he gently kissed her pulling her tightly against him.

"My dear sweet Abby, you drive the darkness away when you sing to me. Your kisses ignite a fire in me that can't be quenched. Your soft touch beckons me to take you to my bed. I'm so in love with you I can hardly contain it." He whispered pulling back to look into her eyes.

She reached up to trace his jawline with her fingers, loving the feel of his stubble. "I love you too, Trent."

He cradled her on his lap as she rested her head on his shoulder. The soft notes of another song drew him into her web of contentment while he rested his cheek against the top of her head.

This was the first time since her fight with Milly that he held her like this. Before long they fell asleep oblivious to the world around them.

GINA STEPPED OFF THE stairs with Lance close behind. She quickly grabbed Lance's arm and shushed him, so he didn't wake them.

She set about fixing breakfast being as quiet as she could as Lance drank his coffee while reading his paper.

Gina's heart went out to them. Memories arose of how she and Lance were before they married. *"I gotta give them credit, I wouldn't have waited as long as they have."* She smiled while putting biscuits in the oven.

The aroma of the coffee drifted into the living room waking Trent. He gazed at Abby curled up asleep on his lap. He loved her so much and wondered how long they would have to wait before they could marry.

Abby snuggled closer shivering a little. Carefully pulling a throw off the back of the sofa, he gently pulled it around her and under his chin. She look so innocent and unfettered by the cares of life.

He thanked God for Gina and Lance's friendship as he nodded into a light slumber. He knew they were trying to keep quiet so they could rest.

Abby slowly opened her eyes feeling warm and safe. Trent's arms held her tightly. The only indication either of them had moved in the night was the throw covering them.

Trent glanced down to see she was awake and smiled at the sparkle and contentment in her eyes. Oh how he wished they were able to shout their wedding date to the world. Despite their longing for each other, he resolve they would wait. His Abby was more than worth it.

He saw Gina peek around the corner and said, "We're awake, come on in."

"I have breakfast ready." She announced.

"We'll be right there." He replied catching the look of pity in her eyes.

Trent gave Abby a sound good morning kiss before they ventured into the kitchen.

"Bout time you lovebirds got up." Lance teased.

Despite nothing untoward happening, Abby's face turned almost purple with embarrassment.

"Okay, papa, leave her alone. Nothing happened." Trent warned.

"Good thing. I would have disciplined you severely." Lance glared at him.

"We're only engaged, not married." Trent reminded him with pain in his eyes.

"I wish we were." Abby muttered under her breath.

"Soon sweetheart, just a bit longer." Trent said with the fear in the back of his mind something would prevent their marriage.

Gina knew he was afraid Abby would leave him, and if she did it would kill him.

"What's on the agenda today?" Lance asked.

"We start closing the cottage up today and leave for home in the morning. The furniture will be here by this afternoon. You and Gina meet Steven at the dock and make sure our supplies are delivered and that Steven hasn't forgotten anything." Trent directed them.

Abby excused herself to take a shower and dress for the day. Gina and Lance left shortly after her departure leaving them alone.

"It's your turn." Abby said carrying a basket of sheets to cover the furniture before they left.

Trent couldn't stop himself and said, "I can't take this anymore. Let's get married today. I don't want to wait another minute."

"What about the promises you've insisted had to be kept first? From the way you made it sound we'd be in danger if someone even suspected we were engaged let alone married." Abby asked taken off guard.

"No one has to know. We can go…" He stopped realizing it was impossible.

"Everyone will know when we file for the license." Abby told him.

"You're right. I'm just tired of waiting. You're right here in front of me, yet so far away." He scrubbed his face.

"Why can't I help you?" Abby asked.

"Because the O'Malley history would scare you off and you'd never come back." Trent's torture laced his voice. "I would rather die than lose you Abby."

"I might have left before, but not now. I have something wonderful in my life now. I've found a family. I love Lance and Gina almost as much as my parents. More than that, I have you Trent. I love you more than you know." She sniffed back tears. "You gave me three wonderful months with my grandmother. Now if I lost you, I'd have nothing to live for."

Trent saw the truth of her words in her teary eyes. "Let me discuss it with Lance and Gina. If they agree, I'll tell you tomorrow while we're traveling back to the island."

Trent barely kept from falling when she threw herself at him squealing, "You won't regret it. I promise!"

Trent went to shower and change praying he wouldn't regret telling her.

Shortly before dinnertime, Lance, Gina, and Steven arrived to help with last-minute placement of the heavier pieces of furniture. Gina and Abby covered everything that they wouldn't use that night.

Gina noticed the atmosphere had changed between the lovebirds, but she didn't pry.

Lance on the other hand couldn't help but corner Trent. "What's going on between you two?"

Trent explained it all to him, including trying to get Abby to elope.

"Well what do you want to do?" Lance asked.

"I want to marry Abby." Trent sighed. "You know the minute she finds out about her ancestor's and that stupid curse, she'll leave. Not to mention what I promised her grandfather."

"Go on." Lance pushed.

"I had no intention of falling in love with her. When I looked in to those mesmerizing green eyes, I lost my heart forever. I'll never love anyone else, and it will kill me if I lose her." He reluctantly admitted.

"Let's look at those promises. First you swore to keep her from getting married and having children while she was on the island. Correct?" Lance asked.

"Yes, I agreed because of what he told me about her life. I did it to protect her." Trent replied.

"Second, you promised to find out why the face in the shadows took his baby given it wasn't an ancestor in the line of Shawn O'Malley." Lance held up two fingers.

"Yes, and we still haven't a clue." Trent sighed.

"Third if you do figure it all out, you have the option of marrying her." Lance said.

"I only agreed to that one to make him happy. Like I said, before I met her I had no intention of keeping that one." Trent shook his head.

"I know, but will Abby believe you?" Lance asked.

"Here I believed my father was the one who put me in a bad situation when I was the idiot who made those promises." Trent sat down with a defeated sigh. "Do you think I could just tell her about the curse and leave out what her grandfather made me promise? Milly already convinced her I was out to steal her inheritance."

"Doesn't she deserve the whole truth?" Lance asked.

"I suppose I do owe her that much." Trent hung his head. "Lance, just shoot me and put me out of my misery."

"If it goes south, Gina will help Abby pick up the pieces and I'll be here for you. You can't keep any of it from her any longer. Otherwise she's gonna start looking into things on her own and we both know that could be devastating. For both of you." Lance said putting a comforting hand on his shoulder.

Chapter Thirty-one

Trent tossed and turned all night giving him a horrible headache, thus he was in a foul mood. He dreaded coming clean with Abby, but at least on the boat she wouldn't have many places to go.

He skipped breakfast to start loading the limo, he wasn't hungry anyhow.

Lance told Gina about his conversation and what Trent planned to do. Gina didn't like the idea, but agreed Abby had the right to know.

The trip to the marina was made in silence leaving Steven to wonder what was going on. The air was electric with tension, and he worried about Abby. Since the night Trent had attacked her, he worried for her safety. Silently he vowed if Abby left Trent, he would help her get away if need be.

Gina and Abby went below deck while the men unloaded the luggage so they could talk.

Abby, Lance, and I have known Trent all his adult life and I want you to know he wouldn't do anything to hurt you." Gina tried to reassure her. "No matter what he tells you please have an open mind and an understanding heart. Trent's motive were all about protecting you even before he met you."

Abby wanted to tell her she already knew what he'd promised her grandfather. Instead she said, "Gina, nothing he says will make me believe he would intentionally hurt me. I know with all my heart he loves me, and I love him too."

The minute they left the harbor, Gina left to join her husband topside while Trent dragged his feet to join her.

Steven watched everyone closely getting more anxious about what they were doing. He didn't know these people all that well since he was Grandmother Abigail's nurse for about two years. Digging deep he pulled every ounce of bravery to the surface to defend Abby if need be.

Abby watched Trent stop and make himself a drink before he turned to look at her.

"Need some courage?" She teased.

"Yes." Trent downed it then sat down across from her.

"I'm ready to hear what you have to tell me." She said anxiously.

"I want you to know I love you with all my heart. Everything I did and promised came about before I met you." Trent said and paused.

"I understand. In all fairness, I didn't intend to fall in love with you either." She said quietly.

Trent cleared his throat and told her everything. The only thing he left out was the incident with Barbara's daughter, still protecting her from O'Malley's indiscretion.

Abby quietly listened having difficulty keeping her emotions passive.

Trent finished avoiding eye contact afraid she was going to leave him in disgust and anger.

Abby reached across the small table and put her hand over his. He finally looked up meeting her eyes in confusion. Dare he hope he still had a chance with her?

"Trent." She spoke softly. 'I already knew what you promised my grandfather."

"Abby I ... Wait... What did you say?" Trent said when she put a finger on his lips.

"When you were attacked, you talked a lot in your sleep. Since your conversation was one sided, I had to piece it together. I also know you're afraid I'll leave you. Don't sell our love short darling. We'll figure this out together. Who knows maybe I'll find something you missed." She smiled. "Besides, we wouldn't want to disappoint Grandmother would we?"

Speechless, Trent went around the table and pulled her into his arms. He captured her lips in a desperate kiss of mixed emotions.

"You know, the day Milly, and I had that fight, she told me you would take me for everything I own, and I would leave the island broken hearted and alone." Abby said. "If you remember, we fought more than once about you buying the island. You acted like you didn't want me here. How was I supposed to deal with all that?"

"I've misjudged you Miss Abby O'Malley. You continue to surprise me." He chuckled.

Trent pulled her across his lap kissing her with more love than he'd ever experienced in his life. Forcing himself to stop, he looked down into her sparkling eyes and said, "My sweet Abby, we'll figure this out together, we'll get married and have a mansion full of kids. Together."

Fully aware that Lance and Gina were anxious to hear how things went, he went to tell them it went better than he expected it to.

LANCE NERVOUSLY PACED back and forth, driving Gina crazy. When Trent appeared they both relaxed and followed him below deck.

Steven's heart fell when Trent emerged with a huge smile on his face. In that moment, he knew any chance of dating Abby was gone.

IN THE FOLLOWING WEEKS Abby and Gina cleaned and sorted through every room of the estate. The music room and sewing room at the back of the first floor were converted into a small clinic for emergencies. Steven informed Trent he'd spoken to his friend Dr. Jason Marcus about making trips to the island for emergencies beyond his capabilities. He also talked with a helicopter pilot about flying Dr. Marcus to the island. Then he requested another nurse to work part time in case one was needed. Trent gave his permission after discussing it with Abby.

Trent and Lance loaded up several wagons of clothing and such to take to the village on the other side of the island the next day.

Abby wanted to go, but Trent put his foot down, "No Abby. It's too dangerous for you to go."

"Why?" She asked almost in tears.

"Because of your history. I'm counting on Gina to go through some of your ancestry while we're gone." He pulled her into his arms. "When you've read what we have, you'll understand."

Although disappointed, she was anxious to begin looking into her ancestry.

The decision to stay one more night with Lance and Gina before their trip was easy.

Abby and Gina cleaned the house from top to bottom before dinner. After they enjoyed their meal and a drink in the living room, Lance decided he needed some sleep, so he and Gina bid them goodnight and left them alone.

Trent tugged Abby down on his lap and started nuzzling her neck and whispered, "Sing to me darling, please?"

"I don't know if I can. I'm too worked up." She said breathlessly.

"One day you'll understand what worked up really is." He kissed her neck again.

"You're enjoying torturing me, aren't you?" She pushed him back realizing he was doing it on purpose.

"Uh huh." He whispered kissing her again with a mischievous smile.

"If you want torture..." She said and kissed him in a blaze of passion. Being aggressive wasn't her strong suit, however, she'd been learning from him.

Trent finally stopped her and said, "I got it, but if you don't stop we're gonna have a real problem."

Settling on his lap she put her head on his shoulder and whispered. "Remember my darling, two can play that game."

She began softly singing his favorite song, but it didn't affect him like it normally did. He leaned his head back and closed his eyes in a desperate attempt to calm the raging fire she ignited in him.

Abby finished the song and kissed him softly. "Goodnight sweetie."

She hopped off his lap and left him sitting completely alone and immensely frustrated.

"I guess I shouldn't have started something we both knew I couldn't finish." He thought to himself as he climbed the stairs for yet another cold shower.

ABBY LAID IN HER BED thinking about Trent. She'd always wanted a big wedding, but being an orphan it was out of the question until now. Since her grandfather left everything to her, she could have the wedding of her dreams. If only...

She sat up in bed with a wonderful idea. The entire second and third floor needed remodeled, and the formal living room and study needed updated.

Oh, Trent would argue, but she purposed to stand her ground. After all, one day he would be her husband and she'd have to deal with him for the rest of her life, she may as well start now.

Happy with her little plan she rolled over drifting into a deep sleep.

TRENT STOOD IN THE cold shower in misery. *"You are an idiot!"* He thought turning the water off. *"It's all your fault for teasing her."*

He would have to be on his guard now that she'd learned her power over him. He dried off and slipped in bed to toss and turn as his desire for her invaded his dreams all night long.

The morning light slowly chased the shadows from his room until it landed on his face. Opening his eyes and wincing from the glare, he rolled over putting his back to the window. More than anything he wanted to sink into the sleep that evaded him. Giving up he threw the covers back and got dressed. He had things to do and laying around wouldn't get it done.

Abby and Gina's laughter greeted him as he stepped out of his room. The tantalizing aroma of coffee and cinnamon rolls drifted over him almost masking the smell of the perfume she wore. His mood darkened as he made his way downstairs.

"Gina noticed right away he hadn't slept well from the redness around his eyes, smiling to herself she knew why.

Abby poured him a cup of coffee before he sat down. She dropped a soft kiss on his cheek as she set the coffee in front of him.

He was thankful when Lance told him all the wagons were loaded and ready when he was. Maybe a few days away would help, but he doubted it.

Abby watched him brood over his breakfast and determined never to tease him like that again, even though he started it.

Chapter Thirty-two

Trent asked Lance to tell Steven to grab some gear so he could go along, while he checked the wagons and the hands going with them. In a last-minute decision, he grabbed four bottles of whiskey to take along.

Steven argued with Lance, "What about the nurse? She's on her way and doesn't have a clue where everything is or what her duties will be."

"She'll have to wing it. Trent's ready to leave so get cracking. And make sure you bring extra supplies. We don't want to get caught without some stuff to fix us up."

Lance left Steven swearing under his breath while packing his med kit. He knew Steven was looking forward to having another female around since Abby was taken.

Lance walked in on Trent and Abby when he got back to his house. Abby was asking Trent about remodeling the mansion.

"Abby, I know you want to do this and why, but it can wait until this is over." He said softly.

"But Trent, when we get married, I want to walk into our mansion and have it ready for us to start our new life together. Besides, you have all this stuff to do, why can't I make plans for me?" She argued. "I want to do this Trent, please."

"How about you wait until we get back and I'll personally find the plans and we'll do it together. For now you are going to familiarize yourself with your family history." He pulled her into his arms.

"Okay, but I'm gonna hold you to that!" She grumbled disappointed.

"I'm just as anxious as you are, sweetheart. It'll happen. It's just gonna take a little longer." He held her tightly.

"I know, I just..." She started shaking her head.

"I believe the answer is right in front of us Abby. We'll find it and everything will be over." He said and tenderly kissed her.

Lance didn't mean to see it, but it brought tears to his eyes witnessing the tenderness he had toward Abby. There was no doubt now, he knew Trent was in love with her.

Abby watched them until they were out of sight. In her heart she determined to find something to end the torture they were in.

"Gina put a comforting arm around Abby and said, Come on, let's go start on the history of your ancestors."

Abby sat on the sofa while Gina placed two well-worn leather-bound books on the coffee table.

"Let's start with this one it is the history of the O'Malley family. When your through with it we'll read Shawn O'Malley's diary. I have to warn you, they aren't pretty." Gina handed the first book to her.

From the look on Gina's face, she thought maybe she didn't really want to know. However, she steeled herself and opened the book praying she would find something to break this supposed curse. She never believed in curses and deep down knew something else was afoot.

"Gina? Do you really believe in this curse?" She asked.

"I never had before, but somethings that have occurred concerning your family made me wonder." Gina answered, hoping Trent had told her about O'Malley's child being kidnapped.

Abby nodded and began reading and finished it just in time for dinner, and Gina insisted the next morning they could read the diary.

They talked and discussed some of what she'd read. The book gave Abby a lot to think about, but nothing that would give her nightmares.

TRENT WAS IN A CAUSTIC mood as he rode his horse alongside the lead wagon. The further away from Abby he got the more his mood darkened. Close to dark, he stopped and told them to make camp. The expression on Abby's face when he mounted his horse to leave clawed his heart. His craving for the whiskey he brought intensified as he grabbed the first of the stash he brought, then walked away to sit on a log with his back to the camp.

Lance watched him intently. The anguish he was in began to worry him. No matter how much Lance talked to him, he wouldn't take her and leave this place. Lance had to give him credit for sticking to his promises, but at what cost.

The men cooked dinner while Trent drowned his sorrows, preferring to be alone.

"What's got the burr under his saddle?" Billy couldn't help but ask.

"He can't wait until this is over." Lance replied.

"I wish it were over too, but there's something else going on. I've never seen him like this." Billy observed.

"Let me put it to you another way, have you ever wanted something so bad you would do anything to get it, but something kept it just out of reach?" Lance asked.

"I get it. Abby." Billy said with a light dawning in his eyes.

"Keep that under your hat. If certain people found out... I don't have to tell you what could happen." Lance said. "You can help me keep an eye on him."

Trent returned, flipped out his sleeping bag and went to bed without a word to anyone.

THE NEXT DAY, ABBY began reading the diary. She had to take a break several times to come to grips with what she'd read.

Abby read all day until just before dinner, she finished and closed the book. Tears welled in her eyes as she looked at her new friend.

"What's wrong Abby?" Gina asked worried.

"That ghoul took my ancestor's baby?" She asked fearfully.

"Yes. From what we can tell that was the first appearance of the face in the shadows." Gina said.

Abby leaned back to calm the waves of disgust from her heart.

"Are you okay?" Gina asked concerned. It was affecting Abby more than she was prepared for.

"How could someone be so horrible?" She asked. "And how could this ghost actually take a child?"

Gina had prepared a light dinner just in case Abby wouldn't feel like eating. She handed the plate to Abby and a glass of wine.

Abby took a sip of the wine and said, "Can I tell you something Gina?" She asked with a well of sadness in her eyes.

"You can tell me anything Abby." Gina's heart went out to her.

Abby hesitantly started her story. "You know I was in foster care for several years. Everyone I was sent to was worse than the last. Unfortunately, some of the foster 'parents' were only in it for the money. They mistreated all of us, some not so bad, others worse. I've had my share of beatings like Trent has." She took another swallow of wine, blinking back tears and told Gina of all the abuse she witnessed.

Gina was appalled that the young woman sitting in front of her had suffered such horrific tragedies in her life. Now she's found that members of her family were as bad if not worse than those people.

"Abby had I known this, I'd never allowed you to read these books. Why didn't you tell Trent?" Gina asked as her heart broke a little more.

"Only you, the police, and the judge know any of this." Abby cried.

Gina sat next to her and held her as she cried. Soon she fell asleep with her head on Gina's lap hiccupping from crying so hard.

Gina lightly stroked Abby's hair realizing she finally found a daughter to love, and the secrets she carried were slowly destroying her. Not to mention she loved a man who couldn't break an idiotic promise if his life depended on it. She worried those secrets and promises might cost one or both of them their lives.

Gina slipped off the couch and put a pillow under Abby's head and covered her with a throw. Unwilling to leave her alone, she settled into the oversized chair across from the couch.

During the night, Abby began dreaming about her time in the foster system. She began whimpering in the darkness.

Gina heard her and looked across the moonlit room to find Abby sitting with her eyes wide open but unseeing. Gina stood when Abby threw her arms up and screamed, "I won't tell! I promise! I won't tell!"

Sam knocked on the door and Gina let him in when Abby screamed. He tried to help Gina hold her down to keep her from hurting herself. Before

Abby awakened from the nightmare, Sam had a bloody nose from an elbow Abby hit him with.

He stuck around until Abby went back to sleep. Gina asked him to carry her upstairs so she could relax and get some sleep too.

Gina walked him back downstairs to the door when he asked, "What happened to that purdy girl?"

"All I can tell you is she's had a rough life." She replied.

"Whoever gave her that rough life needs horsewhipped." He said angrily. "Goodnight Mrs. Gina, don't forget to lock up."

Gina locked the door and turned the lights of when a cold chill washed over her. Pausing to look around she didn't see anything, so she continued upstairs, missing the face peering in the window.

Gina laid down next to Abby pulling a throw over herself for warmth. As sleep overtook her she prayed that God would give her wisdom to help this poor child.

Chapter Thirty-three

Sam knocked on the door lured by the smell of fresh coffee. She noticed he looked a little rough around the edges.

"Want some coffee?" She asked filling a cup.

"Yup, that'd be great." He said and sat down at the table.

Gina set the cup in front of him and sat down with one of her own.

"Mrs. Gina? Is that purdy girl gonna be okay?" Sam broke the silence.

"Yes, she'll be fine. She just has nightmares occasionally." Gina tried to reassure him.

"I ain't never heard nothin so awful than when she screamed last night." Sam shook his head.

"I'm not accustomed to it either. Poor thing has a lot to work through." She said sadly.

"Sad business, that. Din't sleep a wink last night. Kept hearin that scream." Sam yawned.

"I need a favor Sam. Please keep what happened last night under your hat. I want you to stick closer to the house in case I need help again." Gina asked.

"Sure enough, but if she screams like that again, somebody's gonna hear." Sam agreed.

"I'll do my best to keep her from screaming again. Just make sure you stay close." She replied.

"Yes ma'am, see ya later." Sam left her to start his watch.

ABBY AWOKE CONFUSED in a strange room and it scared her. Gina walked into the room as Abby sat up trembling in fear.

"It's okay Abby. You're in my bed. Sam brought you up last night after your nightmare. You're safe." Gina spoke calmly as she would a frightened horse.

Tears fell from Abby's chin realizing telling Gina about her childhood opened the door to the nightmare. Add what she found out about her ancestors, the memories were too close to the surface not to erupt.

Gina held her with no clue of how to ease her pain.

Abby finally sat back and wiped the tears from her soggy face.

"Go take a shower and I'll have breakfast ready when you're through." Gina said as she stood to leave the room.

Abby stepped into the hot shower, letting the water rush over her. *"God? Why was I given this horrible life? What did I do to deserve all this pain? I just want to be happy. Even my engagement, which should be happy, is filled with sadness and secrecy. Trent is a good man. I want to marry him so much. God help us find the answers."*

The hot water mixed with her tears as she wished it would wash away the past too.

Gina was deep in thought when Abby stepped into the kitchen. She quietly poured herself a cup of coffee and sat down in silence.

"I'm sorry Gina. I didn't mean for that to happen last night. It just came out. Normally I keep those memories buried so deep in the back of my mind they never see daylight." Abby looked down at her coffee cup.

"Oh Abby, it's okay. You needed someone to confide in and I'm happy you chose me." Gina's heart went out to her.

"I didn't tell you everything, and truthfully I don't want to tell anyone ever." Abby sniffed.

"Abby, none of what happened was your fault. That guilt lies solely on the people that broke the law. You were punished for being an orphan and it was wrong." Gina covered her hand. "Frankly, I don't see how you haven't gone crazy carrying all that around inside."

"I'm just glad all of that is over except for the nightmares." Abby sighed.

"Abby, I want you to know you have my ear and support as long as you live on this earth." Gina said patting Abby's hand.

Abby smiled feeling just a bit lighter after talking to Gina. Maybe someday she'll have the courage to tell Trent.

"Since I'm finished reading those books, let's go through those boxes Lance brought in." Abby stood up.

"Why not wait until Trent and Lance get back tomorrow." Gina insisted.

"I need to keep busy, besides, there are a lot of papers in those huge boxes." Abby said.

Gina finally gave in. One way or another Abby had decided to end this shadow hanging over her.

TRENT RODE BEHIND THE wagons on their way back to the estate. Normally they would have stayed the evening and left early the next morning, but Trent insisted they leave after unloading what furniture and clothing Abby had donated to them.

The hands knew better than to protest, especially in the mood Trent was in. Since the wagons were empty they made better time and were twenty-four hours ahead of schedule.

Lance and Billy were increasingly concerned about him. He wouldn't eat and became anti-social and restless. As for the liquor he'd brought, he was down to his last bottle.

Billy asked if they could make camp for the evening and Trent nearly bit his head off. After that incident, they kept their distance.

When Trent told them to make camp, Lance decided enough was enough. Long after everyone but the watch crew were asleep, Lance confronted him.

"Trent, we need to talk." Lance insisted.

"What the heck to you want?" Trent snapped.

"You listen to me Trent, you may fire me for saying this, but you need to snap out of it! These men and I have worked for you for a good many years, and some were here before you arrived wet behind the ears. That being said, they don't deserve the treatment they've been getting. They didn't sign on to help you search for the answers you're looking for. They signed on to take care of Abby's livestock and the estate. You've built a good relationship with them over the years, and you're destroying it because you're lonely and angry." Lance tore into him.

"You don't know anything about my feelings." Trent growled. "Take care what you say, or you'll be…"

"I'll be what? Fired? If that's the way you want it fine, but I'll remind you that Abby is now my boss too. I'm quite sure she'll have something to say about it. Besides, we've been through too much together for you to fire me. I want to see you two together as much as you. On top of that, you can't afford to destroy your relationship with your employees. So, pull yourself together and apologize to them in the morning, or so help me when we get back I'll take you to the woodshed!" Lance chastised him again.

"Leave me be! If I want to be angry it's my right!" Trent yelled.

"Your correct, but it ain't your right to tear into the hands the way you've done since we left. Keep it up and you'll be running the island on your own!" Lance warned and stomped off to cool down.

Trent felt like Lance hit him in the stomach, and he was right, it wasn't the hands fault he was alone and angry. He'd have to make amends in the morning.

ABBY AND GINA PUT A big dent in the boxes but grew tired by dinner and after a long talk retired for the night.

The next morning after breakfast, they resumed going through the last of them. Abby seemed a little happier as they went through the endless papers and files.

Sam knocked on the door distracting Gina. When she opened the door to greet him she saw Milly standing behind him.

"What do you want?" Gina stepped outside leaving Abby alone.

"I'm here to see Abby! Why isn't she at the mansion?" Milly sneered.

"That's none of your business and you won't be seeing her anytime soon." Gina said. "Now run along to whatever rock you crawled out from under."

"Oh, I think she'll see me. I have some interesting news for her." Milly smirked.

"I'm sure it will wait for another time. She's unavailable to speak with you today." Gina barely controlled her temper. "Sam, escort this trash back to her boat."

"I want…" Milly squirmed as Sam grabbed her arm and forcibly escorted her to the docks.

Gina closed the door behind her and found Abby staring at a document as the color drained from her face.

"What's the matter Abby?" Gina hurried to her side. "Did you find something?"

"It's a birth certificate. It say's Trent fathered a baby." Abby whispered in disbelief.

Gina went numb, Trent didn't tell her about the baby. "Abby, it's not what you think, the baby wasn't Trent's…"

"It says: Father, Trenton Dale Winthrop." Abby said with a shaky voice.

"But the baby wasn't…" Gina began.

"This says he is! Where's the child?" Abby asked through tears.

"No one knows. The child was taken like Shawn O'Malley's baby. Abby listen… the baby wasn't his it was…"

"Don't Gina! I need some air!" Abby pushed her down and ran out of the door.

Sam came around the corner of the house as Gina burst through the door nearly knocking him off his feet.

"What's wrong Mrs. Gina?" Sam asked alarmed.

"Did you see where Abby went?" She asked looking around for her red hair.

"No, but here come Trent and the rest of them." Sam nodded toward the forest.

Chapter Thirty-four

Abby ran into the mansion and upstairs to her room with tears streaming down her cheeks. Questions bombarded her mind as she flung herself on her bed.

"Why didn't he tell me about the child? Why was Gina covering for him? Where was the child? Was he married to her? More importantly did he love her? Why was he toying with her feelings like this?" The feeling of betrayal washed over her like a tsunami pulling her under a wave of despair.

TRENT ORDERED THE HANDS to search the grounds for her while Gina stayed home in case Abby returned. Lance and Billy checked the stables and docks.

He ran to the mansion hoping she was there. Fear ripped through him that something might happen to her. He wondered what had set her off as a sickening feeling grew with each step he took.

Trent passed through the kitchen into the dining room noting she wasn't in those rooms. He ran into the foyer toward the study, stopping when he heard her crying upstairs. Following the sound of heartbreak, he stopped in her doorway. Seeing her sobbing uncontrollably on her bed ripped a hole in his heart. He'd missed her terribly, and she never left his mind the entire time he was away.

"Abby? What's wrong sweetheart?" He asked softly so he didn't startle her.

Eyes filled with hurt, disappointment, and tears fell on him. To say it hit him hard was an understatement. His chest hurt with each beat of his racing heart.

"You didn't tell me everything, did you?" She asked as anger laced her voice.

"What are you talking about? I told you everything about your family history." He swore.

"You didn't tell me about your child! Were you married, or was it some one-night thing?" She asked accusingly.

"Abby I..." He tried to explain but the words were blocked in his throat.

"Well? Did you or did you not have a child?" She asked hoping he wouldn't lie to her again.

"Yes, it was with Barbara's daughter. The baby disappeared shortly after it was born. We searched for days but we never found it. Barbara's daughter committed suicide a year later. And no we weren't married." He lied covering for her grandfather again.

The hurt in her eyes bore into him nearly knocking his breath from his lungs.

"Why did you hide it from me?" She asked quietly.

"They're both gone Abby. It was a bad moment in time, one that everyone involved wants to forget." He answered.

"Did you love her?" She asked afraid he would confirm what she suspected.

Trent shook his head as he said, "I can honestly say I didn't love her. In fact, I've never loved anyone until I met you Abby."

"Then why hide it from me?" She sniffed.

"I didn't think it mattered. They're both gone and won't be a part of our lives." He replied quietly.

"You had a child who went missing, and you didn't think it mattered?" She asked wondering what kind of man she'd fallen in love with.

Trent didn't say anything, lying to her was driving him crazy, but he had to protect her from her grandfather's indiscretions and...

"Go away! I don't want to talk to you anymore!" She yelled at him.

At least come back to Gina's where you're safe." He finally said quietly.

"I don't want to be around you right now! Just leave me be!" She shouted stubbornly sticking her chin in the air.

"Abby, you will go back to the Elliot's house, I'll come back here to stay. But you will go where it's safe." He growled unyielding.

"I'm staying right here! Go away and leave me be!" She yelled again.

Anger flooded Trent as he desperately tried to control it. He crossed the room intent on carrying her back if necessary. Abby backed away from him as he advanced on her, but he picked her up without any effort.

"I'm not going anywhere with you! Put me down!" She screamed while she struggled in his arms.

Trent looked into her eyes, and saw the anger, hurt and betrayal, yet behind all those emotions he saw love.

"You will do as I say Miss O'Malley or suffer the consequences." He snarled and covered her mouth in a punishing kiss.

Abby struggled to get away from him, but her love for him was so strong, she slowly responded to him.

Regretfully, he pulled away from her even though she'd broken his heart, he had to protect her even if it meant losing her.

Abby misunderstood the look on his face, ran from his presence and didn't stop until she was back in the room Gina had let her use.

Trent showed up a few minutes later, gathered his things, and stormed back to the mansion without a word.

Thoroughly confused and at a loss how to fix things between the two, Lance said, "I'd better go check on him. He'll probably be drunk when I get there."

"I'll talk with Abby. I pray he told her the truth about that baby." Gina said kissing his cheek.

Gina knocked on Abby's door hoping she'd be willing to talk, but her effort went unanswered.

Milly's words reverberated in her ears, *"You'll leave here brokenhearted and alone, pining for a man who took you for everything you own."* In that moment, she decided to leave in the morning. At this point she wished she'd never heard of O'Malley island. Sleep overcame her, albeit a fitful one.

TRENT WAS IN THE STUDY with two bottles of whiskey on the table and one in his hand when Lance found him. He quietly sat across from him watching and waiting for him to open up.

"Well? Aren't you gonna chew me out again? I deserve it!" Trent grumbled.

"I think you're doing a good job of beating yourself up without my two cents worth." Lance said.

He set the empty bottle on the table and opened a new one. "Here's to me!" He raised the bottle in the air and took a big slug of it.

"So, you gonna tell me what happened, or do I have to guess?" Lance asked.

"What's the use? Her grandfather ruined any chance of our being together a long time ago." Trent slurred his words.

"What are you talking about?" Lance pressed.

"Barbara's grandchild." Trent growled.

"You mean you didn't tell her about what happened?" Lance was dumbfounded. "Why not?"

"Because I'm an idiot, still protecting her grandfather. She wouldn't have believed me if I had told her the truth, I could see it in her eyes." Trent said and took another long swallow of the booze.

"You know for someone so smart, you're the dumbest man on earth when it comes to the love of your life." Lance shook his head. "Instead of going to her and making her understand, you'd rather sit here downing all the scotch in the mansion, beating yourself up. You're losing her because you're protecting her from a dead man's moment of weakness!"

"If you're trying to make me feel better, it's not working." Trent slurred sleepily.

Lance barely pulled the bottle from Trent as he passed out. He put his feet on the couch and covered him with a throw blanket. He made good on his promise to leave him where he lie.

⁂

ABBY WOKE UP EARLY with her heart twisting painfully in her chest as she gathered the few things she wanted to take with her. She quickly wrote Gina a note and slipped downstairs. Propping the note against the coffee pot, after one last look around, she left and hurried to the mansion. She was thankful that since Trent returned, they didn't have the guards patrolling.

Abby stepped into her room with a lump in her throat. Quickly packing some of her clothes, along with a few of her most prized pieces of her grandmother's jewelry.

The last thing she did, she put her grandmother's wedding band and the engagement ring Trent had given her on the dresser. Her heart grieved deeply for what she almost had. Of all the losses in her life, this was by far the most heartbreaking.

Even though her heart screamed at her to stay, her mind overrode it reminding her she couldn't trust a man who lied and kept secrets from her.

SOMETHING AWAKENED Trent and he went to check it out. The slight noise of someone in Abby's room drew him to her doorway.

He watched helplessly as Abby took her ring off and lay it on the dresser. His heart fell into his boots when he realized she was leaving, and he couldn't do anything to stop her.

A sharp pain hit him in the back of his head and darkness overtook him. As he fell to the floor drifting into unconsciousness, his last sight was Abby turning and all the color drain from her face.

Abby's skin prickled as she turned to find out what the noise was behind her. That's when she saw Trent fall on the ground and the man who hid in the shadows advanced toward her.

She was so terrified she couldn't move watching him come closer. A hand with a cloth clamped over her mouth from behind. When the darkness began to overtake her, the hideous laughter reached her ears, "I told you I'd make you pay!"

STEVEN HEARD A THUMP as he walked through the foyer to the small clinic Trent had set up behind the formal living room. Quickly going upstairs he found Trent unconscious on the floor in front of Abby's room. He checked the room, but Abby wasn't there, then he checked on Trent.

He hurried downstairs to call Lance, then came back to stop the blood flow from the gaping wound on the back of his head.

Lance and Billy barreled up the stairs and helped him get Trent to the clinic rooms. Soon after he'd stitched him up, Steven brought him around with some smelling salt.

Trent bolted up as Lance and Steven kept him from moving too quickly.

"Where's Abby?" He sounded panicked.

"She's still asleep at my house." Lance said confusion written on his face.

"NO! She was in her room here packing. Someone hit me from behind and… Oh, God! Where is she?" Trent yelled getting dizzy.

"Take it easy Trent. We'll have a look around, if she's here, we'll find her." Lance promised before leaving to investigate.

They looked in her room first. There were no suitcases out, so they turned to leave when Lance noticed something on the dresser shining from the early morning light. Upon closer inspection, he found her grandmother's wedding band and the ring Trent had given her.

"She was here. Billy get to the dock and see if the boats are all accounted for. I'll go round up the hands and get them searching the grounds." Lance ordered, then went down to talk to Steven.

Steven looked up when Lance stopped in the doorway and went to see what he wanted.

"Steven, dope him if you have to, but keep him here."

"Will do." Steven said and went back to check Trent's vitals again.

During their search, they found nothing, so Lance told Billy to round up some of the better hands to go search the forest.

Lance and Gina went to help Steven with Trent while the search continued.

Before she reached the clinic, she heard Steven arguing with Trent.

"Get out of my way!" Trent bellowed.

"You ain't in any condition to go on a search for anybody! You have a concussion!" Steven refused only to be shoved out of his way.

"Trent stop! We're already searching for her. You need to stay here and follow Steven's orders." Lance insisted knowing it wouldn't do any good.

"I'm going! No one is gonna stop me!" Trent bellowed. "Steven if you don't want to eat that needle your sneaking around with, I'd advise you to back off before I shove it down your throat."

"I guess that means I'm coming too." Steven picked up his med kit.

"Gina, you and Sam stay here in case she shows up." Trent ordered.

Gina shot him a loathing look and said furiously, "None of this would've happened if you'd stop protecting a dead man and protected her!"

"I was protecting her from..." Trent swallowed.

"From what?" Gina asked glaring at him.

"From Barbara, she saw we were getting close from the day we met. Barbara still holds me responsible for Susan's death. I didn't want anything to do with her so Barbara took matters into her own hands." Trent explained.

"You knew this all along and never said a word?" Lance asked angrily.

"We're wasting time. Come on!" Trent said pushing past everyone into the hallway.

He divided the hands into three parties and sent them out, one east, one west, one north, and he led the others south.

His fear that she'd been taken grew as each hour passed by, until he knew she'd been taken. He also knew, if anything happened to her, he'd never forgive himself.

Lance and Steven made Trent return to the mansion clinic because he passed out and fell from his horse. He gave the team orders to keep searching.

The men searched the entire island and came up with nothing. After a week, Lance called off the search.

The one thing that puzzled everyone was how she got off the island without a trace, just like the baby that was taken. Fear that the ghoul had taken her gripped everyone.

Trent knew who had her and was at a loss of how to find her.

Chapter Thirty-five

Abby opened her eyes to complete darkness. The air was cold, damp and had a pungent smell. Terror seized her, but she kept silent having learned early on that could lead to dire circumstances.

She moved her hands to find them restrained, while sounds of rodents scurried in the darkness. Occasionally something brushed against her forcing her to recoil on the cot she felt under her.

The constant drip of water and the intermittent sound of waves crashing on rocks led her to believe that she was near the ocean.

The more she struggled against her restraints, the tighter they became. With great difficulty, she managed to sit up, but without light, she was afraid to stand or take a step away from her cot. Without knowing where she was, it could mean life or death.

Tears stung her eyes when she wondered if Trent was looking for her. *"You're such a fool Abby. You love him and now he probably thinks you hate him."*

Her heart was heavy when she visualized Trent on the floor before everything went black. For all she knew he was dead, and she'd lost her only chance for happiness.

Heavy footfalls came from somewhere in the darkness. Quickly laying down, she pretended to be unconscious. She wondered how long she'd been there. Even though she was unconscious at first, it felt like an eternity.

The sound of a key slipping into the door and turning sent a chill up her spine. Then light illuminated the room causing her to flinch.

"Rise and shine Miss O'Malley!" A man's raspy voice seemed to echo off the walls.

When her eyes adjusted to the light, what she saw chilled her blood. Her heart skipped a beat, it was him and he had her at his mercy. The face that glowed in the shadows had kidnapped her. What did he want with her? A scream lodged in her throat when he moved toward her.

Rough hands grabbed her, and he said, "I'm gonna take these ropes off of you and you're gonna behave. If you don't, you can lay here and rot. It makes no difference to me." He growled.

"Who are you?" She stuttered.

"No one you know. Just eat your food and if you're good in a few months I may let you go." He snarled with a wicked smile.

Why are you doing this?" She asked frightened to know the answer.

"You'll understand when the time is right." He laughed fiendishly. "Now eat!"

Abby took a bite of the food. It wasn't very good, but she needed to eat something. She found she was starving, almost as if she hadn't eaten in several days. Maybe if she were obedient she could figure a way out of this.

SEVERAL WEEKS WENT by while Trent searched every inch of the mansion, and every piece of paper he could get his hands on hoping for a clue leading him to her.

"Nothing!" He yelled flinging papers everywhere.

"You can't give in to your fears Trent. We still have a lot to look through." Gina tried to calm him.

"By the time I find her she'll be dead!" Trent growled. "She's not used to fending for herself. How will she survive alone?"

Gina looked at Lance who nodded. She had told him of Abby's story.

"Trent, there's something you should know about Abby." She said.

"What?" Trent looked at her with eyebrows raised.

Gina related the entire evening she spent with Abby telling her how she was raised. "So you see, Abby is quite capable of taking care of herself."

Trent sat back in shock. No wonder she was afraid of thunderstorms.

"Gina? Have I lost her for good?" Trent asked with angst in his voice.

"Don't give up on her Trent. Abby wouldn't have tried to leave if you had been honest with her. The fact that you lied to her about that child is what turned her against you." Gina scolded him. "The note she left said she couldn't deal with your secrets and lies any longer. She felt that if you really loved her, you'd have told her everything."

"What if I'm too late?" Trent asked quietly.

"We can't give up, I'm sure she hasn't where ever she is." Gina insisted.

"It's been a month now, not a sign or clue anywhere." Trent swallowed.

"Here." Lance shoved a glass of scotch in his hand. "That's the only one you're getting so make it last buster. I think you need a change of scenery for a day or two. We need supplies, so tomorrow you and Gina are going to the mainland to get them. I'll handle things here and before your open your mouth to argue don't. Papa says that's an order."

For the first time in a month, Trent smiled. It felt good until he remembered Abby was still missing and his smile fled.

He walked Gina and Lance to the door and watched them leave until they disappeared from his sight. When he went upstairs, he thought, *"What a fool I am. I find the love of my life and let her slip through my fingers."*

When he found her, he determined to never let her go again, if she still wanted him.

⚜

ABBY LOST ALL TRACK of time in the darkness. She was dirty and was told to live with it. Her bathroom was a lone bucket. It made things difficult being in total darkness.

When he brought her food, she made careful observations of her surroundings, looking for an opportunity to escape.

The man brought her daily ration of food and waited for her to eat.

"May I have some water to clean up with?" She asked quietly.

"Maybe if you behave." He grumbled.

"Are you ever going to tell me your name?" She asked.

"It's Harry. Satisfied?" He growled.

"Nice to meet you Harry." She smiled sweetly. "Do you live around here, or is this your vacation home?"

"You think by being nice to me, you're going to escape?" He snorted. "I got plans for you girlie, and I don't care if you're dead or alive when the time comes."

Abby fell silent afraid this time she wouldn't be able to escape the torture she suspected was coming her way.

"What's the matter?" He smiled maliciously.

"Nothing." She said. "I was just thinking it would be nice to clean up a little."

"We'll see, you done?" He asked moving toward her.

"Yes." She answered looking at the cave floor.

Abby's heart sank as Harry took the tray and left her alone again.

While lying in the darkness, she realized there was something familiar about him. Despite the disfigurement of his face, he reminded her of someone. Yes, she'd seen his face many times before, but there was something she couldn't put her finger on. Since she had nothing else to do, she worked on figuring out who he was.

Huddling on the tiny cot, she wrapped the threadbare blanket around her shivering. She knew the ocean was nearby because every once in a while she'd catch the smell of the salty air.

Her mind wandered back to Trent. Closing her eyes she pictured him smiling at her, then his face turned angry and then hurt. She deeply regretted how she left things. Silently crying, she realized who Harry was. He was Trent's father! That's why he looked so familiar.

GINA MET TRENT AT THE dock early the next morning. In no time they were on their way as Lance headed back to the mansion to handle some business.

Trent's mood hadn't improved. He stood at the stern of the ship watching the island disappear on the horizon. Eventually, he joined Gina below deck where she was reading some of the letters from Grandmother Abigail's trunk.

Gina truly worried about Trent, every day Abby was missing, the more withdrawn he became.

Trent sat down across from her with a cup of coffee, obviously wanting to unburden himself.

"What's on your mind Trent?" She asked setting the letter aside.

"You know I hate it when you do that. I forget how well you and Lance know me." He grunted.

"So, what's wrong?" Gina chuckled.

"Gina... I can't sleep, I can barely eat. I miss her so much it's killing me. I want her back, tell me what to do to find her." He pleaded.

"We're all doing everything we can to find her. Don't give up on her or yourself. In your heart, you know she's still alive don't you?" She asked.

"Yes... sometimes at night I feel her heart beating next to mine. I can feel the fear she's in." Trent said as his eyes told her the toll it was taking on him.

"Keep believing you're gonna find her. Trent I know in my heart it's connected to that baby's disappearance. The one question that's been bothering me is, how did that ghoul get in without leaving any evidence behind?" Gina asked.

"If I knew that, we would've found her by now." Trent grumbled. "I hope and pray he didn't get to Abby too."

"Well no ghost, and mind you, I don't believe in them, could've taken her. How would he restrain her?" Gina asked thoughtfully.

Trent mulled over her words trying to make sense of it all.

"By the way, when you told us about protecting Abby from Barbara, you never finished what you were saying. So spill it Buster." She ordered.

"You remember Barbara's daughter getting pregnant?" Trent asked.

"Yeah, so?" She said.

"Barbara wanted O'Malley for herself. When Grandmother Abigail left him she saw an opportunity to step in and comfort him. O'Malley was still in love with Abigail and wouldn't give her the time of day. When her daughter showed up, Barbara saw I wasn't interested and snuck her into O'Malley's room one night and the rest is history. When the baby disappeared, Barbara blamed me because she thought I made sure no one would ever find it to keep O'Malley's indiscretion a secret. Then her daughter committed suicide, she warned me she'd get back at me." Trent seemed to be thinking, "When she saw us getting closer I was afraid she'd hurt Abby."

"What?" Gina could see the wheels turning in his head.

"You don't think Barbara was letting someone in to scare us do you?" Trent asked feeling as though he was close to figuring something out. But what?

"It's entirely possible." Gina agreed.

The only problem with that theory is Barbara's been away for quite a while since we haven't needed a cook. There has to be another explanation." Trent reasoned.

"There's an answer somewhere, we just have to find it." Gina put her hand over his.

"We should be getting close to the mainland. You wanna come with me or do you need to do some shopping?" Trent asked.

"I need some things for the house, I'll meet you back here at four." She smiled still worried about him.

After docking they went their separate ways just as snow began floating from the sky. Christmas had come and gone, and the new year was a few days away.

Trent went to his favorite restaurant where Abby attacked Milly. A smile played on his lips when he sat in his favorite booth.

Abby surprised him that day, now that he knew the story she'd told Gina he understood why.

He ordered his food and lost himself to his thoughts of her. Somehow he felt closer to her while he ate. How he wished with all his heart that when they returned to the island, she'd be waiting for him. He'd wrap his arms around her and never let her go again.

Chapter Thirty-six

"Are you all on your lonesome?" Milly interrupted his thoughts. "Where's that hussy Abby?"

"She's away for the time being, and the only hussy I know is you Milly. Why don't you go torture somebody else?" Trent asked craving solitude.

"Come on Trent, we used to have a close relationship. Why can't we be friends?" She whined. "I'm sure Miss O'Malley hasn't made you feel the way I used to. You always said you loved how I..."

"That's enough Milly. It was a very long time ago and I've moved on so why don't you?" Trent stopped her.

"I just can't forget how we were together, or how much you enjoyed what I have to offer. It could be that way again, you know. All you have to do is keep your dad's promise." Milly put her hand on his shoulder.

"Milly, I'm telling you for the last time, I don't love you! I refuse to live in a loveless marriage." Trent said as his heart burned for Abby. "It's not fair to you or me. So do us both a favor and go find someone else to love."

"I want you Trent, and I always get what I want." She said unequivocally.

"You could've had me, but you chose to cheat on me. That's all it took for me to realize I can't trust you Milly." He reminded her.

"Trent we were young. I was only sowing my wild oats. You can't fault me for getting it all out of my system, can you?" She whined again.

"That doesn't change the fact that I don't love you. Neither of us would be happy, so just drop it!" Trent stood, "I have to go."

Milly expertly tripped and forced him to keep her from falling.

"Oh, how clumsy of me." She feigned embarrassment.

Trent's mind went to the first time Abby ran into him. For a brief moment Abby was in his arms and he kissed Milly thinking she was Abby.

The moment Milly said, "See Trent, you can still love me." Trent realized what he had done. He pushed her away leaving her with a smug smile on her overdone face.

After leaving the restaurant, he went about his business feeling as though he'd cheated on Abby. In his heart he knew no woman would love him like Abby. He'd never be happy with anyone else. Especially Milly Boudreau.

The thought of being in a loveless marriage with her sickened him. From that moment on, he determined if he couldn't have Abby, he'd live a life of loneliness.

He met Gina on the dock feeling worse than he had when they arrived. The liquor store was the last delivery to arrive before he told the captain to get underway.

He went below deck with an armload of booze and proceeded to get stupid drunk.

Gina gave him a little space wondering what had happened. Unable to contain her curiosity, she went below. Watching her husband deal with him for so many years, she followed his example. She sat quietly across from him waiting.

"What?" He grumbled.

"You wanna tell me about it or shall we play twenty questions?" She asked.

"No, and no." He replied.

"Okay, I'll wait until you're drunk and then you'll tell me everything." She said calmly.

"You've been taking lessons from Lance haven't you." He accused.

"Who better to learn from? So, do I wait, or do you want to be coherent enough to know what you're saying?" She grinned.

"Fine. In a word Milly." He growled.

"What about her?" She asked feeling Milly was getting to him.

Trent took another long drink from the bottle in his hand and told her what happened. He hoped it would make him feel better to tell someone, but it made him feel infinitely worse.

"So, just because she managed to get you to kiss her, you feel like you cheated on Abby?" She understood.

"I did! I don't care if I thought I was kissing Abby or not! I still kissed her!" He shouted feeling ill.

"For what it's worth, I'd say your longing for Abby tricked your mind and Milly just happened to be there. Just to be clear, you only kissed her. You didn't hop in bed with that bimbo." She pointed out.

"Tell me we're gonna find her. I need some hope here. I don't think I can take much more of this." He said and downed the rest of the bottle.

When they arrived on the island, Trent staggered to the mansion with his load of booze.

Gina told her husband what happened, and she was terribly worried about him. "I've never seen him like this. I'm afraid he's gonna hurt himself Lance. You didn't see the look in his eyes while he told me about it."

"I'll take care of it. Get Sam and Billy to help unload the supplies. It's gonna be okay my love." Lance pulled her into his arms and kissed her.

Lance made his way to the mansion wondering how to handle this new development. He remembered when he and Gina nearly split up over the death of their child.

Gina left him to stay with her mother for a few months. It nearly drove him insane after a couple of days, so he made her come home. It took a while, but they worked through it.

This situation was completely different. Trent couldn't go get her since no one knew where she is, or if she's even alive. How was he supposed to give him hope when everyone else had given up on her?

His mind was whirling in what if's and how to's when he stepped into the study. Trent was in his usual spot, downing his second bottle by the look of the empty one on the table. God only knew how many he had drank on the trip home. It surprised him the man was still conscious.

Sitting across from him as usual, he waited for Trent to start talking.

"You know I've already gone through this once today from your wife." He grumbled already stupid drunk.

"So why are you waiting to tell me about it?" Lance grinned with pride for his wife.

"You taught her well, and I know she's already spilled her guts to you. That's why you're here. Am I wrong?" Trent looked at him with red blurry eyes.

"You're not wrong. However, what you're doing ain't getting you any closer to finding Abby. The rate you're going by the time you do find her you'll be an alcoholic. Then you'll be no good for yourself, or worse for her!" Lance scolded him.

"You wanna know why I get drunk? So I won't feel. So I can forget. Lance it's been so long, I fear she may be..." He choked.

"You can't think like that. The booze is clouding your mind." Lance said. "Do you love her?"

"You know I do! I'll never get to tell her the truth about everything. Yeah I shoulda done it in the first place, but I'm an idiot." He slurred.

"Then don't give up on her. I'll give you odds she's out there frightened and most likely in pain. The one thing that'll get her through this is her love for you and holding you in her heart." Lance reasoned. "You need to stop this stupid juvenile tantrum and help me, and Gina find her! We haven't given up and of all people you shouldn't either."

Trent flung the bottle in his hand at the fireplace shattering it into a million pieces. When he tried to stand, he was too drunk.

Lance barely caught him an told him to sleep it off. They would start fresh in the morning.

ABBY OPENED HER EYES when she heard Milly's voice arguing with Harry. She started a few days ago making daily visits spewing out threats and insults.

"I want her right where she is. I'm breaking Trent down. He actually kissed me yesterday." She crowed.

Abby felt like someone threw a bucket of ice-cold water on her. *Was Milly breaking Trent down? Was he giving in to her?* Somewhere deep in her heart a small voice told her no, but was what Milly said true?

Refusing to let Milly see her cry, she bit her cheek when the door opened.

"My, oh my, don't we look horrid!" She wrinkled her nose in disgust. "Trent would run the other way if he saw you now."

"You might be surprised at what Trent would do Milly." Abby raised her chin in defiance.

"You're the one in for a surprise, after a nice long chat yesterday, we shared a long passionate kiss. I believe he's coming around to my way of thinking." Milly bragged. "Here you thought he loved you. The truth is he's always loved me, you mean nothing to him."

"That's your story. Why would I believe you?" Abby hissed angrily.

"Let's just say in no time I'll be wearing his ring. And you, well if we did let you go, he'll never want you again. Although if he never saw you again, he'd be a tormented man." Milly snickered. "No matter, I'll make him forget all about you."

Although she showed no emotion, Abby began to lose hope fearing for her life. With her out of the way, Milly would wear Trent down. He was only human, and Milly was gorgeous. He may never love her like he did Abby, but she'd certainly satisfy his physical needs.

"What's wrong? Are you finally beginning to see the position you're in. Trent will be mine and you'll die a lonely death pining for him, knowing that I'm the one he holds in his arms at night." Milly laughed gleefully.

"You may succeed in what you're doing Milly, but remember this, when he holds you, he'll be thinking of me. I'm the one he loves. You'll never own his heart because it belongs to me!" Abby warned her.

"Who needs love when you can have power? With you out of the way, I'll be the new owner of the island. Trent will happily give it to me." Milly said gleefully as she left with Harry locking the door behind them.

As the darkness closed in on her, Abby curled up on the cot crying uncontrollably.

TRENT MOANED WITH THE mother of all hangovers when he opened his eyes. He hated to admit it, but Lance was right. It was time to shape up if he wanted to find his love. In his heart he could feel Abby was still alive somewhere out there, holding onto the hope he would locate her.

When he finally stepped into the hot shower, he kicked himself for wanting to give up. A clap of thunder rattled the old mansion. He stumbled from the shower and threw on his clothes.

He didn't know where Abby was so he couldn't comfort her during the storm. Trent tore through the mansion and ran into the deluge of rain toward Lance and Gina's.

He burst through the kitchen door nearly scaring the older couple to death. "Lance! I can't help her! When she hears this..."

"Calm down Trent. Abby is stronger than you think." Gina said.

"The best thing we can do is keep searching." Lance said.

Gina saw Trent about to explode so she said, "I have an idea. Why don't you two go find the blueprints for the mansion, that way when Abby gets home, you two can start remodeling."

"I don't even know where to start looking." Trent disagreed.

"Just do as I ask. I'll come make dinner there. Lord knows what needs to be thrown out in that refrigerator." She chuckled.

Gina watched them step out into the pouring rain sure that they would find something.

ABBY PRAYED TRENT WOULDN'T succumb to Milly's evil machinations and give up looking for her. The first clap of thunder was so loud it shook her to her core. It didn't help that it echoed through the cave.

"Stop it Abby!" She yelled. "You can't fall apart, you have to be alert!"

With the next clap of thunder she closed her eyes and clamped her hands over her ears. In her mind she heard Trent whisper, *"Abby, I love you. I'm here and I'll never leave you."*

Forcing herself to calm down, she rocked back and forth on the cot hugging herself and pretending Trent was there.

Chapter Thirty-seven

Trent found the blueprints in a file cabinet stored in the attic. He took them downstairs to the study when he smelled his favorite food. Lasagna with garlic bread. Gina learned how to make it when she met a distant cousin of his. Somehow when Gina made the dish it was even more delicious.

Lance followed him to the kitchen with his stomach grumbling.

"I found them." Trent laid them aside and sat at the small table to the right of the door in the kitchen.

Steven came in the back door with an attractive young woman on his arm.

"Hi, Steven, who's this?" Trent asked raising a brow.

"This is Lisa Jones, our new part time nurse." Steven said.

"Welcome to O'Malley Island, Miss Jones. I hope we don't keep you too busy around here." Trent said flashing her a heart stopping smile.

"Thank you, Mr. Winthrop. I hope to live up to your expectations." She returned his smile.

"Would you like some dinner?" Gina asked. "We have plenty."

"We just ate with the wranglers. I'm going to show Lisa the clinic." Steven declined.

After dinner, the Elliots went home, and Trent went upstairs to bed. He deliberately left the liquor alone remembering what Lance said.

ABBY CURLED UP ON THE cot with a stomach ache. She missed Trent terribly. She even missed Gina, Lance, Billy, and Sam. They'd become her family and it was killing her to be away from them.

The cold finally became more bearable leading her to think spring was just around the corner.

She had no idea what time it was or if it was day or night outside. With every visit from Milly she decided it must be day time.

Abby became increasingly afraid of what Milly's plans were for her. The woman became progressively deranged when she showed up to torment her. Thankfully, when winter came, the only person she saw was Harry and he didn't stick around long enough to talk.

Heavy footsteps alerted her to Harry's presence. She wasn't hungry, but she had to eat some of the food, or she'd die. If it were up to Milly, she'd have died of starvation months ago. Harry stepped in and fought her over it.

He opened the door to find her sitting on the edge of her cot. Her delicate face was stained with tears that streaked through the dirt on her face. No one deserved this kind of treatment just for loving someone.

Harry had to be careful around her because his cold heart had begun to thaw toward her. He suspected there was more to Abby O'Malley than met the eye.

Abby was pleasantly surprised when he came in carrying a bucket of water and clean clothes for her.

"I thought since you haven't given me any trouble, you might enjoy cleaning up a bit." He said placing the items on the table with the lantern. "I'll be back in an hour with your food."

The minute his footstep were far enough away, she dipped her hands in the water surprised to find it hot. She wasted no time in stripping off her clothes and tossing them into a corner.

Soon she was scrubbing her skin raw to rid herself of the months of dirt and grime. She even managed to wash her hair, albeit it was matted in places it still felt good to run the now warm water through it.

Quickly dressing she just sat down on the cot when she heard Harry returning with her food.

When he set the food on the table she asked, "Would you stay and talk with me Harry?"

"Why?" He asked suspiciously.

"I'd like to know about the weather, what day it is, or if its spring yet. I just need some conversation." She turned her green eyes on him.

"Okay. It's Wednesday, March eighteenth, and it's sunny out. Anything else?" He asked as his heart melted a little more. She looked so small and scared. If only...

"Is Milly going to kill me?" She asked sadly.

"I don't know yet. She's a real piece of work that one. I've never met anyone so ruthless, not even me." He shook his head.

"Why did you promise her that Trent would marry her?" Abby asked not thinking.

Harry's eyes flashed with surprise and then anger. "How did you know I was his father?"

"Once in a while I can see him looking at me through your eyes." She admitted figuring she may as well go for it.

"Well he isn't. You best forget trying to be nice to me in an attempt to escape." He growled.

"I know you're not gonna let me go so easily. You still want to torture your son." Abby said.

"Milly's doing a good job of that on her own. Besides, I got my revenge on him when I took his child." He chuckled.

Abby's heart broke, so it was true. Harry is the man scaring her all these years. Now that she'd seen him he wasn't all that scary. In fact, she suspected age had mellowed him a little.

"What did he do to make you hate him so much?" Abby asked hoping he wouldn't hurt her.

"He killed the love of my life! She died giving birth to him." Harry said with a far-off look in his eyes.

"How was it his fault? He was a baby for God's sake." Abby asked feeling sorry for both of them.

"The doc said he was too big for her to carry, and it did something inside of her. She bled to death having him." He said with sorrow in his eyes.

"I'm sorry, I shouldn't have asked." Abby looked at the floor.

"It was a long time ago. Ain't nothing can be done about it. Between losing that child and Milly taking you away from him, I think he's suffered quite enough." He said. "Just so you know taking you was all Milly's idea. She has an evil mind surpassing even mine."

"What did you do with the child?" Abby asked.

"Milly took it to the mainland and sold it to somebody." He said not thinking.

"Can I ask what happened to your face?" Abby quickly changed the subject.

"I fought off a feral wolf." He said. "I won. Are you done talking now? I got things to do."

"Yeah. I'm sorry I've kept you. Maybe we could talk more tomorrow." She smiled hopefully.

"It's not likely, but we'll see." Harry said and locked the door behind him leaving her in total darkness once again.

Abby sat against the cave wall with her feet in the cot thinking about their conversation. It's no wonder that Trent was rough around the edges. It's a wonder he even talked to her let alone fell in love with her.

Abby sat up with a light in her brain. Milly had Harry take that baby and she sold it. She wanted it out of the way.

A cold chill of fear slithered around her. Milly had Harry take her because she was in the way. Only this time she feared instead of selling her, there was a real possibility the woman would have her killed.

Abby prayed earnestly that Trent would find her before Milly could harm her any more than she already had. She laid down and closed her eyes trying to feel Trent. To let him know she was still alive, what she was feeling and how much she loved him.

She couldn't explain it, but many times, she felt his desperation as he searched for her. His love for her kept Abby from going mad in the darkness.

TRENT PULLED ANOTHER trunk in the attic to the center of the room and stopped.

"Trent? What's wrong?" Gina asked watching him stand still.

"She's alive! I can feel her loneliness. Her heart is broken because I haven't found her yet." Trent finally said, "Gina? I'm not going crazy..."

"It's possible, the connection between the two of you is strong. Maybe she's figured out a way to send her love to you. I've heard of stranger things." Gina said.

"That's nuts Gina, and I think you've finally lost it Trent." Lance turned to get Steven.

"Where are you going?" Gina asked.

"I'm getting Steven. Trent's losing his ever-loving mind." He said.

"No I'm not losing my mind, but I am losing her." Trent said as the feeling faded.

"This is the last trunk and we've gone through everything in this mansion." Gina said.

Trent knew he wasn't dreaming. He really felt her. That knowledge gave him a renewed sense of hope as they continued to search.

Chapter Thirty-eight

Milly kept the pressure on Trent tempting him every time she caught him alone. He made sure someone was around him most of the time to run interference when she showed up.

She could see him weakening and soon she would break him. Somehow she had to make him forget about Abby. The only solution she could see was to get rid of her. She had to give them both credit, they never wavered in their love for each other. It was a good thing she wasn't out for love, all she wanted was power.

Her plan was to get Trent to marry her, then she'd release Abby and she'd run crying back to wherever she came from.

Happily climbing the hill to the mansion she believed would soon be hers, Milly was in a particularly good mood today. She could feel things were going her way, and hopefully today was the day Trent would crumble and ask her to marry him.

Trent saw her coming up the hill. Milly had something to do with Abby's disappearance and he'd use her to get Abby back or die trying. All he had to do was play along with her. It disgusted him to think of how far he may have to go to get Abby back, but to him it was worth it.

Lance and Gina helped him devise a plan after they'd found letters between Milly and Barbara in her cottage. He'd found one in the pantry which prompted that search.

In them Barbara kept Milly informed of everything Abby was doing. That's when Trent decided Barbara's services would no longer be needed.

The discovery of the letters gave them all the pieces of the puzzle, everything from kidnapping Abby to convincing Trent to marry her. They still had one piece missing. Where was Abby?

Milly slipped in like usual with the key Barbara had given her. Quietly she opened the door to the study to find Trent alone by the fireplace with a glass of scotch in his hand.

"A little early to be hitting the bottle isn't it?" She asked sweetly.

Trent had a couple before she got there to be able to pull their plan off. Milly disgusted him so much it churned in his stomach. His mind raced, *"How could I have actually liked her all those years ago?"*

Getting Abby back had to be his focus and at this point he would do anything to make that happen.

"No. I'm having a rough time today. It's been almost five months since Abby disappeared. I've given up trying to find her. For all I know she's gone back to her home in the states." He sighed.

"I'm so sorry Trent, but I did try to warn you. She was only toying with you." Milly couldn't hide her glee.

"I'm closing the mansion and moving to the mainland." He said barely hiding the smile when her expression changed.

"There are too many memories here. Besides, Abby left the entire estate to Lance and Gina. Lance doesn't need me to be his manager any longer."

"The color drained from Milly's face. Quickly regaining her composure, she said, "How could she! Why would she cut you out of her will like that? You took care of her grandparents and everything!"

"She did leave me Grandmother Abigail's cottage. I figure with all the money I've saved over the years I can live quite comfortably there. Although I would need the love of a good woman by my side. What do you say Milly? Would you be my wife?" He asked trying to keep from choking. "I've been lonely a long time and you've always been around to make me see what I'm missing."

He took her in his arms before he chickened out and kissed her long and passionately. The plan was in motion, and he hoped he could see it through.

Milly felt as though she was in a dream as she returned his kisses. She had missed him, but the object of her desire was the power he wielded. So she wouldn't be queen of the island. Trent was a wealthy man in his own right.

"You know if we want I can arrange for us to be married tomorrow if you like." He kissed her again.

"I... I..." She stammered taken off guard.

"What's wrong?" He nibbled her ear.

"What about Abby?" She stepped back.

Trent reached for her, "What about her? She's long gone." Trent said.

"I guarantee she'll be around to see us marry." Milly sighed as he kissed her neck. "Love me Trent."

He kissed her again thinking *"I'll teach you Milly Boudreau. You have no idea who you're dealing with."*

"You're mine and she'll never have you." Milly said. "Trent please!"

"Tell me where Abby is, and I will." Trent said softly.

"I have no idea where she is." She looked away to hide the truth.

"If you want her to suffer, take me to her so we can give her the good news." Trent nuzzled her neck.

"What's gotten into you? I thought you loved her." Milly's eyes held suspicion.

"She was leaving me when I was hit from behind. Maybe it was a lover I didn't know she had on the side." He kissed the soft spot behind her ear driving her nearly insane. "I was a fool to think she had any real feelings for me."

"Oh, Trent, I'll take you to her. Just don't stop." She begged.

"Anything you want my pet, but I want to wait until our wedding night." He pulled away from her.

"We've been together before." She protested.

"I want my wedding night to be special. After all we'll be together forever. I can have the minister here in the morning if you want. I don't want to waste another minute." He insisted pulling a diamond ring out of his pocket and putting it on her finger.

She agreed to meet him at one p.m. in the rose garden. After one last kiss, she left strutting down the hill to give her family the news. *"I did it! I won! All Trent's power and money are mine."* She thought smugly.

Trent had done well, now he wanted a shower to wash the filth from him. The sick feeling in his gut had almost given him away but he managed to keep it under control. For Abby. He kept telling himself while kissing Milly. He needed mouthwash and now.

Lance and Gina appeared in the foyer after they saw Milly leave.

Gina took one look at his ripped shirt and said, "Trenton Dale Winthrop! You didn't!"

"No I didn't. She was begging me by the time I got some answers from her." He scowled. "Although watching her squirm was kinda satisfying."

"Well spit it out! Where is Abby?" Lance lost his patience.

"Down Papa. We're having a wedding tomorrow at one p.m. When the ceremony is over, she'll let her go. She thinks that if we're married Abby won't want me and leave." He explained. "The preacher will be my friend who happens to be an international sheriff. When Abby is safe, he'll arrest her."

"Brilliant. But what if she waits a day or two before releasing Abby? Milly's going to expect... well... you know." Gina turned a pretty pink.

"Don't worry Gina, trust me I'll handle it." Trent laughed. "When I'm finished with Milly Boudreau, she'll never want to see me or this island again."

The level of determination in Trent was one Lance or Gina had never seen in him before. The man before them had become obsessed with finding the love of his life and bringing her home.

"Now, if you'll excuse me, I need a shower. I feel like I've been rolling around in a sewer and I need to brush the taste of that tramp from my mouth." Trent said disgusted.

Lance laughed so hard tears gathered in his eyes. Gina pulled on his arm wiping tears from her cheeks, "Come on laughing boy!"

The hot water cascaded over his body carrying the stench of Milly from his person and down the drain. He let his thoughts wander to Abby and imagined holding her in his arms safe and secure. When he felt her love for him he vowed that soon she would return to him where she belonged.

※

ABBY QUIETLY SAT ON her cot with her eyes closed thinking about Trent. She could feel his love for her and felt a renewed confidence that gave her hope. The feeling was so strong, she knew something had changed and she would soon be with him.

When the feelings faded she prayed, *"God lead him to me soon, please."*

Footsteps echoed through the cave, but they weren't Harry's. The key turned in the lock and Milly stepped inside leaving the door slightly ajar.

"I see you're still alive on this glorious day Miss O'Malley." She said with glee.

"Where's Harry?" Abby asked standing to her feet.

"He's taking care of a few things for me. You see, I'm to wed Trent tomorrow." Milly waved the ring under her nose.

Abby eased toward her, "You always get what you want don't you. Even if you have to cheat to do it."

"Have you given up? I figured you'd put up a fight for him." Milly taunted. "Is the competition too strong for you?"

"We both know if I weren't in here there would be no competition. You had to cheat to get what you wanted." Abby said moving closer. "I'll tell you this, it will backfire on you. Wait and see."

"It will be over soon, and I'll be rid of you." Milly smirked. "Even though you left everything to the Elliot's, Trent and I will have a very comfortable life in your grandmother's cottage."

Milly didn't see Abby move until it was too late. Even in her weakened state, she packed a punch which landed on Milly's nose sending her to the floor. Abby ran out of the door and locked it behind her.

"No you won't Milly." Abby shouted and ran toward the faint light at the end of the passage. The fleeting comment about the Elliots came to mind but she didn't have time to analyze it. Right now she had to get away before Harry came back.

She hoped the conversations she and Harry had over his last few visits had softened his heart toward her. During his time with her, he apologized for taking her and said that he was sorry for what he had done to Trent. He was afraid Trent would never forgive him, not that he expected him to because of all the pain he had inflicted upon him. Now, she hoped if he did catch her, he would let her go back to Trent.

Nearing the mouth of the cave, she saw part of a beach. She slipped out and saw Harry tying off a boat and ducked behind some huge boulders.

After he passed by and she was sure he was inside, she ran for the boat. One moment before she tried to jump in, Harry caught her. She fought kicking and beating his back, but his hold on her was too strong, and she was too weak from being held captive for so long.

Milly waited fuming with rage until Harry dumped her on the cot.

She shoved him aside screaming, "You think you're going to get free? Think again you orphan!"

Abby flinched as Milly slapped her hard across her face.

There was no way the young woman would take that lying down. Before Milly blinked, Abby was all over her, beating her with her fists until Harry yanked her off of Milly and put her back on the cot.

"Calm down Miss O'Malley! Don't make me tie you up." He barked.

"Do it! Tie her up! I don't want her to move! Starve her!" Milly screeched in anger.

"I ain't gonna do nothing of the sort. It was your fault this happened. You couldn't wait until I got here to shove that ring under her nose." He turned on her. "Now you've got what you want, let her go. You don't need her anymore."

"Not until after the ceremony tomorrow. I want her to see him kiss me and listen to the minister present me as Mrs. Winthrop." Milly's malicious smile turned Abby's stomach.

"Why do you hate her so much?" Harry asked.

"She's standing between me, and all the money and power Trent has." Milly watched Harry's expression change and an evil smile formed on her lips. "You don't know do you? He's become a very wealthy man. Unfortunately, I was stupid and cheated on him. Now I've had to trap him and with your help, Harry, I've finally got him right where I want him."

"You're a real piece of work, Miss Boudreau. Someday you'll find you've made a grave mistake crossing my son like this." Harry growled.

"Why would you care? You just do as your told or you won't get your money. You know you can go to prison for kidnapping if you don't keep your promise." Milly hissed.

"Tomorrow get her cleaned up and bring her to the mansion. I want her to watch from her room while the ceremony is going on. And gag her so she can't scream." Milly said leaving the cave.

Harry closed the door and locked it before turning to Abby. His heart broke for the young woman crying her eyes out because of the evil witch who just left.

Despite his unfounded anger toward his son, he felt for him. This young woman was truly in love with him, and even though he didn't know much about his grown son, he was sure Trent loved her.

A long-forgotten memory of what it felt like to love someone with your whole being, only to have it ripped away cut into his heart opening old wounds. Truthfully, they'd never completely healed. However, since talking with Abby, he realized Trent was not at fault when his wife died. At the time it was easier just to blame an innocent baby. She made him see what kind of man he had become, and it wasn't pretty.

He sat on the cot beside her and pulled her close letting her cry on his shoulder.

Beautiful eyes filled with pain and tears looked up at him. "Harry, please. Please let me go, I love Trent. If he marries her..."

"I can't do that Miss Abby. But somehow I'll make this right." He said softening toward her even more. "Can I get you something?"

"My freedom." She whispered through heavy tears. Witnessing the hurt and pain in her eyes he felt the dagger go into his heart and twist.

Harry left her with the lantern this time thinking, *"At least she won't be alone in the dark anymore."*

Chapter Thirty-nine

Abby sat with a heavy heart waiting for Harry to show up with the water and clean clothes. When he entered he had brought soap and towels too.

"Clean up and we'll leave." He said and locked the door behind him.

When he was sure she was decent, he opened the door.

Abby sat on the cot all bright and shiny except for her matted hair. Even so, she was a beautiful woman, and he knew his son had great taste.

"We'll be leaving in a few minutes." He cleared his throat. "I have news."

"Oh? Did Milly fall off a cliff somewhere? Maybe a feral wolf got her?" Abby smarted off. "Although I'd feel sorry for the wolf, it'll probably die of rabies."

"You're a little fireball aren't you?" He laughed. "I'll put a stop to the wedding. But you have to promise me to do exactly what I say."

Abby nodded as a tiny ray of hope slipped through the darkness around her.

"Do you love him enough to fight for him?" He asked.

Without a thought she said, "I love him enough to die for him, Harry."

The depth of heartbreak and sadness in her eyes nearly broke him.

"If it means leaving him with Milly, if that's what he really wants, I'll leave him to her. But know this, if I even suspect he'd rather be with me, yes, I'd fight for him. And believe me what Milly experienced yesterday will pale in comparison to what I'd do to her if she got in my way again." Abby continued.

The fire in her eyes convinced him of her sincerity.

"I will make sure he doesn't marry her." Harry insisted..

"Why are you willing to help me after all this time?" Abby asked confused.

"I've gotten to know you Miss O'Malley. You've broken through the hard shell I've carried all these years. You made me realize I was punishing my son for something that wasn't his fault. In my grief it was easier to blame him than come to terms with his mother's death." He explained, "My son made a wise decision when he chose you. That witch Milly doesn't deserve him, you do. I know Trent will never forgive me, but maybe I can make some of the misery I've put him through go away. He deserves to marry the woman he chooses, and not one that's forced on him."

Abby put her hand over his massive, calloused, wrinkled hand and said, "Thank you dad."

Those words broke the deep dam of resentment and pain in his heart, and he cried. She comforted him as he came to terms with his wife's death, and how he'd treated his own flesh and blood.

"Are you feeling better?" Abby asked softly out of concern.

"I've never cried in front of anyone before." He looked away ashamed.

"You know Harry, I've always believed that a man who can show his emotions is more of a man." Abby told him.

"If I were younger, my son would have a fight on his hands keeping you Miss Abby O'Malley." He chuckled.

"So fill me in on your plan." She smiled with hope shining in her eyes.

"There's a reason we could slip in unannounced in the mansion. There is a secret passage leading from this cave to the basement. The interior was built with double walls to hide the passages to every room in the mansion." He explained. "The times when you saw only a face in the shadows floating with no body, were only projections from projectors around the mansion to make it seem like a ghost."

"How do you know all of this?" Abby asked in shock.

"Barbara stumbled onto the entrance to the caves. She's angry with Trent for refusing to marry her daughter. When he rejected her, she made her daughter slip into the old man's room one night. The girl got pregnant, and Trent promised your grandfather he'd claim the child was his to keep the curse from harming the child." He said.

Abby gasped, "I found the birth certificate with his name as the father. He lied to me and said the baby was his. The morning you took me, I was leaving him."

"I'm sorry Abby, the baby wasn't his." Harry put an arm around her. "I didn't know until Barbara told me. I don't think she ever told Milly.

"What else don't I know?" Abby swiped at a stray tear.

"Milly was furious when she found out the girl was pregnant, and Trent claimed it was his. She contacted me through her father." He said. "Somehow she found out about the supposed curse and hatched the plan to kidnap the child while making it look like the curse was true. Milly paid me to take the child, then blackmailed me in to promising to make Trent marry her. If I hadn't made the promise she would've told everyone I took the baby and drowned it at sea. As if! I agreed because she had me over a barrel. Two years later, Barbara told me that the old man forced Trent to say the child was his."

"So are you going to take me to the mansion to stop the wedding?" Abby asked.

"Yes. I'll leave you there, but you gotta stay outta sight." He insisted. "The wedding won't start until she sees me open the well house door. Trent can't see you until the wedding's over. I'll make sure there's no I do's exchanged."

"Harry, I know Trent, if he suspects anything he'll have the hands out with guns to stop anyone from pulling anything. You could get shot!" She shook her head.

"It's a risk I'm willing to take. It has to be this way. I'll not put you in harm's way, not anymore." He said regretfully. "It was bad enough that Milly tormented you every day. You are smart enough to know she won't let you live knowing Trent still loves you. Besides, I owe him. This is the only way I can make up for some of what I've done to him.

TRENT STEPPED INTO the shower willing his stomach to stop churning. So much was at stake, and he had to be on his A-game if he were to pull this off. Tonight he would have Abby back in his arms.

His men were out of sight all over the estate waiting. Their orders were to capture the accomplice alive if possible. Under no circumstances were they to harm anyone unless absolutely necessary.

Even though it was a sham wedding, the idea of Milly being his wife sickened him. Thank God her advances toward him had no effect. His heart and soul belonged to Abby.

He put his tux on to find it hung loosely on him. The last time he'd put it on, the fit was almost too tight. Now he had to add two notches on his belt to hold the pants up.

Noting the time, he went down to the study where 'Minister' Martin waited to carry out the plan. Although this charade cost him a bundle of money, he couldn't wait to see Milly's face when the plan succeeded.

Lance and Gina waited anxiously for him in the foyer. Gina's beauty was the prime example of what a young bride should strive for. Her soft silvery hair was swept up in a loose bun with small ringlets at her temples. The elegant gown that flowed over her like it was part of her gave off and air of sophistication. For an older woman she still had it and her husband made sure everyone knew she was his.

"Is everything in place?" Trent asked.

"Yup, they all have their orders." Lance said looking him over. "Are you ready?"

"Ready for this to be over." He swallowed and added, "If you two hadn't been here I..."

"Don't you make me cry Trenton Winthrop." Gina waved her hand in front of her eyes.

"I thought that's what women did at weddings." Trent teased.

Gina punched him as the front door flew open. Milly stepped inside wearing an old-fashioned wedding dress yellowed with age. It looked as though it had been worn on more than one occasion.

"Well? What do you think?" Milly twirled. "It was my great-great-grandmothers. I've always dreamed of wearing it on my wedding day."

Trent swallowed the bile that arose in his throat and crossed to take her in his arms. "It's perfect."

Gina barely stifled a laugh while Lance stepped into the study to hide the smile he couldn't suppress.

"Shall we get started?" Milly asked anxiously.

"Right this way darling." Trent managed.

"Oh, Trent. I want to get married in the rose garden." Milly whined.

"If that's what you want. Shall we?" He motioned for the small party to follow.

HARRY WAITED IN THE well house for Milly to take her place and look toward him. Abby was safely in her room peeking through the curtains. When she saw Milly, her heart sank. This woman was going to marry the man she loves, and at this moment she was helpless to stop it.

When Milly saw Harry a smug smile formed on her lips. Everything was going as planned. She had Trent exactly where she wanted him, and the icing on the cake, Abby would see it all.

The minister began the ceremony, then Harry made his move. He ran from the well house and tackled Trent who thought he was seeing a ghost.

"What're you doing?" Milly yelled.

"Putting a stop to this charade!" Harry growled, pulling a gun from his belt as he scrambled to his feet and aiming it at Milly.

"That's not the plan you idiot! What did you do with Abby?" Milly screamed at him.

"She's safe from you Milly, I don't care what happens to me, but you'll never harm my son or future daughter-in-law again." He yelled. "You're a sick twisted human being. I'm sorry I ever got involved with your family and for what I've done to my son, which is something I'll regret for the rest of my life. However, I can rectify some of that right now." Harry raised the gun a little higher when a shot rang out and Harry fell to the ground.

Trent heard a scream from the back door of the mansion as Abby flew to Harry crying.

"What the…" Trent gasped seeing her hold his father crying hysterically.

"I shoulda known you would get to him. But who cares. Trent is marrying me, so preacher get to it!" She ordered.

"Not so fast Milly, this man isn't a preacher. He's and international marshal, this was a set up to get Abby back. I knew it was the only way to make that happen. Your narcissistic attitude wouldn't allow you to miss seeing the agony on Abby's face and eventually mine." Trent enjoyed the expression on her face change when reality set in.

Milly grabbed the gun Harry had dropped and screamed, "If I can't have you no one will!"

She pulled the trigger and Trent fell as she turned it on Abby. A shot rang out one moment before pulling the trigger. Milly fell dead at the marshal's feet.

Total silence followed as the reality of what just happened sunk in to the shocked people around the rose garden.

Chapter Forty

Trent lay next to his father bleeding profusely from a stomach wound as Steven applied pressure on it while Lisa was attending to Harry.

Harry looked at him with tears in his eyes and said, "Son, I'm so sorry for the misery I've put you through in your life. Your lovely Abby showed me how foolish I was. I wish I had more time to make it up to you." He coughed as blood trickled from the corner of his mouth.

He looked at Abby and smiled. "Take care of him Abby, he needs a strong young woman like you to keep him out of trouble. Thank you for giving me the greatest gift anyone has ever given me.

Abby had his head in her lap while tears dripped from her chin. "I've been honored to know you dad. I'll never forget you, or what you've given me." She bent down and kissed his cheek. "I only wish you could be here for our wedding."

Harry coughed again as Trent reached out taking his hand, "I love you dad, and I forgive you. Thank you for bringing my Abby safely back to me."

Harry smiled with relief and peace filled his heart. Another cough and he took his last breath.

Trent watched the life fade from his father's eyes before darkness consumed him.

Steven kept the pressure on his wound as two hands carried him to the clinic area of the mansion.

Abby followed them as grief and fear gripped her heart. She'd lost her father-in-law to be and now she was in danger of losing her future husband.

Gina put a comforting arm around her as they stood watching Steven and Lisa work on Trent.

"Abby let's get you cleaned up. It's going to be a while before they're through." Gina suggested.

In a state of shock, she nodded her head and numbly allowed Gina to guide her upstairs to her room. She stepped into the hot steamy shower and mechanically washed the last of the cave away. Rinsing her hair she closed her eyes and relived every moment of the afternoon as she watched helplessly while people she loved were hurt and dying.

Why did the loved ones in her life always seem to leave her in tragic circumstances? Her mind ticked off every person one by one.

Unknowingly she sat on the shower floor with her head on her knees as soul crushing grief rocked her tiny body.

Gina found her, turned the shower off, helped her to her feet and wrapped a towel around her.

Abby seemed to be in a trance as Gina helped her into her clothes. She checked her over for injuries with the love of a mother. The poor girl was deathly pale from long months in total darkness. Black shadows framed her eyes, and her clothes hung on her because she'd lost so much weight.

Gina began trying to work a comb through her thick tresses while her own heart was broken after witnessing the tragedy that rocked everyone's world that day.

Noting the lost look in her eyes Gina said, "Abby it's going to be okay. Trent won't leave you now that he has you back and Milly is gone for good."

"It's too late. He's going to leave me like everyone else I've loved in my life. My parents, Grandmother, and now Harry. Trent is in danger of dying too. I feel like I'm supposed to be alone for the rest of my life." Abby mumbled through bitter tears.

"Don't give up on him now Abby. He almost went crazy trying to find you." Gina told her.

"I'll try. We need to go back down there in case he needs my blood." Abby said.

"Let me finish your hair first." Gina tried to get the comb through a big knot. "I think it would be easier if we cut your hair."

While Gina found some scissors, Abby closed her eyes to remember the first day on the island. She had been so excited to start her new life. When she met Trent the cozy smells of the study fled her mind when he kissed her hand. Strange and exciting new feelings rushed through her. Later she discovered she loved him, one that was so strong she could feel him when they were apart.

Gina did the best she could with what was left of Abby's hair. She added a little makeup to hide the circles under her eyes and the paleness of her skin.

"There, pretty as a picture." She smiled.

Abby glanced at the mirror, but she wanted to be downstairs. She managed a weak smile to make Gina feel better.

They went back to the room where Steven was finishing up with him. Looking up he gave her a thumbs up, but his eyes told a different story, he was worried, and Abby knew it.

"How about we get something to eat. I'm sure you're hungry." Gina coaxed her.

"No, I want to be here with him. If he doesn't make it…" The words died in her throat.

"Okay, would you like me to bring you something?" Gina offered as her worry increased.

"I couldn't eat right now. Go ahead and take Lance too. Steven and his helper are here." Abby told her walking into the room to stand by Trent.

Her mind went over every moment she experienced since they'd met.

Steven shook her from her thoughts saying, "He's gonna make it Miss Abby. It was close, but I think he's gonna pull through."

"Don't lie to me Steven. You're terrified he's going to die." Abby insisted.

Stunned she read him so easily, he said, "I've sent for Dr. Marcus on the mainland. He should be here in the next half hour. I've stopped the bleeding and we have enough blood until the doc gets here, and he's bringing more with him. Trent is strong and he's stable for now. Let's have a look at you. I have a feeling you need some attention too."

"I'm fine, I want to stay here and I'm not leaving!" Abby insisted defiantly.

Steven knew enough about her to leave her alone. "Okay, but I'm getting you something to eat, your weight is way too low. A blind man can see it without examining you."

Abby started to protest, but Steven insisted she eat something, or he would sedate her and put a tube in her arm.

When he left, she turned her attention to Trent. Grief turned to fear that she might lose him. She closed her eyes and prayed, *"Dear Lord, please let me have more than memories of him."* When she opened her eyes, she brushed a lock of hair from his pale face as tears filled her eyes.

When Steven came back, Dr. Marcus was with him. The doctor immediately began assigning Steven and Lisa different duties as he prepped for surgery.

Abby stepped into the hall out of the way, watching everything they did.

Lance and Gina forced Abby into the dining room to get her to eat something, since she refused what Steven brought her.

Barely touching what was given to her, she wanted to go back to the clinic and no one stopped her.

Three hours went by without a word while Abby stood at the door watching, waiting.

The doctor worked even quicker than Steven had. That gave her a little hope that he just might make it.

Finally, the doctor went to the sink to wash up. Abby followed every move the man made in agony waiting to know Trent's condition.

Steven and Lisa busied themselves cleaning up and moving some equipment around.

"I'm Dr. Jason Marcus. If I remember right, you're Miss O'Malley?" He asked introducing himself.

"Yes." Abby whispered afraid he would give her bad news while wondering how he knew her. "How is he?"

"He's got a good chance of pulling out of it. That bullet did some major damage when it hit him. You can thank Steven for stabilizing him so quickly, otherwise you'd be burying him." He said.

"Tell me the truth, I want to know." Abby feared he wasn't telling her everything. For some reason, she couldn't read his eyes like she could Steven's.

"Miss O'Malley, with proper care, which Steven and I are giving him, he'll survive. However, the bullet lodged against his spine. I got it out and didn't see any damage but that doesn't mean there isn't any." Dr. Marcus said.

Abby's eyes widened and filled with tears, "You mean he may be paralyzed?"

"I'm saying I don't know. It'll be a few days before we know anything. He's going to need someone by his side to give him support either way." He tried to ease her worry.

Gina stepped behind Abby at the end of the conversation. Her heart fell as she heard what Abby was told. She knew Trent was a stubborn man and if he was paralyzed he'd give up. Abby would be his only hope of recovery.

Gina reached her hand out and patted Abby's shoulder in comfort.

Everything started spinning as darkness engulfed Abby. Unable to bear another tragedy in her life, her body surrendered. Dr. Marcus caught her before she hit the floor. He carried her into the other bed in the room noting how underweight she was. Barking orders to Steven, before long Abby had several I.V. bags hanging off the pole attached to the bed.

Exhaustion, malnourishment, dehydration, and stress almost cost Abby her life and quite possibly still would.

Gina ran to find Lance who was helping the hands finish moving the bodies on the lawn even though the sun went down an hour ago. The marshal witnessed everything and finished getting everyone's statement, except from Abby and Trent.

Sam had shot Harry, and Billy took great satisfaction in shooting Milly.

Lance feared the worst when he saw Gina's pale face. When she reached him, she threw her arms around him sobbing. She told him what was going on with them.

Billy and Sam heard everything an assured Lance they could handle the rest of the cleanup.

They reached the room as Dr. Marcus stepped into the hall.

"How is she?" Gina asked anxiously.

"She's malnourished, severely dehydrated, and completely exhausted. All the stress this young lady is under almost killed her. What the devil is going on around here?" He demanded.

Lance took him to the study to tell him everything while Gina stood watch at the door of the room, silently praying for God to save them. Her mind went back to the day she lost her sweet little girl so many years ago. Little Gracie would be about Abby's age now.

Dr. Marcus listened intently to Lance's story, shaking his head when Lance finally finished. "Those two really have had a tough road. I'm surprised they've made it this far. It will be their love for each other that will ultimately bring them through this or kill them in the process. I can only treat their physical wounds, but those two have deep psychological scars that may need serious attention before they recover completely."

"You take care of the physical stuff, Abby and Trent will take care of the rest. I've had enough time with them to know if they don't give up on each other, they'll make it." Lance said a little cranky from the long day.

"I'm just saying they may need someone to talk to about these last few months, and from the scars on their backs maybe over their entire lives" Dr. Marcus reiterated.

"I'm sure they'll be just fine." Lance said convinced if they pulled through the problems they now faced, they'd be fine. The nightmare was over except for their recovery.

They returned to the medical room and Dr. Marcus went to check on them.

Gina and Lance waited in the hall holding each other. The state they were in, they feared Milly had gotten what she wanted after all.

Chapter Forty-one

Gina hurried through her chores the next morning so she could check on the progress of her children.

Lisa looked up from checking their vitals when Gina and Lance stepped into the room.

"How are they?" Gina asked while her eyes fixed on them.

"They're stable but critical. Dr. Marcus should be here soon to recheck everything. He checks on them close to every four hours." Lisa informed them. "He left orders for us to wake him if anything looks wrong."

Gina silently prayed fervently asking God to watch over them as they healed.

She sat in one of the chairs across the room where she could keep an eye on them, remembering Trent's first days on the island. He'd just graduated high school when O'Malley hired him as a field worker hauling hay.

Lance liked him from the start. Gina knew he had always wanted a son, and Trent needed a father figure. The two of them quickly became quite close. Lance tutored him in every area of the ranch and its operations.

Gina happily watched the bond between them flourish, even as she desired a little girl to love. Accepting Trent as a son was easy, but that longing burned heavily in her heart.

The moment Abby O'Malley crossed the threshold of the island, her dream of a daughter came true. After her grandmother died their connection grew even more.

Even though they weren't her blood, they were still her children, and she always believed no parent should lose a child.

Lance sat beside her and gave her a peck on the cheek.

With tears gathering in her eyes, she said, "Lance I can't lose another child. If we lose them, I..." Her voice broke.

Lance put his arms around her while she cried, fighting the lump in his own throat.

Oh, he put on a good front, but he wasn't as strong as everyone thought. Deep down he knew this may change everything.

Dr. Marcus stepped into the room and checked them, the equipment, I.V. bags, everything while the Elliot's looked on waiting for word of their condition.

"Mr. and Mrs. Elliot. Thank you for allowing me to stay here until my work is done. They are still critical, however, they are improving slightly. The wounds Trent suffered would have killed most men. I have to give him credit for his sheer stubbornness to live." He said. "Abby, she's well..."

"She's what?" Gina panicked.

"She's severely dehydrated and malnourished but improving. Her state of mind concerns me. If she believes he's going to die, she may feel like she has nothing to live for." Dr. Marcus stated.

"Would you do something for me?" Gina asked.

"That depends on what it is." He raised a curious brow.

"Put their beds together and put her hand in his." Gina said.

"What good would that do?" He asked surprised by the unusual request.

"Those two have a special bond. While she was gone they could sense each other's feelings. That's what kept them going all those months." Gina explained. "If they had skin to skin contact, it might be enough to bring them out of whatever dark place they are in."

"I guess it can't hurt, but if there's any sign of distress, I'll separate them." He replied skeptically.

Steven, who was even more skeptical, helped move the beds together. While Dr. Marcus monitored their vitals, Steven put Abby's hand in Trent's.

The look of surprise on Dr. Marcus face was comical when their vitals immediately improved.

"Well I'll be. You were right!" He exclaimed.

Lance followed Gina into the kitchen for some breakfast when Billy and Sam showed up asking how they were. Lance let them know they were hopeful they would recover soon.

Billy asked, "What do we do with Harry and Milly's bodies?"

"Make a coffin for Trent's father and we'll bury him next to Grandmother Abigail. He would have the Marshal take Milly to her parents when he got up.

After a cup of coffee and a small breakfast, no one was really hungry. Gina went back to keep watch over Abby and Trent while Lance went to the study to take care of some business while seeking solitude.

Marshall Martin made his way to the room where the two victims were resting to find out if he could get their statements.

"They gonna make it?" He asked Gina.

"Yes, they're still critical but they'll make it in time." Gina told him.

"Well, when they're better gimme a call. I'll make the trip back to get their statements. Is Lance around?" He asked.

"He's in the study, I'll take you to him." Gina stood.

"Nah, you stay here. I'll find him. Good day ma'am." He tipped his hat and strolled down the hall.

Lance gave the marshal instructions about Milly and let him know they'd bury Harry here. The marshal told Lance to give him a call when the victims were able to speak with him before he left.

Lance placed a call to Abby's guardian, though he wasn't her guardian any longer. He told Lance he and his wife would arrive in two days.

After taking care of the minor details of the ranch, Lance raided Trent's scotch. He sat in Trent's spot when he tied one on. Taking a large gulp of the bottle, he let his tears fall down his weathered face.

This was so much worse than when his little Gracie died. He gave her all the love he had before her short life ended.

Trent and Abby had become the children he'd been denied. They had wrapped their lives and love around his heart.

Billy stood in the doorway waiting to let him know everything was taken care of. When he saw the bottle in his hand, Billy backed away quietly closing the door behind him.

He went to find Gina instead, he knew Lance was taking all this hard. If it went south… he didn't want to think about it. He and Lance had a good relationship, but when Trent arrived, the two of them became more like father and son. When Abby arrived she was the missing piece of the puzzle.

The entire staff beginning with Trent had new life breathed in them, changing everyone's life forever.

The tiny redheaded stubborn woman had even wormed her way into Billy and Sam's heart. He silently prayed that whatever happened the two lovebirds would be together.

Gina turned to see Billy step into the doorway. She could tell he was as upset as the rest of them, but he'd hide it from everyone until he was alone. If she were honest, she had adopted every one of the hands, being particularly fond of Billy, Sam, and Charlie.

"Miss Gina, I came to see how Mr. Trent and Miss Abby are." He said quietly looking past her into the room.

"They're still improving a little more each time the Dr. checks on them." Gina put her hand on his shoulder.

"Good, that's good. Uh," Billy swallowed at the lump in his throat. "Everything's taken care of. Mr. Lance was well... Drowning his sorrows a bit. I didn't want to bother him."

"Thank you Billy, I'm sure Lance would be grateful you left him to his time alone. He's having a difficult time too." Gina put him at ease.

"Yes, ma'am." Billy responded seeing the pain in her eyes. "I'll gather the men and we'll say a prayer for them."

"There's a ray of hope Billy, they're on an uphill battle, but they aren't slipping." Gina told him.

Billy smiled and went back to the barn where the other hands were waiting and praying for some word on their condition.

By the end of the day, Gina was exhausted, and Lance was stupid drunk. Sam helped Gina get him upstairs to bed. She understood how deeply he felt about the kids, and he was using the universal pain killer to ease his agony.

※

STEVEN HAD JUST TURNED his shift over to Lisa when he spotted Gina slip in and sit down.

"Are you alright Mrs. Gina." He asked.

"The same as everyone, waiting and praying." She replied tired even though she slept last night.

"I gotta say, Mrs. Gina, that was a genius idea you had. I never would've thought something like that could produce the results it did." He shook his head in amazement.

"All I know is, Trent told me he could sense her feelings while she was missing. Every time he wanted to give up, I witnessed him sensing her feelings and we'd continue searching." She explained. "They have that once in a lifetime bond that won't be broken."

"All I know is it worked. They've been improving ever since I put her hand in his." He shook his head.

"That's what true love is Steven. When you meet that one person who can make you so angry you want to kill them one minute and the next you're unable to tear yourself away from them because the fire of love burning in you won't let you leave. No matter how you try not to fall for them you fall that much harder." She explained.

"Is that what happened to you and Mr. Lance?" He was captivated by her answer.

"Yes. When you find the love of your life you'll fight for it no matter how long it takes or what you have to go through to be with them. Someday when this is over, you'll find out the whole story behind Trent and Abby's love. Theirs is a love worth fighting for." She said as a tear escaped.

DR. MARCUS DECIDED to bring them around the next morning since their progress was better than anticipated.

Gina insisted he turn their heads so they would see each other when they came out of the effects of the anesthesia.

Although skeptical, he agreed since Gina knew them so well.

Abby's guardians arrived late the night before just as worried as everyone else.

Four hours passed without a blink or twitch from either of them.

Abby was the first to come around. Slowly opening her eyes, she saw Trent's boyish features resting peacefully. Still groggy, she stared at him too terrified to move fearing it was only a dream.

Trent moved a little as he opened his eyes to find the emerald, green eyes of his love staring at him intently.

She was beautiful, but he saw how pale and thin she was from what Milly had done to her and it broke his heart. He squeezed her hand and she responded with a smile as relief flooded her.

Everyone in the room hugged each other with relief, even Dr. Marcus discreetly wiped a tear from his eye.

Lance rushed out to tell Billy, who waited in the kitchen with Sam for the news, while Gina watched happily.

Dr. Marcus stepped to Trent's bedside and said, "Welcome back to the world of living you two. You had everyone on the entire island worried about you."

Trent swallowed hard and whispered, "How long?"

"You've been out four days. Miss Abby close to three days now." He said. "Trent I need you to try and move your feet for me."

He could see there wasn't any movement which concerned him a little. There was the possibility it was cord shock and not anything worse. The poor guy had been through enough.

"Trent, you have some major healing to do, so don't move around too much. We won't worry too much about your legs, it could be cord shock which will take some time to recover from." Dr. Marcus informed him. "We'll keep an eye on it, just concentrate on getting better."

Trent didn't care about anything at the time, he had his Abby back and wasn't letting go of her again.

Chapter Forty-two

Abby didn't wander far from Trent's bedside. Now that she had returned, she wouldn't leave his side again.

Walter observed, when he first met Trent, the spark of attraction between them, but with the man's attitude, he figured Abby didn't have a prayer. To say he was surprised when Trent told him they were engaged was an understatement.

Walter and Deidra Hartman, Abby's guardians stayed until they were sure she would recover from her ordeal before they left the island.

Everyone was worried about Abby being so thin and getting her to eat more than a bite or two was a monumental task. Trent threatened to stop eating if she didn't eat more.

Gina kept a close eye on her, including waiting in her room while she showered. She insisted on brushing her short hair and covering the remaining effects of her ordeal.

Trent was very appreciative when he saw her walk in. Abby dropped a soft kiss on his lips causing the heart monitor alarms to go off loudly.

Dr. Marcus rushed into the room to see what was happening. When he saw the faint smear of lipstick on Trent's lips with a smile he teased, "Miss O'Malley, you'll refrain from kissing my patient, he's in no shape to endure that kind of excitement."

Abby looked at the floor and turned a beautiful shade of red as Trent chuckled.

"You stop it too, you pull those stitches inside and it might be curtains for you." He grinned.

When Dr. Marcus left the room he grabbed Abby's hand and kissed it. "I love you my sweet Abby."

Unable to contain his curiosity, Trent asked Abby about her time with Harry and what happened while she was held captive.

Abby swallowed, remembering how gruff Harry had been when he abducted her.

"Let's wait for a little while. Harry's death is still too fresh to talk about." Abby managed.

She spoke with such sadness he said, "It's okay. I'll wait as long as you need me to. You gave me a precious gift. I waited for years to tell my father I loved him. His love for my mother was so great, he couldn't deal with the thought she'd never be by his side again. He may have abused me, but I still loved him because he was my father."

Abby felt sorry for him wishing things had turned out differently. She loved Harry in the end as her fiancé's father. In time, she felt Harry had come to love her as a daughter too. Milly caused the starvation and filth she had to live in while she was held captive.

Many times since Harry had kidnapped her, Abby thanked God that he had been there to protect her from Milly's lunacy and torment she put her through with each visit.

"Penny for your thoughts." Trent squeezed her hand.

"I was thinking about Harry. I may as well tell you." She took a deep breath and told him the entire story. How she was afraid of Harry until she figured out who he was. The many times he protected her from Milly's tirades and kept her company sometimes. How she almost escaped after he gave Milly that ring."

"So you were on the island the entire time?" He asked wondering where.

"A cave on the north end of the island. It connects to a tunnel that leads to the basement and the well house." She explained. I was kept in a dark hole with a heavy wooden door. I was alone in total darkness until the day Milly showed me that ring. That's when Harry changed his mind about us."

"What changed his mind?" Trent asked.

"Harry told me that baby was my grandfather's child and the reason you took responsibility for it to protect it. I was leaving you because I couldn't believe you were so unfeeling about your own child. Can you forgive me?" She said wiping away a stray tear.

"I'm still keeping promises and secrets for a dead man. Today it ends Abby. I want you to know how much I love you." He kissed her hand.

"You have to know Trent, you're dad cried when he talked about your mother, and how he treated you. He told you the truth, he wanted to make everything up to you. In his mind the only way was to stop Milly's plan before you said I do." Abby told him. "Harry asked if I was willing to fight for you. Without hesitation I told him I'd die for you. That's when he decided to keep me out of harm's way. He said you were very wise when you chose me. Even if it meant his death, he would see to it Milly wouldn't have you because you belonged to me."

Deep sadness crept into Trent's heart. More than anything he wished he had more time with his father.

Abby continued with a tiny gleam in her eye, "He even said if he were a little younger, he'd give you a run for your money."

The expression on his face made Abby burst out laughing.

"What's so funny?" He glared at her.

"As if! I'd never take your father over you Trent." She giggled. "I love you in a whole other way. I did love your father, because without him you would have never been born. Yes, he took me away, but that was Milly's idea not his. Once he got to know me he realized I was in love with you, and in his heart he knew you loved me. He was still in pain from losing your mother. When he told me he was bringing me back to you, I could see in his eyes it was do or die trying. He sacrificed his life for our happiness. How could I not love him?"

Trent quietly mulled over what Abby told him. It took this wonderful, infuriating, mysterious, irresistible, stubborn young woman to break through his dad's hard shell changing their lives forever.

Gina and Lance popped in to see how Trent was fairing. After an argument, Gina coaxed Abby into the kitchen to eat something.

"So, how are you really?" Lance asked.

"Obviously, I'm healing, but no luck with the legs yet. Dr. Marcus has given me a little hope. He thinks it's cord shock and it takes a little time to recover from it." He explained as worry lines formed around his eyes. "What if it doesn't wear off Lance? What if I'm paralyzed? Do you think Abby will want to stay with a cripple?"

Lance barely contained the flash of anger that hit him and said, "Trent that girl has been through hell and back. She hasn't left your side unless we forced her to. No woman in her right mind would've done that to be with you. I believe with all my heart she'd love you if you'd lost both arms and both legs. You've already lost your mind thinking she'd leave you."

Trent winced and said, "Ouch! I think I prefer you yelling at me."

Lance chuckled, "Yeah, well... I gotta be nice since you're laid up, but when you're back on your feet, the gloves are off."

Trent shared his laughter wincing in pain.

"Dr. Marcus is staying until he knows one way or the other about my legs. You know, I've been thinking of hiring him for stuff like this. Steven's a good RN but he was in way over his abilities when I got shot. I'm happy he had the foresight to have Dr. Marcus on his way as a precaution. I'd be dead and lying beside Harry out there if he hadn't..." Trent swallowed.

"I think that's a great idea." Lance agreed.

"Lance... Is Abby okay?" He asked growing somber.

"She's recovering, stubborn as ever, but she'll be okay if we all encourage her and love her." Lance assured him.

"If things go south with my legs..." He managed.

"Stop that! If Dr. Marcus is hopeful, then you should be too. Don't worry until he does." Lance growled. "Besides, if that should happen, we'll put ramps up for you to roll around in your wheelchair if need be. We'll cross that bridge if we come to it and that's a big if."

Trent put a good front on in front of everyone, but in his heart he was terrified he'd never walk again.

Abby returned shortly after Lance and Trent finished their little chat. Soon after Gina left to do some chores and cook dinner for everyone while Lance did the daily paperwork and checked on the hands.

Abby read Trent like a book and asked, "What's on your mind?"

"Nothing, just some business we need to discuss." He lied.

"Trenton Dale Winthrop! Don't you dare lie to me again!" She exploded.

Dr. Marcus rushed into the room when he heard the commotion. "What in heavens name is going on in here?" He demanded checking the monitors.

"Abby called me on the carpet for lying to her." Trent explained embarrassed.

"Well, Miss O'Malley, kindly keep it down to a dull roar, he needs rest and relaxation right now. And you're not doing yourself much good yelling at him like that. You're still recovering too. So please remain a little calmer or I'll sedate you." He insisted with a twinkle in his eye.

"I'm sorry. He just makes me so mad. I'll try to be good." She hung her head as her cheeks heated.

"I'll let it go this time." He said and turned back to Trent. "You quit lying to this young lady. Seems to me after what she's gone through to be with you, she deserves the truth about whatever you're trying to keep from her."

"Yes sir." Trent felt ashamed. He was right. Abby had been through hell to be with him, and she deserved the truth.

Dr. Marcus left them thoroughly chastised like two little kids.

"Abby... I'm... I'm scared." He finally got it out.

"About what?" She asked.

"What if I don't get my legs back? What will happen to us? Will you even want a cripple for a husband?" Trent asked clearly troubled.

"My darling Trent, we'll get married and deal with it and anything else that comes our way. Just because you might be paralyzed doesn't mean anything to me. Not when it comes to my love for you. It just means I'll love you that much more." She pulled his hand to her heart.

Relief flooded through him as a lump grew in his throat. He reached up and pulled her lips to meet his not caring if the monitors went crazy again.

Dr. Marcus knew if Abby wasn't having a meltdown Trent was okay. He smiled and continued the work he was doing.

Chapter Forty-three

Dr. Marcus saw improvement in Trent's reflexes, however he had no movement yet.

"You're going to need some intense physical therapy to get your legs moving again. I have a therapist in mind to help you. His name is Micky Jarvis, the best in the business." Dr. Marcus said.

"Are you sure it will help?" Trent asked skeptically.

"Either way, you have to keep your muscles from atrophy." He replied.

"Okay." Tren sighed. "I have a proposition for you. We are in need of a doctor to settle on the island. We have around a hundred employees as well as natives on the other side of the island who would benefit from your services. You would have your own house and we will build a clinic fully stocked with whatever you need." Trent explained after Abby agreed with him.

"That's a compelling offer, may I take time to speak with my family before I give you an answer?" He asked thoughtfully. He'd always dreamed of having a small practice enabling him to help the poor. This would be the perfect opportunity to live that dream.

Turning to Abby he said, "You my young patient, are looking better, but you're still too thin. If you ever want to be strong enough to get married and have children, you need to gain some more weight. Are you taking the vitamins I gave you?"

"Yes, and I'm trying to eat more but my stomach won't hold it." She said.

"Then we need you to eat smaller portions every three hours." He insisted.

The expression on Abby's face changed, hating the thought of eating more food, but he was right, and she knew it. "Okay, but I won't like it."

"No one asked if you liked it or not. Just do it, or I'll feed you myself." He crossed his arms over his chest. "Now if you excuse me I have phone calls to make. We'll discuss your offer in the near future."

Abby went to Trent's side. He was able to have liquids now. Gelatin wasn't his favorite, but he suffered through it. He longed to put his arms around his love again. Oh he could give her a hug with one arm but having both arms around her had always made him feel complete.

"Abby tell me more about the cave." He asked.

"The place I was had a heavy wooden door and no lights." She said. "I was in the dark for most of the time. At first they kept me in the dark for most of the day and night. The only light I received was when Harry brought my one meal a day."

"Where did Harry stay?" He urged her to continue.

"I don't know. He had to be close. When he first brought me water to clean up with it was hot. He gave me the impression those caves run all over the island." She told him.

"When I'm better we'll go exploring, I want to know what's down there." He said thoughtfully.

"By the way, where is Barbara?" Abby asked realizing she hadn't seen her.

Trent told her about the letters and how she helped Milly. Abby couldn't believe the woman had duped everyone.

Lance and Gina knocked before stepping into the room. Gina insisted Abby help her with dinner so Lance could talk with Trent.

"What's wrong?" Trent asked recognizing that look.

"Barbara sent word she's ready to come back, what do you want to do?" He asked.

"How much does she know?" Trent asked as anger flared in him.

"I believe she knows Milly is dead, but I can't say how much more she may know." He shrugged before turning serious. "What concerns me is Milly's family, they may retaliate now that things have settled a bit." Lance said. "I don't know how they could without us seeing them coming though."

"Abby told me there's a cave system under the island. There are passages running to the basement and the well house, maybe other places as well. That's how Harry was able to move around so easily. From what Abby said, there secret passages all through the mansion." Trent apprised him. "I think Barbara found the one in the basement and told Milly."

"And if Milly knew, so does her family." Lance finished his thoughts.

"I want you to take Billy and Sam down there and find out where they lead and if anyone's hiding there." Trent spoke decisively. "Be careful, you won't know what you may be walking into. If you find someone, keep out of sight, and get back here. Don't confront them."

"Okay, but wouldn't it be better to take more men?" Lance asked.

"No, the more people down there the easier it would be for you to be found out. I'm also letting Barbara go. We don't need someone like her working here any longer." Trent said.

"Sure thing, I'll be back when we're done." Lance turned and left.

ABBY FORCED DOWN ALL she could hold of the spaghetti she and Gina made for lunch. Dr. Marcus purposely joined them to make sure Abby cleaned her plate.

"Miss O'Malley, you need to eat more of your spaghetti. You need the carbs." He insisted.

"I'm so full I'll be sick if I take another bite." She looked at him with pleading eyes.

"Okay, but in three hours you will drink a supplement shake I had delivered for you." He relented.

Abby agreed so he wouldn't make her eat anymore. She felt tired so she visited Trent and then went upstairs to rest.

While she slept, eyes peered from the closet watching, planning. Soon the young heiress will have nothing left to her name.

LANCE, BILLY, AND SAM met in the basement early the next morning with side arms and lanterns. Billy located the entrance and Lance led the way inside. Lance warned them earlier they had to be extra quiet since they had no idea what they were walking into.

The passages were man made, each of them hewn out of solid rock leading three different directions. The cave that connected them had magnificent columns stretched from the floor to the ceiling.

Lance chose the passage on the left or what he sensed was north. They soon found where Abby had been kept. Billy opened the door, they found the cot, table, and the few other items she'd been allowed.

"This has to be where they held Abby, poor kid." Billy growled. "I'm glad I got to shoot that witch."

Lance shushed him motioning them to follow the passage until they heard voices. As soon as he heard he ocean waves he knew where he was. As they neared the mouth of the cave, the sound of voices stopped them.

"You was smart to show Milly all them passages. Trent and that O'Malley girl are gonna pay for what they done to Milly." A deep voice said.

"Are you sure you have enough guns to take care of them?" Barbara's voice rang out.

"Yup, we got a good bit of guns and ammo under the well house and were putting some under the gazebo and barn. They won't know what hit them." The man laughed.

"You make sure Trent knows he's paying for the death of my poor daughter and grandchild. If he woulda done what I wanted, none of this woulda happened." Barbara ordered bitterly.

"Let's get the rest of this stowed away." The man said grunting as though he picked something heavy up.

Lance led the way back to the basement thankfully without being discovered.

"I'll go tell Trent what's going on. You two board this up good so they can't sneak in here again." Lance said leaving them to it.

Lance was thankful Gina had Abby in the kitchen preparing dinner when he went to see Trent. He quickly informed him of what they'd found and heard.

"So Barbara's been showing the Boudreau family how to get around the island unseen." Trent growled." You and the men need to get that stash of ammo and guns before they get organized."

"Should we get marshal Martin involved?" Lance asked.

"It wouldn't hurt for him to know. That way we won't have to explain stuff later." Trent agreed.

"Until what's over?" Abby asked from the doorway.

Lance turned surprised that Abby and Gina had snuck up on them.

"Lance, go tell Gina and get the hands busy rounding that stuff up." Trent said.

When everyone left the room, Abby's heart told her something bad was happening again.

"Trent?" Abby questioned with worry furrowing her brows.

"I sent Lance into the caves you told me about. They heard Barbara and someone from Milly's family talking about weapons and making us pay. They don't know we've discovered their plans which gives us the element of surprise." Trent explained.

Abby's worried expression turned to shock. Not only from the fact that Trent didn't lie to her, but that more danger loomed in her eyes.

"I thought this was over since Milly died. Why are they still coming after us?" Her heart sank as she wondered if this was what the future held for them. Since they met, life had become turmoil, terror, and trouble.

"Your grandfather was the baby's father. I made sure my name was on the birth certificate as a favor to your grandfather. Barbara was furious and I suspect she told Milly who automatically assumed I was the real father." Trent explained. "You already know don't you."

"Yes, Harry took the child and Milly said she sold it." Abby admitted.

"I had a feeling Harry told you what happened to the baby in more detail." Trent said. "Don't worry sweetheart, we've got this. No one on this island will ever let anything happen to us again."

"I suppose we ought to warn Dr. Marcus and Steven about what's headed our way, they're gonna need supplies." Abby said accepting the inevitable.

"Let me know what?" Dr. Marcus asked coming into the room with a mug of coffee.

"You're gonna need more supplies Doc. It looks like all hell is gonna break loose around here again. Get anything your short on, or think you'll need." Trent said. "Charge it to the O'Malley's account."

"What do you mean by all Hell?" He asked.

Trent explained what Lance discovered.

"You two attract trouble like static electricity. No wonder you need a hospital on this island, from what Steven's told me and from what I've witnessed. The troubling part is that it all started when Miss O'Malley showed up almost two years ago." He teased.

Abby glared at him as her temper quickly surfaced.

"Just kidding Miss O'Malley. From the bits and pieces I've picked up, this started long before you were born." He calmed her. "I'll get Steven and Lisa so we can order everything to be delivered tomorrow. Or will that be too soon."

"I'm sure it will be fine. Our tormentor's have no idea we've discovered their plans." Trent said and added, "You may want to find another doctor to come help if you know of one. We'll take care of paying them."

Chapter Forty-four

Trent hid his anger over being so helpless. He needed to be on his feet to help protect Abby.

Abby clutched his hand, and he could feel the fear rolling from her in waves. He managed to pull her into his arms and held her tightly.

"Abby, I'm scared too, even more so since I can't help defend us." Trent admitted.

She looked up at him love radiating from her eyes as she whispered softly. "It's okay Trent, it's my turn to protect you now."

She kissed him as he pulled her closer. Lost in his Abby, his legs began to tingle.

Trent pulled away and said, "Abby! The feeling is coming back into my legs!"

Dr. Marcus rushed in to see what all the ruckus was about. He listened carefully as Trent told him what he felt.

Dr. Marcus checked his reflexes once again and performed some other simple tests. He concluded the shock was beginning to wear off. In essence the nerves were beginning to wake up.

"Micky is clearing his schedule so he can give you the intense therapy you need." He said then turned to Abby, "Miss O'Malley, whatever you're doing to make him continue to improve like this, by all means keep it up." He teased noting the smudged lipstick on Trent's lips.

She lit up like a Christmas tree causing the men to chuckle.

After Dr. Marcus left, Trent pulled Abby close and whispered, "Miss Abigail Jane O'Malley, I would consider it an honor if you'd marry me."

"You've already asked me." She said confused.

"This time we aren't keeping it a secret from anyone. Besides, you left this here when you were abducted." He said holding the ring he'd given her on Valentine's Day.

Tears gathered in her eyes as she accepted the ring and replied, "Trenton Dale Winthrop, yes, I'll marry you."

Trent kissed her and whispered, "Abby you'll never regret marrying me once I'm back on my feet."

She whispered back, "I already have regrets, but that hasn't, nor will it ever kill my love for you."

Gina heard their conversation as tears gathered in her eyes. A silent prayer went up that God would protect them from anymore heartbreaks.

Lance and some of the more trusted hands found the stashes of weapons and removed them to the hayloft in the barn before the Boudreau's returned.

"Man, they got enough stuff to conquer England." Billy sighed with exhaustion.

"Well, we have it all now. They're gonna have a big fight on their hands if they do anything." Lance said wearily. We gotta guard this stuff. Everybody is on twelve-hour shifts until this is over. Divide the men in half, five men in the barn, six in the mansion and the rest patrolling the grounds. Gina and I are moving to the mansion until we put this to rest."

"Will it ever be finished, Mr. Lance?" Sam asked weary of fighting. "Seems like we get something figured out and something else comes up."

"Hopefully soon. The curse was a fable that Milly found out about. She forced Harry to kidnap that child nine years ago now. According to him Milly sold it to someone on the mainland, though we'll never know for sure." Lance explained. "Once this is over, it should be the end of it for good."

DR. MARCUS CHECKED in the orders of supplies that came in. Since Trent expected more casualties than the small room in the back could handle, some of the hands helped move furniture out of the rooms on the third floor and put extra cots in them. Two rooms were made into sterile rooms for operations. A good friend of Dr. Marcus, Dr. Adrian Goldstein, arrived with extra blood, pain medication, and every other medicine they may need.

They moved Trent back to his room and the Elliots moved into the room next to him. The other hands were spread throughout the mansion covering entrances and exits.

Abby wound up staying in Trent's room for the time being. She had better protection there and could help take care of him.

Trent was still bedfast, but he was beginning to move his feet slightly.

Abby slept curled up next to him feeling safe for the first time in a long while.

Trent felt whole again having her next to him. Her breathing was so soft, he would wake up fearing she was gone. When she moved, he relaxed and went back to sleep.

They prepared for any and every scenario they could think of. The ammo was divided between the hands, and extras were brought to the mansion readily available to everyone there. Although the danger they faced was real, tension eased when the hands began patrolling.

However, they had no idea someone unexpected lurked in the shadows orchestrating everything.

ABBY AWOKE THIRSTY around one a.m. and slipped quietly out of bed trying not to wake Trent. Sam stopped walking the hall when she stepped out of the room.

"Miss O'Malley? What is it?" He hurried to assist her.

"I'm just going downstairs for some water." She turned toward the stairs.

"Would you like me to go with you?" Sam asked quietly.

"No thanks, I'll only be a minute." She smiled.

In no time she closed the door safely back in Trent's room. Trent was awake and smiled as she crossed the room when the hair on her neck stood on end. Trent gazed past her with fear and panic filling his eyes.

Abby turned to find Barbara standing near the fireplace with a butcher knife in her hand.

"So, you're still sleeping with him are you?" She hissed with anger boiling in her eyes.

"Why are you so angry with us?" Abby asked loudly hoping Sam would hear and come running.

"Ask Trent, he's the one who cheated my daughter out of her baby and it's inheritance. He made my daughter commit suicide. He's the one who arranged to have my grandchild taken. Then you show up and get everything!" Barbara snarled.

"What makes you think Trent did all those things." Abby asked.

"Milly told me he arranged everything." Barbara's voice rose.

"I'm sorry Barbara, but Milly lied to you. Harry did take your grandchild and Milly sold it to someone." Abby told her hoping Sam was close enough to hear their raised voices.

"Why should I believe you? You killed Milly!" She said a little louder.

"No, Milly got herself killed. She shot Trent leaving him paralyzed and one of the hands shot her to save my life." Abby insisted.

"Serves you right Trent. I'm gonna leave you alive and kill Abby in front of you. She has to die, and you can't do anything to stop me! You'll always regret not being able to save her and know that you're the one who caused all of this!" Barbara said with a wicked grin and wild eyes.

"Barbara, I only did what Abby's grandfather asked of me. The rest was all Milly. Harry told Abby everything." Trent tried to remain calm even though his insides quaked in fear. "You wouldn't want your daughter's death to be for nothing. Doing this isn't honoring her memory and revenge won't bring her back."

"What would you know about honor? You're nothing but a selfish pig! My daughter was beautiful and much better than Milly and certainly better than this floosy!" Barbara's voice carried louder.

"I know Harry sacrificed his life for Abby and me. He stopped the wedding that Milly forced me into. She picked up his gun and shot me then went for Abby. Two people are dead because of the memory of a curse and lost children weren't laid to rest. Stop it here Barbara, don't let it go any further." Trent pleaded.

"Shut up!" Barbara shrieked lunging at Trent in a mindless rage.

Abby stepped between them, and the knife Barbara held went into Abby as Sam and another hand rushed into the room. Abby collapsed to the floor while the men tackled Barbara. Sam hurried to Abby's side and turned her. The knife was still inside her.

Lance and Gina appeared in the doorway awakened by the commotion. Gina screamed as Lance ran to get Dr. Marcus.

Trent forced his legs to the edge of the bed and slid down next to Abby on the floor. Pulling her gently across his lap, he said through tears of anguish, "My sweet Abby, don't leave me, I want to hear you seeing to me again. I love you, please don't leave me, I want to be with you forever."

Dr. Marcus sent Lisa to help get Abby upstairs with instructions to leave the knife in her.

Before they moved her, she looked up at him and whispered through the intense pain she was in, "I saved you my love."

With a shallow breath she passed out. Steven arrived in time to help Sam carry her upstairs to save her life.

Trent leaned against the bed as her words sounded in his ears. The familiar cold long fingers of fear and anguish wrapped around his heart squeezing it again.

Sam and Lance came back to take him upstairs. Gina was already pacing as they placed him on the sofa they'd moved in the hall earlier.

"Gina? What's going on in there?" He asked in a state of panic.

Dr. Marcus is taking good care of her. You know he's a fantastic doctor or you wouldn't be here now." Gina placed a calming hand on his shoulder even though her insides quaked with fear.

"Gina, she told me she saved me before she..." He choked.

Gina sat next to him holding his hand. "Trent, she'll beat this, look what she's already been through with you. She's tougher than we realized."

"How much more can her body take? She's still recovering from months of abuse at Milly's hands." He said swallowing hard. "I won't survive if..."

"Don't lose faith in her now." Gina squeezed his hand.

When Gina went downstairs with Lance to make lunch, Trent sank back on the sofa and prayed, *"God, I don't know why all this misery has come to my sweet Abby, but please save her. I love her and want to make her life better and happier. I know you're up there and I know you can hear me, please save her."*

Two hours passed without a word from that sterile room.

Gina paced enough for her, and Trent combined. Another hour came and went, driving Trent to the brink of insanity.

Dr. Marcus stepped from the room to update them on her condition.

"Doc?" Trent spoke with trepidation.

"She's weak, but I'm confident she'll survive. How did it happen?" He asked.

Trent told him the story reliving the incident in his mind. Her words before she slipped into unconsciousness rang out in his heart.

"Is she really going to be okay?" Trent asked with hope in his eyes.

"Miss O'Malley is going to be just fine. Now let's get you back to bed." He insisted.

"No! I want to be with her. Let me stay, please." Trent demanded.

"Okay, we'll get the wheelchair I ordered for you after they unpack it, and let you sit with her." His eyes twinkled. "By the way, how did you wind up in the floor with her?"

Trent hadn't given any thought to moving off the bed and onto the floor. "Everyone was so busy helping Abby, I must've made myself do it."

"That's what I thought. You're coming along nicely. Micky should arrive in a day or two. Then you'll wish you hadn't moved at all." He chuckled.

Two of the bigger men held him up by her bedside so he could hold his songbird's delicate hand.

Dr. Marcus motioned Dr. Goldstein over to observe the connection between his two patients.

The moment he clasped her hand, the monitors showed a stronger heartbeat and her oxygen levels increased closer to normal.

"Have you ever seen anything like that before?" Dr. Marcus asked.

"Never. What happened?" Dr. Goldstein asked.

Dr. Marcus asked Trent to let go of her hand as Steven pushed the new wheelchair into the room.

"That's amazing!" Dr. Goldstein exclaimed.

"I've never seen anything like it either. If I hadn't witnessed it with my own eyes, I wouldn't have believed it." Dr. Marcus said.

LANCE AND SAM WERE down the hall out of earshot when Lance asked, "How did she get past you? Six men and at least twenty outside and no one saw her?"

"Beats me, maybe there's another entrance to the mansion from the cave. If so, we gotta find it quick since we don't know if she brought company." Sam straightened in alarm.

"Get some of the men in search this place from top to bottom. I'll go get Billy and a few of the other men, I have a bad feeling about this." Lance said hurrying downstairs.

Sam and Billy started in Trent's room tapping walls and searching for hidden buttons. Sam ran his hand under the mantle of the fireplace and hit a switch. The wall beside the fireplace slid silently behind it.

"Found it!" He yelled.

They followed the passage as it wound down to the basement. The opening to the passage they'd blocked hadn't been disturbed. Billy sent Sam for help as he began looking for another opening.

During his search, a sound behind him drew his attention. Abby's guardian had a gun trained on him as he turned.

Chapter Forty-five

"Mr. Hartman." Billy stated as understanding dawned in his eyes."
"That's right, I'm the one who orchestrated this entire thing." He said smugly.

"Why would you put Miss Abby through all this?" Billy's hand moved toward his side arm.

"I wouldn't touch that pistol if I were you." He glared at him. "Mr. O'Malley paid me to keep watch over her when her parents died. When things in her last foster home became too dangerous for her, I asked why he wouldn't just bring her here. That's when he explained about that silly curse. That gave me an idea. So I arranged to become her legal guardian. When her grandfather died, I would insist she allow me to run things, and I could take everything she owned. I didn't count on her falling in love with Trent."

"He loves her too." Billy informed him.

"I figured he would after meeting the first time. I did some digging and ran across Milly and Harry. Because of her greed and lust for power, she was elated to help me." He snorted. "All I had to do was sit back and watch the fireworks. The icing on the cake was she wanted Trent. With him out of the picture, Abby would insist I handle everything when I arrived to comfort her."

"How'd that work out for ya?" Billy smirked.

"None to well as you already know. I underestimated her powers of persuasion. She appealed to Harry's love for his dead wife and turned his heart back to Trent. That little vixen could charm a snapping turtle out of its shell." Mr. Hartman scowled. "One would think with all she has gone through in her life, she would have gone crazy, but she just keeps coming back for more. Fortunately for me, it all ends today. The Boudreau brothers should be here any minute now. I'll be the new owner of the O'Malley Island, of course I'll change the name to Hartman's Island."

"I really hate to tell you this, but there's one thing you didn't count on." Billy said with a cocky grin.

"What would that be?" He asked cynically.

"Them." Billy nodded toward Sam and the others.

When Mr. Hartman looked away, Billy tackled him.

In that moment, another entrance opened, and the Boudreau brothers and several men poured into the basement.

After the brief battle, most of the intruders were either injured, running back into the tunnel or dead.

Some of the O'Malley employees were seriously injured with one fatality. Mr. Hartman shot Billy when he lunged for him. Sam saw it and shot Mr. Hartman between the eyes.

Sam heard gunfire coming from the tunnel and signaled the remaining men to follow him. He stopped when Charlie popped out of the entrance and several men flooded the basement.

"Why are you coming through there?" Sam asked confused.

We heard the gunfire, so I figured we'd come this way and sneak up on em." Charlie grinned. "Worked too. When y'all went gun happy, we got the ones that ran."

Sam had to give it to Charlie, he may be a little slow at times, but the boy was sharp."

Lance stumbled downstairs as Sam started ordering the hands to help the wounded upstairs.

Lance, ya better let Doc know he's gotta lotta work to do." Sam told him.

Lance ran back to deliver the message and to let Trent know what happened.

"Lisa busied herself assessing the injuries and putting the more seriously wounded first. Dr. Marcus, Steven, Dr. Goldstien, and his nurse worked feverishly to patch everyone up.

Sam stopped in the hall dreading the conversation about Billy, but he had to tell them. Now that he was gone, Sam was the head wrangler.

With a deep breath, he walked to the door of Abby's room while his heart sank into his boots. Billy had been his best friend since their rodeo days together.

Trent knew something was wrong when Sam stepped into the room.

"Don't keep us in suspense boy, tell us what happened!" Lance grumbled.

"Billy didn't make it." He managed. "Mr. Hartman shot him when Billy tackled him. When they hit the floor, I shot Hartman when he tried to get up, then another passage opened, and bullets went ta flyin. Most of the intruders got hurt or kilt. The rest was caught and tied up."

Trent's jaw dropped, "Did you say Mr. Hartman? Abby's guardian?"

"Yup, I heard it all." Sam said and told them what he'd heard while they were sneaking down the stairs.

Trent didn't quite know what to say. This came from left field taking even him by surprise.

"So the man Abby kept seeing in the shadows must've been someone he hired. O'Malley was trying to frighten her away even when she was eight years old." Trent reasoned it out.

"You don't know that for sure Trent. Besides it's finally over once and for all. You and Abby can get married and live a happy life." Gina smiled.

"Lance I want every entrance from that cave found and sealed, along with the hidden doors through the mansion. No more surprises." Trent insisted.

※

OVER THE NEXT FEW WEEKS, Billy was laid to rest alongside Harry.

Abby continued to recover from the incident with Barbara, although she still had some pain, and her weight was concerning the doctor.

Trent began his physical therapy remembering what Dr. Marcus told him, which proved to be true. Micky worked Trent hard to get his muscles to loosen and relax a little.

Marshal Martin transported Barbara and the surviving intruders to the mainland after he called for reinforcements to handle the twenty or so prisoners. Barbara had gone insane from the agony of failing to get revenge on Trent. The judge sentenced her to a mental institution.

Dr. Marcus accepted the position Trent offered him. His family moved into Barbara's small cottage while a new home was built on the plot of land Abby agreed to let them have. Building plans were made for the new clinic and hospital for their approval.

Steven and Lisa eloped, then returned as Dr. Marcus staff.

Lance helped Trent keep things running smoothly while he put in the work with the therapist.

Sam and Charlie stepped up to fill Billy's boots which was a monumental task. Sam took Billy's death as hard as Gina. They had known each other for years on the rodeo circuit in the states, and he missed his friend.

Abby and Gina planned an engagement party and hired a new cook along with two housekeepers. They made a trip to the mainland for an extended shopping trip leaving the men at home.

After a few days they returned with armloads of new clothing, window treatments and would receive several pieces of new furniture for the formal living room.

Abby had some of the older pieces removed and given away.

The day of the party was almost on them keeping Abby so busy, she barely noticed Trent's absence. Micky and Lance had kept his secret from everyone as a surprise for Abby.

Deliveries had been coming for several days thanks to the cook and her friends who owned a catering business.

Excitement grew as the day grew nearer. Abby wanted to show off the gown she'd bought. Never in her wildest dreams had she thought to own such an expensive, beautiful gown.

The deep emerald, green gown was a shade darker than her eyes. The bodice came together with a teardrop shaped crystal stone, framing it just below her bustline. The chiffon skirt floated around her like a cloud. Gina raved about how perfect it was for her. She had told her about the necklace Trent had given her, and how perfect it would be to wear with the dress.

Dr. Marcus happily declared her fully recovered and at a healthy weight. She was happy he wouldn't make her eat more food than she wanted anymore.

Abby talked non-stop to Trent about the party. He was thrilled to see her so happy. For the first time since she'd come to the island, she glowed. Trent vowed he'd do everything in his power to keep that glow on her.

The day of the party, Trent remained in his room waiting for Lance to arrive with the tux Trent ordered. The surprise he had in store for Abby made him giddy inside. In just a few hours he would spring it on her.

When he was dressed, to keep his secret Micky and Sam helped him downstairs to the wheelchair waiting for him at the bottom.

Gina fixed Abby's hair so that it fell in soft curls about her shoulders. Putting the final touches of makeup on and spritzing the new exotic perfume she bought, Abby turned to look a Gina.

"Abby, you look gorgeous. Trent better watch out, all the men in the room will be after you." Gina teased.

Abby laughed, "Maybe it'll be enough incentive for him to get outta that chair."

"You know you're an amazing young woman Abby O'Malley." She hugged her. "Are you ready to make your entrance?"

Butterflies stirred in Abby's stomach as she and Gina walked down the hall arm in arm until they reached the landing. Gina stepped back so Trent could see Abby make her entrance alone.

Lance tapped Trent on the shoulder and nodded toward the stairs. Trent turned his chair to find a perfect Irish Rose standing at the top of the stairs.

The room fell silent as she descended them slowly keeping her eyes locked on Trent. She crossed the foyer, took his hand, and asked, "Are you ready?"

For a moment he was so captivated by her he couldn't say anything, and her perfume assaulted his senses with a vengeance.

"Trent? Are you ready?" She repeated happily satisfied with his reaction.

"Uh hem, I am." He smiled and pulled her into his lap. Carefully rolling the chair into the formal living room. They stopped in front of the fire place to make their announcement. Abby held his hand when he squeezed it an let her go. It was time for his surprise.

Abby before we make our announcement, I have a surprise for you." Trent said sheepishly.

Confusion settled on Abby's face as her heart raced.

He locked the wheels in place while Sam and Micky made a big show of helping him stand to his feet. Sam took the wheelchair away for the last time. Micky let go as Trent walked to her. Pulling her into his arms he kissed her passionately in front of everyone. Soft music began playing as he pulled her close for their first dance ever.

Abby looked up with tears in her eyes and asked, "How long have you been keeping this from me?"

"Close to a week now. I still have some work to do, but the chair is gone. Shall we make our announcement unless you'd prefer to wait a little longer." He teased.

"I can't wait another minute, let's do this!" Abby insisted.

Cheers went up when they officially announced their engagement.

Gina wiped tears from her eyes admiring how beautiful they were together before she caught Lance a little misty eyed too.

The party guests began to leave in the wee hours of the morning, thankfully they had plenty of rooms for those who wanted to stay while others opted for helicopter rides back to the mainland.

Trent and Abby were still dancing when the last guests left. Totally oblivious to the empty room around them as they swayed to the soft music. Lost in the freedom of showing their love publicly.

Abby's eyes sparkled with tiny diamonds of love in an emerald sea. After a soft passionate kiss, he stepped back and said, "I think it's time for you to go to bed."

Before she could answer, he swooped her into his arms to take her upstairs.

"Trent! You shouldn't carry me! Your legs..." She protested.

"It's okay. Micky said I still have a little weakness, but he said I have no restrictions. Besides, I won't miss another chance to pick you up and hold you again." He smiled at her.

Opening her door, he carried her to the small loveseat and sat with her on his lap.

"Sing to me sweetheart, I've missed it so much." He begged her.

Abby lay her head on his shoulder and began singing softly.

Trent closed his eyes and allowed her soft voice to permeate his soul. While she sang to him he floated away from everything.

Chapter Forty-six

Tiny rays of sunlight filtered through the lace curtains awakening Trent. They'd fallen asleep holding each other again.

He looked down at her peaceful face, happy she had recovered from her ordeals. It dawned on him he had a lot to be thankful for. Over the last two years they could have lost their lives, but God helped them through it all. Now the danger had passed, and they would be married on October first.

A smile graced his face when he remembered the day Abby turned his life upside down two years ago. In a matter of days she captured the hearts of almost everyone on the island.

Abby's eyes fluttered opened to find him staring at her innocent face with a smile.

He kissed her deeply and said, "Abby, we have guests and I need to change."

"October first can't get here fast enough for me. October second you won't get away from me so easily." She teased.

Thankful their guests were still sleeping, they changed and met downstairs in the dining room. The caterers had just finished setting up the elegant breakfast when they arrived.

They helped themselves to the delicious pastries and coffee before sitting down. Their conversation revolved around their wedding plans.

Slowly their guests trickled in as the aroma of the fresh coffee and delicate pastries permeated the entire mansion luring them downstairs before they prepared to leave. There were many comments about the hospitality they'd received and the wonderful time they had. Each guest was handed a wedding invitation as they left.

Finally the last guests were on their way to the docks. Abby let out a sigh of relief.

What's wrong Princess?" Trent asked gathering her close.

"I'm not used to this kind of life. I grew up poor and alone. To have this many people to entertain was an eye-opening experience." She leaned against his chest.

"You'd better get used to it, I'm gonna show you off every chance I get." He kissed her forehead.

IN THE ALMOST THREE months before the wedding, Abby was so busy she didn't have time to wish they were already married.

Gina proved to be more than a friend, she'd become a mother to her happily helping Abby pick everything out for her wedding.

Trent oversaw the final phase of the remodel Abby asked for. She elected to restore her grandparents room along with the furniture. The room was ready to move into one week before the wedding.

"Gina, you have to see our bedroom! I never dreamed it would be so beautiful!" Abby exclaimed pulling Gina down the hall.

Gina gasped as she walked into the room. It was like something out of a luxury magazine. Hugging Abby, she thought if anyone deserved this kind of luxury Abby did.

They made the trip to the mainland to pick up the tuxes and dresses from the tailor, who designed a one-of-a-kind dress for Abby. When she stepped out with it on, Gina's eyes misted. No other dress would hold a candle to this one.

It was a mermaid dress in white silk with a right shoulder beaded brocade sweeping across her back to her left hip with a bow connecting it to the skirt that flowed into a sweeping train. Her left shoulder and most of her back was bare. Embarrassed by the scars on her back, Abby worried about others seeing them.

Gina took her to a makeup specialist who would be there on the day of the wedding.

When the day arrived, everything was perfectly set waiting for the bride and groom.

Lance was touched that she had asked him to give her away. Gina was her matron of honor, with Sam being Trent's best man.

The wedding was held in a huge tent with a spectacular view of the ocean. The inside of the tent was like an autumn wonderland. Fall flowers were on every surface and ribbons floated on the soft breeze gently blowing through the tent.

Abby insisted framed pictures of the seven people who were a big part of their lives be placed on the unity table.

Jacob and Trisha O'Malley, (Abby's parents) Harold and Margie Winthrop, (Trent's parents) Jacob and Abigail O'Malley, and Billy Watson, surrounding the unity sand.

Trent and Abby were nervous something else would go wrong before the wedding started. Neither gave into the fear. This was their day, and nothing would stop it now.

Abby looked at Gina with trepidation and said, "Gina tell me this is really going to happen."

Gina smiled holding up her dress, "Let's get this fabulous dress on you, the love of your life is waiting."

Abby smiled back still nervous, but Gina's calming presence seemed to ease the knot in her stomach.

Gina left her alone for a moment to check herself one last time in the mirror. Taking a deep breath, she followed a minute later.

Lance waited patiently in the foyer to escort her to Trent's side. When he looked up his chest popped out with pride as Gina descended looking as lovely as a bride in a stunning burgundy dress. She waited with him for Abby to make her way down to them.

Unable to take his eyes off his wife, Lance looked up when Gina nodded toward the stairs. Abby came down gracefully as Lance's eyes beamed with pride.

Gina made her way down the aisle catching comments about how beautiful she was, giving her the satisfaction of knowing she chose the right dress.

The music changed and everyone stood turning to look at the bride entering on her proud papa's arm.

Trent was so mesmerized he forgot to breathe as she floated down the aisle toward him.

Lance placed her hand in his and said quietly, "Treat her right, or you'll have me to deal with."

They turned toward the minister, and the ceremony began with a short sermon about why two people come together as one. There was a short pause as their favorite song played softly in the background.

The minister said a few more words and gave Abby the microphone. The music to the new song she'd learned began to play. Her sweet voice flowed from the speakers as she sang the most beautiful song Trent had ever heard.

The crowd wiped tears by the time she finished and handed the microphone back to the minister, who handed it to Trent. He smiled when Abby's expression changed into confusion.

"I've been working on this for three months now. I think Lance and the wranglers will be glad this is the last time they'll hear it."

A chuckle ran through the crowd when Sam nodded his head vigorously.

The music began and his baritone voice rang out in a love song.

Tears spilled from Abby's eyes when he took her hand and held it next to his heart.

When he finished he kissed her softly and handed the microphone back to the minister amidst cheers from the guests.

The minister explained that Abby and Trent had written their own vows and held the mic for Trent as he took Abby's hands in his.

"My dear sweet Abigail Jane O'Malley, the day you crossed the threshold of my dismal existence was the best and worst day of my life. Because of promises and secrets, I almost lost you several times over the last two years. Somehow you managed to come back to me each time a little more beautiful than before. You gave me a gift that I never even imagined receiving from anyone let alone dream could ever happen. Somehow you made a man hardened and calloused to love, breakdown and not only love me for the first time in his life, but to actually tell me he did." Trent took a moment to swallow. "Before he died, I was not only able to forgive him, but to tell him I loved him too.

You rocked my world when I looked into your gorgeous eyes, feeling something I'd never felt in my life. I tried to keep you at a distance, but the more I tried to keep you away the more you wound up in my arms. During all the hardships we've endured, somehow you reached deep inside me and pulled out the love I'd buried from everyone. Despite all the lies, secrets, and the actions of two very disturbed people, you fell in love with me. Even when you knew it would most likely leave you brokenhearted and alone. You gave me the gift of life when there was no one else who could, letting a part of yourself mingle with the stubborn, broken man you see before you.

We have a special bond that I won't let be broken, I'll cherish every second of everyday with you. I'm complete when you're in my arms. The sadness and despair you've lived with for so long will be a long-forgotten memory as you become my siren, my friend, my lover, and my wife. I'll love you throughout eternity, both in life and in death. I love you my sweet Abby." He said tears streaming down his cheeks not caring who saw him crying, he meant every word.

The minister choked back the lump in his throat and turned to Abby.

"Trenton Dale Winthrop, I had no idea what I was letting myself in for when I came to O'Malley Island. The first day I was so excited to be on this big adventure away from the tormented and sad life I'd endured. When you took my hand and kissed it a bolt of electricity shot through me. Then we argued and I thought there was no way I'd ever fall for someone as callous and hard-hearted as you. Then you helped me through a night of terrifying memories, showing me a tender side of you that made me fall hard. When I looked at you as you went through the healing process after you were attacked, I saw a frightened, innocent little boy who bore some of the same scars I bear. My heart told me to love you, but my mind was screaming no. Through all the trials we've been through over the last two years, the one thing that kept me from giving up was feeling your arms around me even when you weren't there.

You gave me the gift of a lifetime when you brought me to my Grandmother Abigail. I didn't have long with her, but the time I did have was because of your kindness to both of us.

Your selflessness and determination brought me out of the depths of despair and loneliness that had been my life. You gave me hope things could be amazing for us, even in the midst of the dangers we faced there was you.

I promise from this moment on, I'll always love you. I'll be your songbird, your best friend, your lover, and your wife. There'll never be another man for me. My heart is now and forever yours. I love you."

There wasn't a dry eye in the place as everyone knew their story.

The minister cleared his throat after a brief pause. "Trent here's the ring for Abby."

Holding her hand, he slipped her grandmother's ring on her finger repeating his vows to her.

Abby place her grandfather's ring on his finger repeating her vows to him.

Together they walked to the unity sand. Pouring it together in a big vase as soft romantic music played over the speakers. They looked at the pictures of their lost loved ones thanking them for their love and sacrifices for them.

They returned to stand before the minister who said, "I now pronounce you man and wife, you may kiss your bride."

Their lips met amidst an explosion of cheers from the guests. The sun stretched out the last fingers of sunlight setting the horizon ablaze seemingly signifying their fierce intense love for each other. They turned and were introduced as Mr. and Mrs. Trenton Winthrop.

Epilogue

The celebration of their marriage was met with joy and fun. Many toasts were made, and many jokes were told throughout the meal. When it came time for the cake, Trent carefully fed her a piece of cake making sure he didn't get any on the gorgeous gown she wore.

Trent didn't move quick enough when he caught the glint in her eye just before she smashed the cake in his face. He took it all in stride but whispered teasingly, "You'll pay for that later."

The traditional toast was made, and they found themselves alone on the dance floor for their first dance as husband and wife.

Time seemed to stand still as they moved together, everything fading around them. Totally absorbed in each other until the song ended.

Lance tapped him on the shoulder and said, "I believe the next one is mine as 'Father' of the bride."

Trent smiled and said, "Careful papa, I might think you're after my lady."

"Trent, I…" He stuttered before squaring his shoulders, "I'll have you know if I were a little younger and hadn't already found the love of my life, I'd give you a run for your money!"

Trent burst out laughing handing Abby over to him. He crossed the room and grabbed Gina twirling her around the dance floor like a pro.

The party broke up a little before midnight when all the guests boarded their speedboats or took the helicopter back to the mainland.

Trent picked his bride up and carried her across the threshold and up to their room.

Pulling her close he kissed her passionately taking his time enjoying his new bride. Their tormented love was finally satisfied.

Abby had taken Trent's cold lonely heart and coaxed a tiny spark into a blazing inferno within him. Lost in the fog of her scent attacking his senses, he became impassioned making her his forever more.

Afterward, Abby lay in his arms thinking as he dozed. Theirs was a true love story that would be told for generations to come. She was no longer alone in the dark and the face in the shadows was no more.

The End

Don't miss out!

Visit the website below and you can sign up to receive emails whenever R. J. Stevens publishes a new book. There's no charge and no obligation.

https://books2read.com/r/B-A-YSVZ-NCIMD

BOOKS 2 READ

Connecting independent readers to independent writers.